Starting Again

The Heart of Bath, Book 3

Jenny Worstall

ARE YOU SIGNED UP FOR DRAGONBLADE'S BLOG?

You'll get the latest news and information on exclusive giveaways, exclusive excerpts, coming releases, sales, free books, cover reveals and more.

Check out our complete list of authors, too!

No spam, no junk. That's a promise!

Sign Up Here

www.dragonbladepublishing.com

Dearest Reader;

Thank you for your support of a small press. At Dragonblade Publishing, we strive to bring you the highest quality Historical Romance from some of the best authors in the business. Without your support, there is no 'us', so we sincerely hope you adore these stories and find some new favorite authors along the way.

Happy Reading!

CEO, Dragonblade Publishing

CHAPTER ONE

Marianne

January 1817

"NELSON! NELSON, STOP that at once, do you hear? Naughty boy!" Lady Barrington hurried across the grass towards her pet, wagging her finger. "No! Leave his shoes alone. You must not behave in this way."

Marianne ran after her aunt, watching in dismay as the pug set about destroying the fine evening shoes of the handsome young gentleman standing on the Crescent Lawn. The gentleman offered little resistance, merely laughing as he attempted to pat the dog.

"There, there! You and I should be friends, little one. 'Tis a dear wish of mine that you should stop attacking me whenever we meet. What is bothering you?"

Perchance Nelson was confused as to why the unknown gentleman was wearing full evening dress – for 'twas early morning and the sun was still struggling to cast its beams through the dense clouds and announce that the day was breaking. Perhaps the pug also wondered why the young man was not wearing more substantial outer clothing to protect against the chill wind – and why his hair was damp.

"Ah, Lady Barrington," the gentleman said. "How charming to see you. I do hope you have had a pleasant Christmas."

Then he directed his gaze at Marianne and she felt her insides turn to liquid. That look! His dark tumbled hair and easy smile – a face made for pleasure and amusement. But something about his piercing blue eyes spoke of hidden depths, possibly of a sadness or dissatisfaction, but with what, 'twas not possible to say. He seemed an intriguing character – and one Marianne would do well to avoid.

"Indeed, I have had a splendid Christmas," Lady Barrington said to the gentleman, "and the highlight was the arrival of my niece a few days ago. 'Tis a blessing to have a young person in the house now all my dear daughters are married and living far away. Mr. Templeton, may I present Mrs. Marianne Pembroke? Marianne, this is Mr. Edmund Templeton. He is a near neighbor of mine – and I believe you met his parents last night at my twelfth night party."

Edmund bowed to Marianne, then reached for her gloved hand and raised it to his lips with practiced ease.

"I am delighted to make your acquaintance, Mrs. Pembroke."

Marianne's heart danced – she could do nothing to prevent it – and she felt afraid.

"But Mr. Templeton, I have a bone to pick with you." Lady Barrington shook her head. "For you did not accept my invitation to yesterday's party."

"A thousand apologies, Lady B, but I was already engaged for the evening elsewhere. Be assured, however, that turning down your invitation caused me great pain. I adore visiting your beautiful home at Number 4 and felt utterly heartbroken that I had to miss your bountiful hospitality last night."

Lady Barrington smiled almost girlishly at these compliments. Heavens! Was no one immune to Mr. Templeton's charm? No one, it seemed, save Nelson.

"And moreover," Edmund continued, "I know how forward I have been in addressing you as Lady B instead of Lady Barrington. I hope you will forgive me?"

Edmund fixed Lady Barrington with such a winsome smile that 'twas all Marianne could do to keep from bursting out laughing. Her aunt was a formidable woman – everyone agreed on this – but she was putty in Edmund's hands, enjoying every moment of his flirtatious nonsense.

"I should give you a good trimming for choosing to celebrate twelfth night elsewhere," Lady Barrington said, "for the party would have been even more enjoyable if you had attended. However, you make your apologies so prettily that I find I cannot be cross. And of course you may address me as Lady B – as often as you wish."

"Thank the Lord," Edmund said. "You cannot know how relieved I am to have caused no offense."

His eyes – possibly looking a little tired from lack of sleep – then turned to Marianne. "Welcome to Bath, Mrs. Pembroke. Is this your first visit?"

"'Tis not my first, but I have not been here for some time."

I spent most of my last visit crying – 'twas a very distressing period that I wish most fervently to forget.

Nelson squared his shoulders and gave Edmund a hard stare – then he growled and lunged at his shoes again.

Lady Barrington looked horrified as the soft leather received further extensive scratching.

"Mr. Templeton! How can I apologize enough? This is very much out of character for Nelson, for he is usually such a friendly and sociable dog."

Again, the blood-curdling growl issued forth from deep within the pug's throat – and this time, it sounded like a threat.

Edmund smiled. "Pray do not concern yourself, Lady B. My shoes have survived. Nelson is quite right to be wary of me; I am sure that he only wishes to protect you and Mrs. Pembroke."

"We have no need to be protected from a fine young gentleman such as yourself, Mr. Templeton. I would like to invite you to tea tomorrow so that you can make friends with Nelson. He is always more relaxed in his own drawing room, sitting on his cushion by the fireside." Lady Barrington put her head to one side and gave Edmund a smile that was almost coquettish. "Might we prevail on you to accept? Will you be able to squeeze us into your busy social life?"

"I would be absolutely delighted and can scarce wait for the hours to pass till 'tis time to attend." Edmund gave a small bow. "But now I am afraid I must leave you all, for my parents are expecting me at breakfast. Farewell – until tomorrow."

"I do believe Mr. Templeton will be heading straight for his bedchamber to catch up with his sleep after he has breakfasted," Lady Barrington remarked as Edmund strode away. "I wonder how many parties he attended last night; he certainly knows how to enjoy himself. These young men! How they find the stamina I will never know."

Marianne studied Edmund's retreating figure. Such confidence! A fleeting frown passed over her features. Was Mr. Edmund Templeton perchance a little *too* pleased with himself? And did his teasing way of conversation mask a heart of flint? But he had such a handsome countenance, 'twas hard to think ill of him.

Beware, Marianne! Remember your resolve.

Nelson gave a short series of joyful, wheezy yaps and then turned his face to the chill January wind sweeping across from the river and scampered into the distance.

"Marianne, my dear," Lady Barrington said. "Would you mind chasing after him? I find I cannot keep up with the dog as I used to."

"Leave it to me, Aunt. I am sure I can catch him."

Heavens! I have only been here a short time, but I have already lost count of the number of occasions on which I have had to pursue this little rascal. I hope he does not leap from the ha-ha as he attempted yesterday, for 'tis quite a sharp drop.

Marianne felt a little weary too, as the party the night before had not finished until the small hours – but in Lady Barrington's household, one was expected to rise at the same time every morning – early – no matter what time one had reached one's bed the night before. Marianne did not mind, though, for the walk was refreshing and would make the coffee and freshly baked rolls waiting for them at Number 4 taste all the sweeter.

Eventually, she caught up with Nelson and scooped him up into her arms. He was quite out of breath, but there was no sign of his former bad temper.

"What is it you do not like about Mr. Templeton, I wonder?" Marianne whispered into his ear.

She carried the dog back to his mistress.

"Thank you, my dear." Lady Barrington held out her arms. "Come to me, little one."

Nelson allowed himself to be deposited in Lady Barrington's arms, and she wrapped him in her fur stole.

"I do hope you are enjoying Bath, Marianne," Lady Barrington said as they began walking back to her home. "Tell me honestly, what did you think of last night?"

"'Twas incredible," Marianne enthused. "I have not been to such a large gathering for a long time."

"I thought that would be the case, for your parents do not have a very active social life. And when your mother and I were growing up, I was always the one wild for company – she was quite shy. I think you take after her, my dear, do you not?"

"Perhaps; I must admit to feeling a little nervous occasionally when I meet new people."

"We will have to cure you of that – after all, you are here for a purpose."

Oh, Lord! Not this again. Marianne had endured several talks from her aunt already on the subject of matrimony.

"Yes," Lady Barrington continued, "you have been languishing long enough in Clifton with your parents, wasting the best years of your life. Now you are here in the heart of Bath, you have the opportunity to mix with the cream of society. Tell me truthfully – did any of the young men you met last night catch your eye? Is there anyone you would wish to see again?"

This was a forthright way to speak, indeed. Perchance Marianne might answer in an equally direct way? Should she say that she did not give any of the single men last night a second glance in case they felt encouraged to woo her? She could not bear to – for if there was one thing she was sure of, it was that she fully intended never to marry again after her previous marriage had been cut short so tragically but a year and a half ago.

Marianne opened her mouth to speak. Then closed her lips again, for what was the point? Her aunt was a determined individual and had already said many times that this was to be the year of Marianne's second marriage.

"What about Mr. Templeton?" Lady Barrington said. "He has excellent prospects, for he will inherit his father's title and fortune one day – though, God willing, that will not be for many years. But if Mr. Templeton is not to your taste, no matter, for in truth, he does not seem in a hurry to settle down."

And I have no wish to remarry. Even if I did, I suspect Mr. Templeton and I would not suit, for I find it hard to think what we might have in common – I am not so green, but I know that his seeming interest this morning was merely the typical flirtatious behavior of a man about town. Doubtless he has scores of ladies lined up who adore him and long for his attentions. They are welcome to him!

"There are many other eligible gentlemen for you to meet in Bath." Lady Barrington tickled Nelson's ears. "And now the business of Christmas is over, we can start planning which balls you will attend. I believe you are very fond of music, too?"

"Oh yes. I would adore to go to some concerts. And the theatre, if that is a possibility. I have heard how splendid the Theatre Royal is."

"Concerts, theatre, balls, dinners, and gatherings – 'twill all be so exciting! And, hopefully, fruitful. I think I might ask a few more people for tea tomorrow. Perhaps Mr. Templeton's sister, Mrs. Fitzgerald, might be free."

"Ah, I met her in passing yesterday," Marianne said. "She was going into Number 3 when I was coming out of your house, and we exchanged a few words. I liked her very much."

"She has a charming husband – Mr. George Fitzgerald. They married last summer, and I should now call him Doctor Fitzgerald, for he has recently qualified as a medical man. 'Tis so confusing, for his father is also Doctor Fitzgerald and is a very much respected personage in the city; Doctor Fitzgerald senior is my physician and has also attended a few times to treat Nelson."

"And he did not mind?"

"Mind? Why should he? What do you mean?"

"Oh, I simply meant because Nelson is a dog." Marianne blushed and hoped she had not caused offense.

"Lord bless you, no! Doctor Fitzgerald senior is a notable animal lover – as is his son. Besides, Doctor Fitzgerald knows how much I dote on Nelson and, as my physician, is always keen to keep Nelson in good health – for if Nelson is ill, then I rapidly become unwell too, such is my affection for my pet."

Marianne reflected that 'twas good to hear of Lady Barrington's more sensitive side; generally speaking, she was considered rather a dominant character with a mission to convert all to her way of thinking. Marianne would have to be strong – and courageous – if she was to stick to her plan of remaining unwed.

For I will never marry a second time; I cannot face the agony of loss again.

Edmund

LADY TEMPLETON REGARDED her son quizzically. "Sit down, my dear. How delightful to see you at breakfast; this is indeed a rare occurrence."

"Good morning, Mama." Edmund looked down at his evening clothes. "Perhaps I should go upstairs to change first? I seem to have dressed in the wrong attire."

"You need not try to pretend you have not been out all night. I know your habits."

Edmund gave a snort of laughter and sat down at the table. A footman moved to fill his coffee cup.

"Thank you," Edmund said. "Yes, fill it right up if you would be so kind. Ah! 'Tis nice and strong."

Edmund spread his toast liberally with butter and quince jelly, and wolfed it down appreciatively. Then he accepted a second cup of coffee and flopped backwards in his chair.

"Are you feeling better, my dear?" Lady Templeton smiled. "I remember how proud your father was at your age that he could forgo a night's sleep to attend social engagements and carry on relatively normally the next day."

Edmund grinned and helped himself to a large piece of honey cake. "And pray, where is Papa?"

"Your papa was reluctant to rise early this morning. We did not arrive home from Number 4 till the new day was well underway."

"Ah yes. I have just encountered Lady B on the Crescent Lawn and was thoroughly reprimanded for not attending her twelfth night gathering."

"Perhaps you should have gone," Lady Templeton said. "There were many interesting guests, and we all had such fun with no end of music and cards – then we played charades."

"I will wager that was amusing! Lady B has just introduced me to her niece – and has asked me to take tea with them tomorrow."

Ah, Mrs. Pembroke with her Titian locks and scintillating green eyes. There is something very special about the lady – Mr. Pembroke is a lucky man. I expect I will meet him when I go to Lady B's for tea tomorrow.

"Mrs. Pembroke is very good company," Lady Templeton said. "We chatted yesterday for quite some time about novels and the theatre. Between you and me, I think she is in Bath to find a husband."

"She is a widow?"

Now that is interesting! There is no Mr. Pembroke on the scene to object to a flirtation.

"Yes. She was married but a short time, a matter of five months, I believe. Captain Pembroke was killed at Waterloo, along with far too many others." A tear rolled down Lady Templeton's cheek. "Oh, I can scarce bear to think of those dreadful times."

"Pray, do not distress yourself, Mama." Edmund put his hand across the table and gently stroked his mother's fingers as she tried to compose herself. "All turned out for the best for Henry in the end, did it not? He is safe with us in Bath again, married to his dear Kitty, and proud father to little Isabella."

Edmund's younger brother, Henry, had managed to survive Waterloo under the most extraordinary circumstances in 1815 and had then had a hair-raising adventure returning to England, pursued by his mortal enemy, Lord Steyne. William Carter, Henry's manservant – and the illegitimate half-brother of Lady Templeton – had saved Henry's life on more than one occasion. 'Twas most fortunate that Carter had worked for the government as a spy for many years and so possessed special skills of survival.

"We owe dear Carter such a great debt of gratitude," Lady Templeton whispered. "And though he does not wish us to broadcast the fact to the world, never forget that he is your beloved uncle."

"Indeed, Mama, we all hold Carter in the highest regard, and he will always take his rightful position when we are *en famille*. That will never change, whatever the circumstances. But how I long with all my heart for him to be publicly accepted as your brother by the *ton*."

"As do I, but timing is critical in these matters, and Carter himself is reluctant to be the cause of any stain upon the family."

"The *ton* are but hypocrites! And Carter is worth more than the lot of them."

"You are a dear son, Edmund, and I appreciate your loyalty.

Now, have another slice of cake and I will tell you more about Mrs. Pembroke. Her aunt is very keen to introduce her to the cream of Bath society and plans she will stay for a good few months, possibly longer."

"Does the length of her visit depend on whether or not she finds a husband in the city?"

"There is no need to be facetious, Edmund; matrimony is a serious business, and a lady must plan for her future."

Unmarried – and not looking for flirtation, but a husband. I must be wary! How sick I am of being pursued by young women – aided and abetted by their relatives – all because they want the Templeton title and fortune. So many see me as a gateway to a new life, not as a potential future spouse they can respect; 'tis hard for me to judge who might be genuine.

"I found Mrs. Pembroke to be a woman of good sense and refinement," Lady Templeton said, "perhaps a little shy, but that is no bad thing. And although her parents have somewhat fallen upon hard times, she is Lady Barrington's niece and thus part of a well-connected family. 'Twould not be beneath you to marry her. And she is exceedingly pretty – and still quite young – three and twenty, I believe."

"Mama!" Edmund put his napkin down on the table. "I do wish you would not talk about matrimony as if it were some sort of cold transaction where a man may select a partner according to a woman's breeding, character, and looks. Does the woman herself have no say?"

"Of course she does! But Edmund, you know where your duty lies."

"Yes, yes, I know that one day I must choose a bride who will be worthy to become the next Lady Templeton. When that day comes, I will seek advice from you and Papa and then ask for your blessing on our union – but that time is far distant. There is no need to discuss the subject as endlessly as you do. I resent being put under pressure – for I am not yet ready for matrimony."

Lady Templeton took a sip of coffee and then placed the cup down very firmly on the saucer. "You have been saying this for many moons, and you are now five and twenty. 'Tis high time you settled down. Mrs. Pembroke is a very suitable candidate and would be an honorable addition to our family – but if she does not appeal, then you must look around the ladies of Bath in earnest, or perhaps we should take a trip to London, for your father and I think the time is right . . . and we both think you should begin to take more interest in learning to manage the Templeton estate, for 'tis wrong to leave all the burden with your papa."

Edmund closed his eyes and let his mother's words drift across him, then his head slumped forwards.

Lady Templeton laughed. "Are you really falling asleep?"

"No, of course not." Edmund gave an exaggerated shake. "I do beg your pardon, Mama. I merely nodded off for a minute due to the immensely tedious nature of the conversation. But on second thought, perchance I should retire to my room, for I feel uncommonly tired."

Just then the parlor door opened and Lord Templeton appeared.

"Good Lord!" Edmund said. "Papa! You look even more exhausted than I do."

"How very pleasant to see you, too, Edmund," Lord Templeton said. "Did you have an enjoyable evening? We missed you at Lady Barrington's – you would have –"

"Yes, yes," Edmund cut in. "Mama has already given me the lecture about missing the party."

"But I have a special reason for saying this," Lord Templeton said, "for there was the most amiable young lady there, a Mrs. Pembroke. Your sister Selina was very taken with her, and I believe they have already become firm friends. I do hope you will make her acquaintance soon, for your mother and I think you would suit."

Edmund chuckled. "Too late again, for Mama has already

broken the news that the pair of you have decided to marry me off to Mrs. Pembroke. And as a matter of fact, I have already made her acquaintance outside on the lawn this morning when the infernal Nelson savaged my shoes for some ungodly reason."

"Nelson has never been that fond of you, Edmund," Lady Templeton observed, handing her husband a slice of pound cake.

"'Tis not my fault the pooch has no taste," Edmund said.

He then proceeded to give a hugely embellished account of how Nelson had attacked his evening shoes with great vigor and determination – and an awful lot of noisy wheezing and snarling which Edmund took pleasure in mimicking.

"Please, desist!" Lady Templeton said. "'Tis far too comical for this hour of the morning; we are trying to have our breakfast in peace."

But Edmund was in full flow, his tiredness forgotten, and he would not pause his farcical tale of woe.

"See here?" Edmund lifted up a foot to show the damaged leather. "What on earth is wrong with the idiotic pug that means he turns into a rabid beast bent on destruction when faced with a pair of handsome evening pumps?"

Lord Templeton laughed heartily, then the laugh turned into a cough. Things went from bad to worse as he started clutching alarmingly at his chest and went puce in the face.

"Water! Some water, for pity's sake," he gasped.

Edmund leapt to his feet and held a glass to his father's lips.

"Quick!" Lady Templeton began to wring her hands. "We must send a servant for a doctor!"

"'Twould be better if I ran to Number 3," Edmund said, "to see if George is at home."

"Yes, of course," Lady Templeton said. "Speed is of the essence. I do believe your papa is suffering with his heart. Here, my dear, let me help you lie down on the carpet – perhaps on your side?"

Edmund raced towards the door of the parlor, knocking over a small mahogany box on the desk in his haste.

"Edmund!" Lady Templeton shrieked, "Pray do not stop to pick up the alphabet letters, for pity's sake!"

"Sorry, Mama!" Edmund fled from the house, then around to Number 3, urgently beating on the door.

"George! George! Are you there? Let me in, man, for God's sake!"

When the footman opened the door, Edmund ran into the parlor and found his sister, Selina, and her husband, George, at breakfast.

"Selina, 'tis Papa!" Edmund said. "Come quickly, George – there's not a moment to lose. Your medical skills are required."

George stood up immediately. "I have my bag ready by the door. Describe your father's symptoms as we run and try not to panic; these things often seem worse than they are."

George and Edmund hared along the pavement with Selina not far behind, and very soon George was examining Lord Templeton. He turned his father-in-law onto his back, then loosened his cravat and shirt, and with sincere apologies for the intrusion, placed his ear on Lord Templeton's chest in order that he might listen to his heart.

"What is going on?" Lady Templeton's eyes filled with tears. "Is this it? Is he dying?"

Selina held a finger to her lips. "Shush, Mama! George must have total silence to be able to make a diagnosis."

The seconds ticked past and then George, his brows knitted together in concentration, proceeded to take his father-in-law's pulse. Eventually he nodded, and looked round the room with a cheerful smile before turning back to his patient.

"I am glad to say 'twas a false alarm, Lord Templeton, and you are free to stand up. If you would care to take my arm and Edmund's too, ah – gently does it. And feel free to take a few slow sips of water. I am pleased to report that your heart is strong and steady, as is your pulse. 'Twould be advisable to let my father know of this episode as he is your physician, but my diagnosis is that the act of eating a piece of dry cake and laughing at the same time resulted in digestive discomfort, which in turn caused understandable and natural alarm."

Lady Templeton shed more tears, this time of gratitude as she hugged her husband.

"What a relief!" she cried. "You have no idea, my dear George, how grateful I am to have my son-in-law the doctor living so close by."

"Yes, thank you very much, George." Lord Templeton wiped his brow. "I feel completely restored – albeit rather foolish to have created such a stir. 'Twas all because Edmund made me laugh by talking about Lady Barrington's rascally pooch in such a humorous way."

"I will remember, Papa, not to attempt humor when a family member is eating pound cake in the future."

"You will do more than that, Edmund," Lord Templeton said, "for although this was a false alarm, nevertheless it has got me thinking. No one lives forever, and before I die, my greatest wish is to see all my children happily married and with their own families."

He clasped Lady Templeton's hand. "We have been blessed in recent years, for not only do we have our dearest Henry married to Kitty next door at Number 2, but we have you, Selina, married to George, and living at Number 3."

Lord Templeton allowed his gaze to fix upon his firstborn. "And as for you, Edmund, well, you must see where my mind is travelling with this."

"Yes, yes I know. You would like to see me settled, preferably with an heir to inherit the Templeton name and fortune – possibly even residing at Number 4, although I am at a loss to understand how that might be achieved, for you do not own that house."

"An heir and a spare," Lady Templeton murmured. "That is the safest."

"Two spares, at least." Selina's eyes danced with mirth. "You need to hurry up, Edmund."

"I can recommend marriage," George said as he gave Selina a particularly smoldering look.

"But really," Edmund protested, "I cannot be expected to marry purely because my family think 'tis the right time – surely? Besides, I have not found the right lady yet."

Edmund's voice trailed off as he looked around the room. His parents were still holding hands after their shock, and George and Selina were gazing at each other in the sort of sentimental way people do when they have been married for scarcely seven months.

Unbidden, a vision of a flame-haired lady flooded into Edmund's mind.

Mrs. Pembroke! I must be on my guard, for I have no inclination to marry anyone for a good few years yet – despite my family's sincere wishes and best encouragement. And I certainly have no desire to marry someone who has come to Bath with the express wish of hoping to snare herself a rich husband, however pretty she might be.

Marianne

"I AM SURE there is something going on at Number 1," Lady Barrington said as she stood at the window of her parlor.

Marianne took another sip of her breakfast coffee. What could her aunt be looking at now? In the past few days, Lady Barrington had spent an inordinate amount of time at various windows in the house, observing the life outside and passing judgement. She had even been known to open the sashes, despite the cold, in order to lean out with an ear trumpet to hear better what passersby were discussing.

"Well, my dear," Lady Barrington said as she sat down at the breakfast table again, "I have just seen Mr. Edmund Templeton running along the pavement and then beating at his sister's front door."

"Perhaps he is going on a visit?" Marianne said.

"'Tis a little early for a visit, do you not think? No, I believe it presages something more urgent. An emergency?"

"Possibly."

'Tis is none of our business – but I do wonder what could be happening.

Lady Barrington resumed her position by the window, a plate with two pastries in her hand.

"Ah ha! He is running back to Number 1 now – and he has Mr. Fitzgerald, I mean young Doctor Fitzgerald with him, as well as his sister Selina. Come, my dear." Lady Barrington beckoned to her niece. "Pray join me."

Marianne needed no further invitation – after all, 'twas a little intriguing, and what harm could glancing out of a window do? Hastening over, she endeavored to stand half-hidden next to the shutter, rather than openly gawping like her aunt.

"Do you think I should go over there?" Lady Barrington said in an eager tone.

"Perhaps not, for it could be a family matter."

"But Doctor Fitzgerald was carrying his medical bag, and that makes it a public matter, surely, for any member of the public could see him if they happened to be in the street."

Marianne coughed. "I merely meant that if a member of the Templeton family or staff were ill, would that not make it more of a private concern?"

Lady Barrington frowned, the word "private" not seeming to register.

Nelson wheezed noisily as he sprang across the room to join the two ladies; he then whined and tugged at the hem of Lady Barrington's skirt until she put down her pastries and picked him up.

"There you are, my little darling. You want to see what is going on, too."

She held the pug's face close to the window pane.

Marianne stifled a giggle. Then she felt a twinge of guilt.

'Twas no laughing matter if something was genuinely wrong.

"I must know what is happening," Lady Barrington said. "Therefore, I will summon Jane."

"Your maid?"

"Yes. 'Tis a short step for her through the back garden and thence round to the servants' quarters of Number 1. Did you know her sister, Martha, works there – and will be able to reveal exactly what has happened?"

Marianne felt a little shocked to hear this and turned away to hide her face.

"My motives are of the highest," Lady Barrington continued. "I never indulge in gossip or interfere with other people's business. However, 'twould be churlish to look a gift horse in the mouth, and I cannot tell you how much better informed I have been since Jane came to work for me a few months ago. Her arrival has enriched my life considerably."

I cannot believe that my aunt thinks 'tis right to use a servant girl as a source of information about her neighbors – and what about the possibility that information passes the other way, too?

Yet, what do I know? This is not the way my parents behave with their maid in Clifton, but this is Bath, and Lady Barrington is a highly regarded member of the ton. *Perchance the situation is quite normal in high society?*

There was a timid knock, and Jane appeared.

"There you are!" Lady Barrington quickly explained how imperative it was that Jane found out from her sister if there was any special news at the Templetons that morning.

"Do you wish me to go round to see Martha now?" Jane said.

"Yes. But first, ask Cook to load up a plate with some of the delicacies left from last night, and take the food with you to Number 1's kitchen as an offering from me. And on your way round, my dear, you may consume one of the sweetmeats from the plate. Do we understand each other?"

Jane grinned, nodded – and scurried away.

"The next item on my list to achieve today, Marianne, is to

sort out a problem that has worried me for some time – and that problem, why, it concerns you."

"I am so sorry." Marianne felt a familiar, panicky feeling. "Have I done something wrong?"

Was she to be sent back to her parents after only a few days in Bath? How could she have caused offense?

"Heavens above, do not look so worried, child; I only wish to sort out your wardrobe."

Marianne looked down at her clothes in dismay.

"Yes, my dear, well might you look worried; in the past few days I have seen you wear far too many grays, blacks and drab colors; 'tis time for you to emerge from mourning. A considerable time has passed since your dear husband departed this life, and you are young, pretty, and very much in need of a new husband."

Lady Barrington's voice softened a little. "I have written to your parents about this, and they are in complete agreement – so what say you? Shall we walk to Milsom Street this morning to visit my dressmaker? I have taken the liberty of making a tentative appointment; we can look at fabrics and have measurements taken. No one wants to rush you, dearest Marianne – but I think 'tis time."

Is it? How can one decide when to stop mourning one's husband? Sometimes, in my darkest moments, I fear even a whole lifetime of sorrow would not be enough of a tribute for my brave Richard.

"I have no doubt you will find Madame Dubonnet an agreeable and sympathetic woman. She is also stylish, knowledgeable, and works very speedily; she and her team will help you present your finest self. 'Twill be like a butterfly emerging from a cocoon. And then you will be able to shine brightly in society like a beauteous and majestic tropical bird, although in the west of England rather than further towards the equator."

Am I to be both a butterfly and a bird at the same time? What an imagination my dear aunt has! And do birds not feast on butterflies on occasions?

"This is vastly generous," Marianne said, "but there is no need for you to spend your money on me, for I have frocks aplenty and they are not all drab – I wore my lavender gown last night."

Lady Barrington sniffed. "Lavender is not your best color. You should wear bright blues and greens, and perhaps the warmth of gold – and russet. Then the gentlemen will notice you."

But I have no wish to attract a husband nor to look like wildlife; I am quite happy being a widow who intends to remain unmarried to the end of her life. However, would it not be rude of me to continue to refuse my aunt? She means well and has a kind and generous soul.

Marianne twisted her fingers together. What should she do?

"I will brook no opposition," Lady Barrington said, "and will see you in the hall in ten minutes time, ready to visit the dressmaker."

Lady Barrington's edict made it easy for Marianne to realize where her duty lay – and that resistance would be futile.

So 'tis decided – I am to emerge from my widow's weeds. Ah well, perhaps 'tis time – for I have become a little weary of wearing muted shades for so long. My dear Richard always said how much he admired me in vibrant colors. But I am not prepared to go along with the husband-hunting part of my aunt's scheme.

Lady Barrington swept from the room. "Come along now," she called back to Marianne. "No dawdling! You need to come upstairs my dear; you have nine minutes left to get ready."

Did not my aunt say but a few minutes ago that no one wished to rush me? And now she is determined we should be out of the house in double quick time. How quickly her moods change! Truly, she has a whim of iron.

Marianne followed her aunt up the stairs and made her way to her bedchamber. She stared in the mirror, noticing how the dull gray of her frock did nothing for her complexion – if anything, it exaggerated the shadows under her eyes.

Lord! Mr. Templeton must have thought me very lackluster this morning when we met. And my hair! It resembles a bird's nest after being buffeted by the cold January wind.

Marianne wound a shiny red curl around a finger, coaxing it into a tighter spiral before releasing it, then moved on to the next, working her way around to frame her face until satisfied with the effect. She bit her lips gently and pinched her cheeks to create a rosy look, then wrinkled her nose, annoyed to see a tiny dusting of freckles even in the middle of winter.

Richard always admired my warm coloring, but not all men look favorably upon redheads, especially redheads with freckles. I wonder what looks the tall, dark, and elegant Mr. Templeton prefers?

Marianne took a step back from the mirror and gasped. What in God's name was she thinking? She had no interest in what Mr. Templeton, or any other man, thought of her looks. That part of life was closed to her – forever.

Lady Barrington's voice could be heard from the corridor. "Marianne! Two minutes left! I am about to descend the staircase."

"I am coming!" Marianne changed her shoes, pulled her black pelisse from her closet and snatched her reticule, feeling inside quickly to see if all was there. She smiled as her fingers met the reassuring smoothness of the tiny leather pouch she carried with her constantly – and would until the day she died.

Downstairs in the hall, Lady Barrington was talking to her maid.

"Well done, Jane," Lady Barrington said. "You are a quick worker, and I thank you for your diligence. Now go and see Cook and tell her I give express permission for you to have another sweetmeat from last night. I am very grateful, my dear."

Jane hurried towards the back staircase, and Lady Barrington and Marianne set off with Nelson to go into the city.

"Try not to stare as we pass Number 1," Lady Barrington cautioned Marianne. "'Twould not do to be considered over inquisitive."

"Was Jane able to establish the cause of the commotion this morning?"

"She was. There was a concern about Lord Templeton's health which I am very pleased to say turned out to be a false alarm."

"That is good to hear." Marianne hated to hear of anyone suffering illness.

Lady Barrington tucked her arm through her niece's. "But you will be very pleased with what I found out next. The word amongst the servants is that this health scare led to a conversation about the need for Mr. Templeton to marry ere long and produce an heir. His wife will be Lady Templeton – imagine!"

I have no interest in this matter; I am not searching for a husband.

"Well, my dear, Jane also told me that earlier, before the medical emergency, your name was mentioned at the Templeton breakfast table as a fitting bride for Mr. Templeton. What do you think of that?"

Marianne's eyelids began to sting. She was determined not to give way to her feelings, but the tears started to escape nonetheless.

"Look at me, Marianne," Lady Barrington commanded. Marianne held up her head and regarded her aunt through a watery haze. "Ah, I see I have been a blundering idiot – as usual. I apologize unreservedly, my sweet child. I know first-hand what the pain of losing a dear husband is like. Please, forgive me – and I promise to stop talking about your marriage prospects until such time as you are ready. Or, at least, I promise to try my best to be more circumspect. Now, let us walk briskly. Would you like to hold Nelson's lead? He does so adore you."

Marianne nodded her acquiescence and Nelson gave her a baleful look before licking the hem of her dress.

"And on reflection, I think we should browse the bookshop, and then visit a teashop before we venture to the dressmaker. I know how much you adore reading, and I always find a hot drink and a sweet treat cure most ills. Come, my dear – place your best foot forward!"

I wish I had even an ounce of my aunt's indomitable spirit, for she knows how to overcome the difficulties of life and find joy after bereavement. How glad I am that I have come to stay with her in Bath. Perhaps here I will learn to control my unquiet mind and find the courage to face my future – whatsoever that might be.

CHAPTER TWO
Edmund

STANDING IN THE middle of his bedchamber, Edmund gave an immense yawn and stretched his arms, arching his back. He then released his body with a mighty sigh.

Ah, but last night had been busy! Edmund had lost count of how many gatherings and parties he had been to, playing cards, flirting, dancing, and drinking. The fun went on till dawn. What a tremendous sendoff he and his friends had given to the Christmas season! And they had ended the celebrations in time-honored fashion by galloping round the city singing lustily before partaking of a quick, freezing swim in the River Avon.

Edmund walked over to the window and looked across to the trees at the top of Beechen Cliff. And who was that in the street below? Why, Lady Barrington and Mrs. Pembroke, if he was not very much mistaken. And that hellish creature, Nelson.

Pressing his nose to the glass, Edmund admired the red curls that were escaping around the brim of Marianne's hat like fiery rays. She was a very handsome woman, no doubt about it, and would have no trouble finding a husband in Bath – but preferably one who did not live at Number 1 Royal Crescent.

There was a knock at the door. "Edmund? May I come in?"

"Of course, Mama – as long as you are not going to nag me."

"Edmund! I have no idea what you mean. I never nag, merely

suggest improvements that would make you even happier with your life – and perhaps give you a sense of purpose."

A sense of purpose? Who needs one of those?

"If you say so, Mama."

Lady Templeton closed the door firmly behind her. "I know you are tired at the moment and hoping for a nap, but this cannot wait."

Lord alive! The same tune from Mama gets mighty dull – and my poor head already has a megrim threatening.

"Now Edmund, we all know that Papa's health episode this morning was not what we thought. However, he is not getting any younger and I would like him to be able to relax and enjoy what years he has left on this earth."

How I long to lie down and close my eyes.

"He has the immense burden of running his estate to deal with – why, the volume of paperwork he undertakes daily in his study is horrendous, and then there are his frequent visits to Templeton Park and his other properties to oversee the staff and supervise their tasks."

"But the staff are all trustworthy and capable, are they not? Why would they need to be supervised by Papa as well as by the steward?"

Lady Templeton smoothed her skirts briskly. "Really, there is so much that Papa must do that you know nothing of – mainly because you have taken pitifully little interest in what is, after all, your birthright. You have a duty to support your father in his endeavors now, just as you will have a duty to take on the full burden following his death."

Lady Templeton held her head high as if declaiming to a public meeting, and Edmund took the chance to surreptitiously lie down on his bed. Ah! That was better – the softness of the pillow and the support of the mattress were heaven sent. As a young blade he had not felt this level of weariness, but now, at five and twenty, his body was reminding him that it was not designed to miss a whole night's sleep without a little protest.

The years were creeping along – perhaps his mama was right and 'twas time for a change? He did feel uncommonly jaded.

Edmund began to enter that blessed state of half sleep where one lingers between consciousness and oblivion.

"No, you shall not lie down, Edmund; you will stand when I address you – and pay attention!"

Edmund slunk from his bed with an ill-disguised pout. There were not many people in his life he would allow to chastise him, but he knew that his devoted mama loved him with a passion and wished only the best for him – even if she could be damned annoying on occasions.

"And this is not all I wish to talk to you about," Lady Templeton continued. "'Tis one thing to leave your father to do all the work – that is bad enough – but you must fix your mind to the future of the Templetons. Think of your heirs – and their heirs. In short, 'tis high time you were married. This summer would be an excellent time for your wedding."

"Mama! Do you wish me to marry the first young lady I see?"

"You did not marry the first young lady you saw," Lady Templeton said, a little tartly in Edmund's opinion. "You have been allowed much liberty in this matter, but now your thoughts should turn to matrimony."

"I have not yet met a lady who is worthy to become the future Lady Templeton."

Lady Templeton coughed delicately. "This is partly, dear Edmund, because you mix with the wrong ladies. From henceforth you will attend only respectable gatherings. I expect you to make an appearance at all the important events in the city for the rest of the season; that is the only surefire way for you to meet your future bride."

Edmund gave a sharp intake of breath. How would he have time for his many leisure pursuits?

"You will not meet a potential bride in your clubs, nor when you gallop around the city in the early hours, or bathe in the moonlit river. You must see that."

"But how the devil? Mama! Who could you have been talking to?"

"I have my sources."

Is nothing private?

"How I wish I were an ordinary young gentleman, able to live an unobserved life," Edmund said. "Many are the times I would gladly have changed places with my brother Henry, for to be the second son is a much more comfortable position."

"I do not think poor Henry was in a comfortable position when he faced his enemies at Waterloo. Do you?"

Edmund hung his head. "I offer abject apologies, Mama; I spoke without thinking."

"I accept your contrition – as you must accept your position in the family as the first-born son." Lady Templeton's eyes misted over. "My dear, sweet Edmund. What an adorable infant you were, and what joy your arrival into this world brought." She reached up and tucked a stray curl behind his ear. "You have grown into an admirable young man, a son to be rightly proud of, and your papa and I love you with a light that will never diminish. But 'tis time for you to mature and fulfil your duty."

Edmund nodded mutely. What else could he do?

"Now, what about a short nap? Then I will send your valet up to help you wash and dress. After that, my dear, you and I will make our way into Bath and see who is around. We will go for a walk."

"A walk?"

This is not how I usually spend my time, walking with Mama.

"Yes," Lady Templeton said. "There are myriad eligible young women in Bath, and many of them are doubtless promenading around the city as we speak, eager to meet you and your friends. You do not want to miss out, do you?"

"This sounds like rather a waste of time to me. Could I not wait and see if the perfect lady might spontaneously appear?"

Edmund flung himself on his bed again, overcome with weariness.

"I believe what you describe as 'the perfect lady' has already appeared," Lady Templeton said. "You met Mrs. Pembroke this morning. She is a most personable young woman, and one I would be proud to call a daughter-in-law. I do not think you will find anyone more suitable, however hard you look. But alas, you have made it plain that you have no wish to woo her; therefore we must start our search of Bath in earnest for your future bride."

Edmund felt his heavy eyelids closing, then, as he began to drift off, he was conscious of his mama kissing his forehead and stroking his hair.

"My darling Edmund," she whispered, "I am not doing this to be unkind. You can have no idea of the delights waiting ahead for you with a loyal wife beside you and children playing at your feet; you will be an exemplary husband and father. I know it."

The last thing Edmund heard before he slept was the sound of the curtains being drawn.

His dreams were vivid – and punctuated by little snores and flashbacks to the previous evening. Ah, but the wine he and his friends had consumed! The parties they had visited, the women they had encountered, the card games they had played – and the feel of the chill river water upon their skin.

"Such good friends I have," Edmund croaked.

Then he frowned, remembering how Forbes had mentioned this would be the last year of hell-raising for him as he would be getting married soon. Shortly after this revelation, Lymington said he was about to undertake some sort of gainful employment. Imagine! The group had been shocked to hear these two appalling pieces of news and had thoroughly drenched both men with river water as a punishment, to the merriment of all.

Edmund shuddered as he lay in a half sleep. He was still determined to put off for as long as possible the evil day when he would have to do some serious work. And as for marriage, why it simply did not bear thinking of.

And yet, would it not be sweet, as Mama said, to have my own children all around me and a loving wife at my side? I have felt a little envious of my dear brother Henry on occasions when I have visited him next door at Number 2, for as a second son he was able to marry for love – to join with his childhood sweetheart. He has never in his life been as happy as he is now, married to dear Kitty. And my niece, little Isabella, is such a diverting creature. I remember the first time I cradled her tiny body in my arms; her sweet trusting gaze awakened my protective paternal instinct.

Edmund turned onto his side. Maybe he would enjoy being married one day – but not yet, for he was still having too much of a good time.

What was this? A trick of the light? A single tiny ray of sunshine penetrated the gloom of his chamber, and through his half-closed lashes Edmund imagined he saw a tiny infant with blue Templeton eyes and a hint of reddish hair.

Edmund sat bolt upright and rubbed his eyes furiously to repel the disturbing vision.

"Are you awake?" his valet said as he finished drawing back the curtains to reveal the daylight. "Lady Templeton sent me upstairs to help you wash and dress."

"The devil she did, Voyle! I have only been asleep for five minutes."

Voyle smirked. "I believe you have been asleep a full half hour. Lady Templeton said she would like to see you downstairs as soon as possible."

Edmund never stayed discontented for long, and with a grin, he swung his long legs over the side of the bed, stood up, and gave another enormous yawn. 'Twas amazing how restorative even a short sleep could be.

"Is that coffee I can smell?"

"Yes, sir. Lady Templeton asked the kitchen to make it double strength."

"Good for Mama!"

"She said you were about to go for a walk." Voyle raised an eyebrow.

"There is no need to be surprised. Mama is determined to

seek out a suitable young bride for me – and we are to start today by parading through Bath. 'Tis her new campaign which she hopes will result in a victory – for her."

"Very good, sir."

Edmund bellowed with laughter. "You know full well this is not a good situation. I am relying on you, Voyle, to be my right hand man in the conflict ahead – for I am determined to hang onto my single life as long as possible."

Voyle nodded. "I will do what I can, sir. And now, if you would allow me . . . ah yes, that's it . . . I trust the water is warm enough? And shall I attempt the *trone d'Amour*? I feel that would be a fitting way to tie your cravat this morning."

"No, Voyle! I cannot abide so much starch round my neck. And I will not wear a style that has *amour* in its name. Make it something more natural, for pity's sake."

"Very well, sir."

Then Voyle combed Edmund's hair into a windswept style and started to apply pomade.

"Enough!" Edmund pushed the fragrant potion away. "I do not want to look as if I am trying to attract the ladies – nor smell like a lemon grove."

Voyle replaced the pomade on the dressing table and grimaced.

"What is it, man?" Edmund said. "You have something to say – I know it. Do not hold back; I will not be offended."

"Well, with the greatest respect, I am worried about the battle ahead, for Lady Templeton is a skilled and practiced strategist."

"Ah, I see your point. Mama possesses the same qualities as a top military general such as the Duke of Wellington himself. Tremendous energy, absolute focus – and a determination never to give up."

"Indeed." Voyle's expression was grave. "To be blunt, sir, with Lady Templeton commanding the opposition, I do not altogether fancy your chances – and think you must prepare to surrender."

Marianne

"HAVE YOU HAD enough tea, Marianne? And what about another of these?" Lady Barrington offered a plate of delicious pastries as the two ladies sat in the window of Hunter's tea shop.

"Thank you, Aunt. You are spoiling me today." Marianne accepted a fruit tart and then looked down at the three volumes of *Pride and Prejudice* on the table beside her. "I am most grateful for this gift."

"You deserve to be spoilt, my dear, after all you have suffered. Now, can you squeeze in another pastry?"

"Thank you kindly, but if I consume any more, I will scarce be able to fit into any of my clothes. I am not accustomed to eating as much as I have of late."

"'Twould do you good to put some meat on your bones," Lady Barrington said, "and besides, your clothes not fitting is of no consequence, for I am about to revolutionize your wardrobe. All your previous clothes can be discarded. 'Tis time for you to cease concealing your beauty by hiding your light under a bushel. You must think of time's wingèd chariot – as time and tide wait for no man – and you should, of course, gather ye rosebuds while ye may."

Marianne felt laughter threatening to erupt; what an amazing blend of quotations – together with a host of mixed metaphors. 'Twas entertaining in the extreme.

"From henceforth, you will dress in a bright array of fabulous colors and sophisticated styles, not the ghastly grays and insipid lavenders of your provincial frocks. 'Tis time for you to shine like a diamond in the firmament of Bath."

I know my aunt means well, but I still question whether 'tis too soon to change my apparel. Perchance I am not ready to cease mourning my

Richard, and to release thoughts of the family I had dearly hoped for with him – but now will never enjoy.

"I, I rather like the subdued shades," Marianne said.

"Stuff and nonsense! As I have said before, lavender does your complexion absolutely no favors. Your skin looks like chalk."

Lady Barrington put her hand over Marianne's. "I mention this for your own good, my dear, not to be unkind. I say! Is that not Lady Templeton passing by – with Mr. Templeton? I must say I am very surprised he is in the city, for I thought he would need a longer sleep." She lifted her quizzing glass to her eye. "He still looks a little tired. What do you think, Marianne?"

Marianne glanced out of the window at the very moment Mr. Templeton was looking in, and their eyes locked together in such a startling way that Marianne felt quite faint. 'Twas as if a bolt of lightning had crashed through the window and ravaged her soul. She had only felt like this once before in her life.

Oh my! How impressive Mr. Templeton looks in his day dress. And the dangerous warmth in his eyes – that suave smile playing about his chiseled lips. I must be on my guard.

"He looks tolerably well, I suppose," Marianne said, her heart quivering.

What a liar I have become!

"Ah, good," Lady Barrington said. "They have seen us and are coming in. They shall sit at our table – I will brook no opposition."

"But should we not be on our way to the dressmaker?"

"Madame Dubonnet will be pleased to see us at any time," Lady Barrington declared. "Ah! Lady Templeton! How delightful to see you. Would you care to join us? We can recommend the pastries."

Within minutes, all were sitting together at the table with a fresh pot of tea. Somehow, Lady Barrington had contrived that Edmund and Marianne were seated next to each other at one end of the table with Nelson at their feet, while she sat at the far end with Lady Templeton and engaged in a loud and animated discussion about the very poor weather that had been inflicted upon them in recent years.

"We had no summer to speak of last year," Lady Barrington said.

"None at all," Lady Templeton agreed.

"How I long for sunshine."

"Ah, yes; I pin my hopes on better things to come this year."

"In all sorts of ways!"

"It seems we must converse with one another," Edmund said to Marianne, "unless you wish to chitchat about the wind and rain."

Marianne grinned. "I am sure we can do better than that."

She was acutely conscious of an appealingly fresh lemon fragrance emanating from Edmund. She was also only too aware of his magnificent body encased in tight pantaloons and a fitted jacket, for he was sitting so very, very close. The tea shop table and chairs were on the delicate side, and a tall, well-built gentleman such as Mr. Templeton would naturally find it tricky to contain his muscular legs under the table, but must out of necessity shift closer until his thighs were almost brushing hers.

Almost! Oh, how I miss the masculine touch – the comfort, the affection – and the passion.

Edmund leaned even closer to Marianne, and she felt his breath on her face, then Nelson growled from underneath the table.

"Do you want to have another go at my boots?" Edmund asked the dog. "Is that it? Go ahead, if it pleases you, but methinks you will find them tougher than my evening shoes."

"Do not encourage him," Marianne said. "He must learn how to behave."

She cast a swift glance at Lady Barrington, who was now deep in conversation with Lady Templeton about the necessity of finding good domestic staff.

"I believe," Marianne said to Edmund in a lowered voice, "that 'tis possible Nelson has been a little indulged in the past, and this may account for his slightly distrustful behavior on occasions."

Edmund shook his head. "You need not apologize. I know Nelson is a sweet-tempered dog but, as incredible as it is to believe, he thoroughly disapproves of me."

"'Tis quite incredible, as you say," Marianne said with a laugh. "What do you think there is about your character that he might take exception to?"

"Why absolutely nothing. Nothing Nelson could possibly have any knowledge of, anyway."

"You forget that Nelson saw you coming back from a night's revelry in your evening dress. Perhaps he was jealous and would have liked to have been out on the town himself?"

"No, that cannot be it," Edmund said, "for I know Nelson will have been the center of attention at Lady Barrington's twelfth night party."

"This is true. He spent most of the evening lying on his silk cushion in front of the fire being admired and petted by the guests."

"That does sound an awfully pleasant way to spend an evening," Edmund said. "Perchance I am the one who should feel jealous."

He reached down to give the pug a gentle caress, but Nelson opened his jaw and Edmund quickly withdrew his hand. "I wish the little fellow wanted to be my friend. What can I do?"

"Try a small piece of pastry?"

Edmund broke off the edge of a tart and held it under the table. Nelson jabbed his head forward to snatch the tasty morsel and then licked his lips appreciatively.

"You can make him work harder for scraps," Marianne suggested.

"Show me."

Marianne held a tidbit just out of Nelson's reach before commanding him to sit.

"Now, paw!" she commanded, and the animal lifted a tiny

paw before Marianne allowed him to accept the morsel.

"You have a way of taming wild beasts that is most impressive," Edmund murmured. "Would that there were someone prepared to take on the formidable task of civilizing me."

Suddenly, to Marianne's horror, she realized that Lady Templeton and Lady Barrington had stopped talking about their servants and were now whispering to each other and exchanging knowing looks.

I distinctly heard the words "wedding" and "this summer." How shameful! Hunter's tea shop is no better than a cattle market.

Marianne felt rage boiling up inside her.

Why does everyone think that the only way for me to live my life is within the bonds of matrimony? I am happy with my memories; they are all I need.

Edmund was pulling uncomfortably at the neck of his cravat – perhaps he thought a trap had been set for him?

Marianne clutched her reticule, pressing her trembling fingers against the fabric until she felt the reassuring presence of what lay therein.

"I think perhaps we must proceed with our errands this morning," Lady Barrington said. "If you would excuse us, Lady Templeton?"

"Of course. We also have many things to do in the city, have we not, Edmund?"

Edmund flushed scarlet.

I wonder what they have planned for the day?

"We are due to visit Madame Dubonnet," Lady Barrington said, "for Mrs. Pembroke has agreed to release herself from her mourning. We are going in search of new outfits – with plenty of color."

What a shockingly personal thing to say! How can my aunt speak of these things in front of people I hardly know?

"And I look forward to seeing you tomorrow, Mr. Templeton," Lady Barrington said.

"Ah, yes, tea in the afternoon." Edmund smiled. "I am looking forward to the event greatly. I believe you said you might also invite Selina and George?"

"Yes," Lady Barrington said. "I have already sent a note round to Number 3 and am waiting on their reply. Ah, Marianne, do not forget your books. And it has been a pleasure, Lady Templeton, to discuss the many interests we have in common. Until tomorrow, then. Farewell!"

Did my aunt wink at Lady Templeton? Oh, the shame! I am seriously contemplating writing to Mama and Papa to ask them to allow me to return to Clifton at the earliest opportunity.

"'Tis not far to Milsom Street," Lady Barrington said once they were outside again. "Come along now, Nelson. You know how pleased Madame Dubonnet always is to see you."

I have to say something! I cannot let my aunt continue under the illusion that she is allowed to dress me up in finery and then auction me off to the highest bidder.

"Aunt," Marianne began timidly. "I wonder if you realize, er, oh, I find this hard to say."

"What, my dear? Please do not tell me again that you are perfectly happy wearing your grays and lavenders."

"'Tis not about the color of my clothes. I wonder if you realize how much I do not want to marry again."

"But this is absurd," Lady Barrington said. "Every young lady wants to make a good marriage; we are nothing without men."

"Would you have married again," Marianne asked, "if your husband had died very early in your married life?"

"Yes! I would have needed to. But I was lucky; your uncle and I enjoyed many happy years of married life and produced four wondrous daughters."

Ah, yes – my cousins Augusta, Amabella, Aurelia and Alicia – and all of them married last year. My aunt is a skilled match maker – and is looking for fresh employment.

"My dear," Lady Barrington continued, "I think I can guess what is worrying you. Do you somehow feel disloyal to your Richard for wanting to marry again?"

"But I do *not* want to marry again."

"Perhaps you are not quite ready? When you meet the right man, that feeling will soon dissipate."

Marianne sighed. How could she explain that it was not simply a question of time?

"And what will you do if you do not marry?" Lady Barrington put her head on one side. "Need I remind you, Marianne, that given your parents' financial situation, you need to make a good match."

"I could become a governess. One of my school friends is a governess and writes to me saying how much she is enjoying it."

"She must be deluded! Being a governess is not pleasant – 'tis a last resort for those without money."

"I believe it can be a worthy occupation if one is fortunate enough to be placed in a good household."

"I will not hear of it! No niece of mine is going to become a governess. You are going to marry, and marry well; that is an end to it. Ah! Here we are at Madame Dubonnet's emporium. How beautifully she has dressed the window. Is there anything here that catches your eye before we go in? My word! Look at that beautiful tippet."

Once inside Madame Dubonnet's shop, Nelson became very excited and nibbled a few stray threads at the ends of some bolts of fabric before retiring to a corner to sit on a velvet cushion.

"Mrs. Pembroke," Madame Dubonnet said, "welcome to my establishment! I am delighted to make your acquaintance. Lady Barrington ne'er spoke a truer word than when she described you as a veritable beauty."

"She will look better once we get her out of these frightfully dreary colors," Lady Barrington said. "What would you suggest?"

"Let me see." Madame Dubonnet regarded Marianne closely. "I suggest Mrs. Pembroke inspects the array of fabrics we have here to see what attracts her. Perhaps the spring green silk might suit? And I think the Prussian blue velvet would be charming. What about this amber silk? I can see that you would dazzle in all the richer, warmer colors – and clear bright ones, too. Take your time! Let your eyes become accustomed to less somber shades. And once you have decided on the fabrics, we can discuss styles. I have all the latest illustrations and some samples, too. Does that sound agreeable?"

Marianne nodded – what else could she do? – and began walking down the aisles looking at the bolts of fabric and feeling the different textures between her fingers.

I have to say there are some dazzling colors here, and if the circumstances were different, I would thoroughly enjoy this treat. Ah! What a gorgeous crimson! Perhaps 'tis indeed time I was out of mourning? And this emerald green silk is sensational.

After perusing the fabrics and discussing styles with Madame Dubonnet, Marianne allowed herself to be measured. Then Madame Dubonnet and Lady Barrington made an extremely long list of all the new items she required, including undergarments.

In vain did Marianne protest that she had no need for such extensive purchases. One or two items would be hugely generous and welcome gifts, but a whole new wardrobe – was this not excessive?

"I have plenty of colorful gowns at home in Clifton," Marianne said. "Perhaps I could ask Mama to send them?"

"But Marianne," Lady Barrington said, "they were all made for you before the battle of Waterloo. They will be hopelessly out of date."

Madame Dubonnet's eyebrows shot up. She was evidently horrified to think someone would wear a gown from seasons ago – when they did not need to.

"'Tis such a waste," Marianne said. "The gowns are perfectly serviceable."

"Then your mama should pass them on to those in need," Lady Barrington said. "You must understand that for all the events here in Bath, you will need to be fashionable – especially if you want to capture the heart of an eligible young man."

"I do not think men notice whether apparel is up-to-date or

not," Marianne murmured.

"*They* may not," Lady Barrington said, "but their mamas do. And the *ton* will judge you."

Madame Dubonnet nodded vigorously.

"That is settled, then," Lady Barrington said. "We will have everything on the list, please, Madame Dubonnet, as fast as you can supply it. Oh, and please add the ermine tippet displayed in the window."

"Aunt!" Marianne exclaimed.

Such extravagance! But, oh, how beauteous the garment is.

"You need to keep warm, my dear," was Lady Barrington's answer.

"An inspired choice," Madame Dubonnet said with a very wide smile. "We will get to work straight away, Lady Barrington, but if 'tis not impertinent of me, I have an additional suggestion."

"Yes? Pray continue."

"It came to me when you said you wanted the items as soon as possible. I happen to have here in the shop a beautiful cerulean blue gown that has already been cut out and partly constructed for a young lady who then unaccountably changed her mind. The young lady is of a similar build to Mrs. Pembroke – and I wondered if you would like me to include this frock in your order."

"Could it be finished by tomorrow," Lady Barrington asked, "in time for my tea party?"

"Certainly! My seamstress will work tirelessly until it is finished."

"Outstanding news! Please proceed. And send the tippet with the gown, if you will."

"Perfect! I will deliver it early tomorrow morning without fail. And if I might ask Mrs. Pembroke to try the half-constructed gown on for minor adjustments?"

Marianne nodded mutely.

"This way, if you please, Mrs. Pembroke. Now, if you could wait a minute while I fetch my best seamstress, we will do the final measurements and fitting."

Marianne found herself alone behind the privacy of a curtain for a blessed few minutes. Reaching into the leather pouch inside her reticule, she pulled out a tiny miniature and kissed the sweet representation of a tiny red-headed infant before returning it to its home.

Richard had known of her pregnancy before he had set off for Waterloo and had been thrilled at their good fortune so early in their marriage. A talented amateur artist, he had endeavored to portray what he thought their child might look like, and had given the miniature to Marianne on the very day he had departed for the Continent.

"If I do not return, my love," he had said, "you will have this picture to give our child. They will know how much I loved them before they were born – and how much I love them still from a better place."

Marianne felt the familiar pain piercing her heart – for not only had she lost her dear husband during the summer of 1815, but also, shortly after hearing the news, her unborn child.

I can never face such a loss again. How I wish I felt differently – but I cannot find the strength. Am I fated to be trapped in this unbearable situation forever?

Edmund

THE NEXT DAY, Edmund burst through the front door of Number 1 with rosy cheeks and windswept hair – and covered in mud.

What an exhilarating gallop I have had this afternoon! I feel full of energy.

"There you are!" Lady Templeton was waiting for her son in the hall. "This is cutting things rather tight; you are due at Lady Barrington's in fifteen minutes for tea."

"I know – that is the reason I came back."

"But you have hardly left enough time to change your clothes."

Edmund grinned. "Why can I not go dressed like this?"

Lady Templeton brushed some dried mud from Edmund's shoulder. "I know you are teasing me, for even you know 'tis not acceptable to pay a visit when one is covered in dirt from head to foot. Now run along. Voyle is waiting to assist you in your room – with plenty of hot water."

Edmund made for the staircase and began leaping up the steps two at a time.

"'Tis important you look your best," Lady Templeton called after him, "for I happen to know that Mrs. Pembroke has had a new frock delivered a few hours ago."

"Of what relevance is that to me? And how the devil do you know she has a new frock?" Edmund asked, leaning over the banisters.

"I have many sources of information, but in this case, I have Martha to thank."

"Your maid, Martha?"

"Yes. She is sister to Lady Barrington's maid, and Lady Barrington and I encourage the free flow of information between our houses, for it can oft be enormously useful."

"Good Lord!" Edmund said. "There are spies within the Crescent – and I had thought Carter was the only one."

How typical of Mama and her dear friend Lady Barrington.

"Anyway," Lady Templeton said, "that is how I know that Mrs. Pembroke has a new frock. Apparently the seamstress worked through the night to finish the sewing. Imagine!"

"This hardly seems fair to the seamstress," Edmund said under his breath, "or necessary."

". . . and Mrs. Pembroke is now officially out of even her half-mourning, and this new dress is only the beginning of a beautiful new wardrobe that Lady Barrington has been kind enough to order for her."

Edmund felt a shiver running down his spine. Needing a new

dress because one was coming out of mourning was one thing – but a whole new wardrobe? Lady Barrington was obviously determined her niece should make a good marriage – and soon.

Might this also be Marianne's aim? What a shame for I enjoyed chatting with her yesterday in Hunter's. If she is indeed searching for a husband in earnest, I would do well to keep my distance – for I do not want any misunderstandings.

"Come along, Edmund," Lady Templeton said. "Hurry! This is an important tea party; from small acorns, mighty oaks grow."

"I am merely going to drink tea, Mama. What are you insinuating with your horticultural talk?"

"You know full well of what I speak. Everything has to start somewhere."

"Maybe. But you might do well to remember that most acorns wither and die before they have a chance to become a mighty oak."

"Well," Lady Templeton retorted, "if Mrs. Pembroke and you are not going to grow into a mighty oak together, we must continue our search for someone you would be prepared to woo. Did none of the young ladies we saw yesterday during our promenade catch your fancy? Edmund! Are you listening?"

Edmund stomped off to his chamber, not caring that fragments of mud were falling from his riding boots with every step.

And now I feel guilty, for I am making work for the servants by dirtying the stairs. Oh, Mama is impossible!

Why can she not understand that I am a person with a brain and heart, not some racehorse that must be perfectly matched with another of the correct pedigree – with our union arranged and observed by others.

Voyle was waiting for Edmund in his bedchamber. "My instructions are to help you dress swiftly, sir."

"Ha! Are these instructions from the military general downstairs?"

Voyle nodded.

"I will have you know that, as planned, my mama dragged me all over Bath yesterday. After visiting Hunter's, we went to the Pump Room where she introduced me to countless young women of her acquaintance, and then we promenaded up and down Great Pulteney Street greeting members of the *ton* before strolling through Sydney Gardens. I was quite worn out with false smiles and empty chitter chatter by the time I got home."

"I had heard something of the sort," Voyle admitted.

"Confound it! Nothing is private in the goldfish bowl that is my life."

SHORTLY AFTERWARDS, EDMUND made the brief journey from Number 1 to Number 4, where he was warmly received by Lady Barrington in her withdrawing room upstairs. Huge portraits of her four adored daughters, Augusta, Amabella, Aurelia and Alicia, dominated the wall opposite the door – and visitors were oft startled on a first visit to see four such robust young women glaring down at them.

Marianne was sitting next to Edmund's sister, Selina, on a sofa. A hostile growl came from the silken cushion in front of the fire and Nelson bared his teeth.

"A thousand apologies Mr. Templeton," Lady Barrington said. "I simply cannot think what has got into him."

"Luckily, I came prepared." Edmund reached into his pocket and pulled out a pungent delicacy; Nelson leapt from his cushion, nose quivering. "Sit! Good boy. Now – paw. That's it! Paw! Clever Nelson. Here you are."

Nelson gobbled the treat and smacked his lips appreciatively.

"Bravo, Mr. Templeton," Marianne said. "You are taming Nelson."

Selina clapped her hands with delight. "Well, I never! You are turning into an animal lover, Edmund. Just wait till I tell George this evening."

"Will he not be joining us this afternoon?" Edmund asked.

"Alas, no," Selina said. "He is seeing a patient on the other side of the city. 'Tis a very interesting case; he has been experimenting with a new treatment of his own devising and is very happy with the relief it has afforded to the poor man's suffering."

When I hear about George's work, I sometimes feel that 'twould be good to have a mission in life. However, this would necessitate being compelled to sacrifice my freedom to do as I please – so on second thought, I am happy as I am.

Mostly.

"Back you go to your cushion, Nelson; there's a good boy," Lady Barrington said. "Mr. Templeton has given you a treat; there is no more."

But Nelson stayed at Edmund's feet, salivating and licking his boots.

"Actually, I do have a few more treats somewhere about my person," Edmund said. "Perhaps Nelson can smell them? I asked Voyle to furnish me with some scraps from the kitchen, you see, in case Nelson took a fancy to my footwear again."

"Oh, yes!" Selina said. "Marianne and I were talking just before you arrived about how amusing 'twas when Nelson attacked your evening shoes."

She already calls her Marianne! They are firm friends on but a short acquaintance. And Marianne is a beautiful name; it suits her well. "You must not spoil Nelson, Mr. Templeton," Lady Barrington cautioned. "'Tis one thing to make friends with him – but quite another to indulge him."

Edmund caught Marianne's eye after this comment and realized he was not the only one to appreciate the humor contained therein.

"Ah, here is Jane with the tea," Lady Barrington said. "I urge you all to eat as many sandwiches and cakes as you can this afternoon, for Cook will be offended if there is anything returned. Now, Selina, would you care to sit next to me? I could do with some advice about a tapestry I am attempting. And perchance Mr. Templeton would like to sit next to Mrs. Pembroke?"

Lord! Mrs. Pembroke does not seem pleased that I am to sit next to her – what have I done to offend her? But now she is blushing. Is she perhaps endeavoring to flirt with me? Devil take it! I am getting mixed messages and must be on my guard in case she turns out to be a fortune hunter like all the rest.

"Did you have a pleasant time after our encounter in Hunter's yesterday?" Edmund said.

"I did, thank you," Marianne said.

What a vision of loveliness she is in her delicate blue frock! Ah, the vibrancy of her complexion, and the lustrousness of her curls are proving quite distracting.

"Is there anything wrong, Mr. Templeton?" Marianne asked.

"Absolutely not. I was admiring your new gown.'

"How do you know 'tis new?"

Edmund grinned. "There is a covert channel of communication between Numbers 1 and 4."

"Ah, I have been made aware of that; indeed I believe 'tis rather an open secret." Marianne frowned. "Life is more public here in Bath than I am accustomed to when at home with my parents."

Oh! I hope I have not offended her by making light of the situation. I would like to tell her how much I sympathize with her wish to keep her life more private – but for now, I will change the subject.

Edmund noticed some slim books on a side table. "Did I not see you with these in Hunter's?"

"Yes. Lady Barrington was kind enough to purchase the novel for me; I have been hoping to read *Pride and Prejudice* for a long time, having heard many good reports."

Edmund picked up the first volume. "I believe my sister talks of this. She says 'tis exceptionally comical."

"Are you fond of reading, Mr. Templeton?" Marianne asked.

"I am sure I would be fond of it, if I did any, but I seem very busy with other occupations."

"How do you spend your time, then?"

"I love horses – especially betting on them. Cards, gatherings, dining at my club, oh, the list is endless; I am always having fun somewhere."

She does not need to hear about my fondness for galloping around Bath at night with my friends and bathing in the river.

"Selina has been telling me about her work with the children of the parish," Marianne said. "She asked me if I would like to help one day."

"And would you?"

"I believe I would. 'Tis always a joy to be with children, and I like to keep busy. Perhaps one day I might become a governess, and 'twould be good preparation."

A governess? My word, Mrs. Pembroke does not sound like a fortune hunter.

"And Mr. Templeton," Marianne continued, "I know you are being disingenuous when you imply that you live merely for pleasure, for I know well enough you must spend much time helping your father."

"Well, I am not tremendously busy with estate business every day."

Dammit! Is she laughing at me? Does she know how much I avoid working with Papa? Perchance Selina has been telling tales.

"But your father owns many properties, does he not?" Marianne said. "Including Templeton Park, which I know is vast. My parents and I drove past it once, for 'tis not far from their house in Clifton."

Why in God's name is Mrs. Pembroke so interested in the Templeton estate? Was the mention of being a governess simply a red herring designed to distract me? Does she mean to marry again – and does she already have me in her sights?

Ah! I have no wish to be cruel to a sweet lady – but I must be forthright and open.

"I have little wish to marry," Edmund said.

Marianne's eyes opened wide and the plate on her lap, complete with cucumber sandwich, threatened to fall to the ground. "Indeed?"

"Yes! I cannot abide the way my family are trying to push me into matrimony. I prefer the single life."

Marianne took a sip of tea. "I have absolutely no idea why you have shared these thoughts with me, Mr. Templeton, but it may interest you to know that I feel exactly the same. Unfortunately, Lady Barrington and my parents think 'tis high time I was married again, but that is not my wish. I have been married once, and that was enough."

I did not expect that! What welcome news! Mrs. Pembroke is possibly the only woman in Bath society with whom I might flirt, confident in the knowledge that there is no ulterior motive to snare me. My joy is unbounded!

"Mrs. Pembroke, please address me henceforth as Edmund; I believe we are going to be firm friends."

"I would be delighted. And you may call me Marianne."

"I thank you!" Edmund picked up the first volume of *Pride and Prejudice*. "And now 'tis time I dipped into this novel that everyone is talking about. Let me see. Ah, yes. I will read you the opening: *It is a truth universally acknowledged, that a single man in possession of a good fortune, must be in want of a wife.*"

Both Edmund and Marianne burst into fits of laughter, causing Selina and Lady Barrington to break off from their conversation about tapestry wools.

"I must know what you have been talking about!" Lady Barrington said.

"Yes, what is the jest?" Selina said. "Do share,"

"We were laughing at something very silly," Marianne said.

"Yes," Edmund agreed. "We seem to share the same sense of humor, and possibly the same ambition and purpose in life, too."

"Superb news!" Lady Barrington said. "I felt sure you two were meant for each other and believe this year is going to be a very exciting one indeed."

CHAPTER THREE
Marianne

MARIANNE CLENCHED HER fists and saw that Edmund had been put to the blush.

Now my aunt imagines wedding bells ringing out for Edmund and myself this summer. And all was precipitated by a line from a novel!

"Marianne," Selina said, "Lady Barrington has told me how beautifully you play the pianoforte. Would you perchance delight us with a piece?"

God bless Selina for coming to our rescue! She has saved us from an awkward situation – for now, at least.

"I would be happy to play," Marianne said to Selina. "Shall we perform a pianoforte duet together?"

Selina smiled. "I am afraid you would not find me a fitting duet partner. Now, if my sister-in-law, Kitty, were here, 'twould be a different matter."

"But you sing so beautifully, Selina," Lady Barrington said. "Perhaps you might perform one of your airs while Marianne accompanies you?"

"That would be most agreeable." Marianne walked quickly across the room, causing the fabric of her new dress to rustle luxuriously.

'Twill be good to put as much space as I can between myself and the man my aunt already considers I will become engaged to. Oh, heavens!

How are we going to be released from this muddle?

Marianne sensed a slight movement behind her on the sofa and saw to her consternation that Edmund had buried his nose in *Pride and Prejudice* and was rocking with laughter.

How quickly he is able to switch his mood from acute embarrassment to comedy – just what sort of character is he? I fear he has a shallow nature which I cannot admire.

"I have a few airs here," Selina said, standing next to the pianoforte. "I brought them in readiness, for Lady Barrington's teas often lead to informal musicmaking."

Marianne perused the music. "Ah! 'Tis an impressive selection."

"Selina, my dear," Lady Barrington said, "have you brought that entrancing song by Schubert you sang last time – the one about the girl sitting at her spinning wheel?"

"*Gretchen am Spinnrade*? Why, yes, I have," Selina said. "Do you know this one, Marianne?"

"Yes; my mama sings this, and I have oft accompanied her."

Edmund seemed to be taking no notice of this exchange and was still snorting with laughter. "I say! I should have spent more time reading. I had no idea novels could be so humorous."

"How glad we are to hear this afternoon has been an opportunity to improve your education," Selina said with a mischievous grin.

"Yes, indeed," Lady Barrington said. "Reading is a much-underrated pastime among young men, Mr. Templeton. And you have Marianne to thank for your enjoyment, for she chose the book. She makes very wise choices – in literature, and generally, in life."

Lady Barrington fixed Edmund with a gaze that was so ludicrously arch and knowing, that Marianne completely forgot she was displeased and found 'twas all she could do to stop herself from bursting out laughing again.

"Come and sit beside me, Edmund – if I may call you that?" Lady Barrington patted the space on the sofa beside her. "You are about to experience a musical treat beyond compare."

Marianne sat down at the pianoforte and launched into the brief introduction of flowing semi-quavers, then Selina's gentle soprano was added to the texture. Nelson sat up and put his head on one side, as if paying attention to the melodious sounds.

And I would not have put Edmund down as a music lover, but he also seems very taken with our performance – and is staring at me in particular with rapt attention.

As the tragic love story unfolded, the rippling accompaniment portrayed not only Gretchen's spinning wheel, but also the turbulent nature of the fictional heroine's inner anguish.

Ah! And I, too, am troubled by swirls of disturbing imaginings from time to time.

"Bravo!" Edmund said at the end, leaping to his feet to applaud.

"Breathtaking, my dears!" Lady Barrington said. "What a heartfelt performance."

"I have no idea what the song was about," Edmund said, "because, to my shame, I know little German, but it was mighty prettily played and sung. Well done!"

"I am glad to see that you appreciate a fine musical performance," Lady Barrington said to Edmund. "We are going to the Pump Room tomorrow to hear the band – there are so many talented players. Would you care to join us?"

My aunt has not mentioned this outing before.

"As long as no one forces me to drink from the fountain in the Pump Room, I would be most happy to accompany you," Edmund said.

"And Selina, you are very welcome too," Lady Barrington said.

"I thank you and would be delighted."

"And afterwards," Lady Barrington continued, "we might visit the Roman Baths. Marianne, have you been there before? I remember your mama once sent you to Bath for a whole fortnight to stay with your dear school friend Charlotte in Laura

Place; you must have done much sightseeing then. 'Twas such a shame that I was away on holiday with my daughters during your visit, or you could have stayed here with me."

The familiar vice closed round Marianne's heart.

Nelson ran across the room and jumped into Lady Barrington's arms. "Ah, my dear little one, my Nelson. Now, what was I saying? Oh, yes. When was your last visit to Bath, Marianne?"

"'Twas in the autumn of 1815," Marianne managed.

"Yes! I remember, 'twas after . . . after . . ." Lady Barrington's voice trailed away and she looked a little confused, then flushed scarlet, evidently regretting starting the conversation.

"I, I did virtually no sightseeing during that trip for v-various reasons," Marianne said. "I look forward to visiting the Roman Baths tomorrow, Aunt. I am sure it will be very interesting. Thank you."

"And does Charlotte still live in Bath?" Lady Barrington said. "She is very welcome here if you wish to offer her hospitality; I would love to meet her."

"Her parents still live in Laura Place, but Charlotte was married last spring – to one of Richard's fellow officers – and is now residing in the Lake District very happily with her husband. We are frequent correspondents, and I am pleased to say they are expecting a joyful event very soon."

"How marvelous," Lady Barrington said, putting Nelson down on the floor. "What joy children bring to a marriage and to the world. The births of my four girls were the high points of my life. How I miss them all now they are married and moved away – but I cannot wait to become a grandmother. Sometimes I amuse myself by trying to work out whether 'twill be Augusta, Amabella, Aurelia, or Alicia who will be blessed with a child first."

Marianne bit her lip. She would not cry, for she had shed enough tears for her unborn child to last the rest of her life. But 'twas so hard when others seemed slow to remember.

"I love to visit the Baths," Selina said, "and imagine how the Romans used to walk around wearing their togas and taking a dip in the steamy waters."

She linked her arm through Marianne's, squeezing quite fiercely.

Selina knows something is amiss and is offering her support – what a true friend. And Edmund is regarding me most sympathetically too.

"We will have fun there tomorrow, mark my words," Selina said, "and perhaps even get Edmund to taste the waters again and see if they are any more agreeable."

"You know I will not be willing," Edmund said. "Why people think the spa water is good for you, I have no idea. And by the way, Selina, I will never forget my tenth birthday party, when you filled the water jug with spa water and slices of fruit, telling me it was a special cordial that Cook had prepared as a celebratory drink. It was beyond vile – and quite spoilt the fun."

"Nonsense!" Selina said. "You thoroughly enjoyed all the attention, with Mama feeding you sweetmeats to take away the horrid taste. Why, you have been dining out on this tale and getting sympathy from ladies ever since."

"Do you have a sister, Marianne?" Edmund asked. "And if so, is she quite as annoying as mine?"

"I am an only child. I oft wished for brothers and sisters – but 'twas not to be."

I love to watch the easy banter between Selina and Edmund; they seem the best of friends as well as brother and sister. Perhaps I will achieve my own easy friendship with Edmund now we have cleared up the misunderstanding of each of us thinking the other is seeking marriage.

Edmund picked Nelson up and held him in his arms facing the mirror on the wall. This allowed Marianne to admire both Edmund's broad back and his handsome visage at the same time.

Ah! Would it not be sublime to be held in Edmund's arms? Lucky Nelson!

"I feel we must bid you adieu, Nelson," Edmund said. "Farwell, little friend. We will meet again."

Now he caresses Nelson with strong, shapely hands. What is this? Have I become envious of a little pug? And am I capable of forgetting

Richard so quickly?

"How pleased I am, Edmund, that you and Nelson are friends," Lady Barrington said. "There has been no unfortunate recurrence of his aggressive behavior towards you. I do hope this means you would like to join us on one of our early morning walks on the Crescent Lawn."

"I would love to join you, Lady B, although the words 'early morning' in your invitation are slightly off-putting to a night owl such as myself." Edmund tickled the dog behind his ears. "And yet Nelson is so adorable that I may find I can make a special effort to rise earlier in the days to come."

"I will hold you to that," Lady Barrington said. "But I am still curious about the reversal in Nelson's behavior towards you. What has changed?"

"I have Marianne to thank, for when we were in Hunter's, she showed me how to make the little chap wait for his treat by raising the paw of friendship. Although quite why being firm with a dog should result in better behavior, I do not know."

"But everyone knows animals – and humans – are far better behaved when they have strict boundaries," Selina declared. "You would do well to remember that, brother."

"I am wounded by your insinuation that I have been brought up with too few boundaries and have been overindulged." Edmund affected a distraught look and drew one arm across his face in a dramatic fashion, which caused all the women in the room to laugh heartily.

And yet, could there be some truth in the notion?

"Marianne, my dear," Lady Barrington said, "I fear my knee is causing me a little discomfort today. Would you perhaps accompany the Templetons downstairs to take their leave, as this would spare me excessive exertion? I would be most grateful."

"Gladly, dear Aunt."

I did not know my aunt suffered from a bad knee; how forbearing she has been.

As the three young people walked to the door, Lady Barrington ran to Nelson. "My sweet one! Have you enjoyed the company?"

Ah! The knee has recovered. How bizarre!

Downstairs in the entrance hall, Selina gave a sharp intake of breath. "Silly me! I have left my music upstairs."

"I can ask one of the maids to collect it," Marianne said.

"No need." Selina was already making for the stairs. "I will go myself – for I cannot quite recollect whereabouts I left it, and it may take me some minutes to find."

I think we are being toyed with.

Edmund raised a sardonic eyebrow. "And now we are all alone, for a few minutes at least. But whether by accident or design, 'tis not possible to say."

"Whatever the reason, I am pleased we have the chance to converse," Marianne said, "for we both know we have to put a stop to this mistaken impression that we two are . . ."

A playful smile on his lips, Edmund moved forward until his handsome form was but an eighth of an inch from Marianne. "That we two are what?"

Can he not hear the beating of my heart? 'Tis almost as loud as the clock behind me marking the seconds – and 'tis going twice as fast.

"I meant what I said to your aunt," Edmund murmured. "We share a sense of humor and a common purpose."

"But she does not realize that the common purpose is that we will neither of us submit to matrimony."

"Nevertheless, we are bound together by these two things. You are not going back on your word, are you, Marianne? You do not want to marry, do you?"

"I never want to marry again!"

Although I find my resolve weakening with Edmund so close beside me. For it has been a long time since I have been alone with a young man, especially a man as devilishly handsome as Edmund, with soft lips begging to be kissed – ah! What sort of woman am I that I can forget my resolution this quickly?

"I do hope I am not interrupting anything," Selina said as she appeared in the hall.

"I see you found your music," Edmund said.

"Yes. It took quite some time. Lady Barrington helped me search the room; we had a good chat too."

"Was the music not on the pianoforte?" Marianne asked.

"Most of it was," Selina said. "One or two sheets had fallen to the floor and wafted into various corners of the room. No doubt Nelson had scattered them with his scampering."

This misapprehension that Edmund and I are a match is too ridiculous. Already, Selina and Lady Barrington are behaving differently – and inventing excuses to thrust us together.

Marianne bid her guests farewell and then, alone at last, leaned against the back of the door in the entrance hall.

I must have a private and uninterrupted conversation with Edmund as soon as possible – for we must work out a way to deal with this misunderstanding to the satisfaction of all.

But how was she to achieve time alone with him? The visit to the Pump Room would not provide any privacy. Instead, they would be stared at and gossiped about by the *ton*; their very presence together would reinforce the unfortunate assumption that they were a pair of love birds, soon to be married.

And that is the last thing in the world that I should ever want.

Is it not?

Edmund

"Sir! Wake up, sir."

"Voyle! Damn your eyes, man. 'Tis not even light yet. How dare you wake me!"

"Sir! 'Tis urgent."

Edmund sat upright in bed. "Papa! Is it Papa? Is he not well? I must get up."

"No, no. I apologize for alarming you unduly. There is an

emergency of a different sort – a note from a lady."

Edmund rubbed his bleary eyes. After leaving Lady Barrington's tea party yesterday, he had met with friends at his club, and one thing had led to another. Gambling, a late night party, an even later dinner – and then he was not quite sure he could remember what had happened after that.

Think, man, think! What did I do last night that might have caused a lady to send a note?

A vague vision of some frolicsome behavior appeared. Ah, yes! Edmund had been near Pulteney Bridge last night and one of his friends had dared him to jump into the river near the weir fully clothed.

"My God, but that was a dangerous notion," Edmund muttered.

"I beg your pardon, sir?" Voyle said.

"Nothing! I was just talking to myself. But Voyle, my clothes from last night – are they wet?"

"No sir. They are a little muddy, perhaps, but no, not wet. If you were asking if you went for a swim in the river near the weir – the answer is no."

"Thank the Lord!" Edmund lay back on his bed again.

"And if you are wondering how you got home, that was Carter's doing."

Ah! Now Edmund remembered. Carter had come across the group of young men as they had been discussing jumping into the river and had given them quite a roasting. He said 'twas high time they all grew up, started acting like respectable members of the *ton,* and stopped taking foolhardy risks and distressing their poor mamas.

"Yes, Carter brought you home, and I helped you to bed." Voyle's thin lips quivered – though whether with disapproval or amusement, 'twas impossible to guess.

"Yes, well, never mind all that now. Tell me again why you woke me so early."

"A note came a short time ago." Voyle held a folded piece of paper which was addressed to *Mr. Edmund Templeton* and marked both *Private* and *Urgent*.

"Who is it from?"

"I am not entirely sure, for I have not read it, but I believe it must be from a lady, because that is what Martha told me."

Voyle can pretend all he likes, but I have no doubt that the whole of the downstairs staff are familiar with the contents.

Edmund opened the note and read silently.

My dear Mr. Templeton,

We need to talk – urgently. Lady Barrington is indisposed this morning – apparently her knee is playing up again – therefore I will be walking Nelson on the Crescent Lawn alone, apart from a maid. I see this as a heaven-sent opportunity for us to converse and to resolve the delicate issue of the unfortunate tangle we are embroiled in.

Yours,
Mrs. Marianne Pembroke

'Twas an odd sort of note, when one thought about it. Marianne had addressed Edmund as Mr. Templeton – depressingly formal – and she did not explain what they needed to talk about, but merely made an allusion to a tangle.

"Who delivered this note?" Edmund asked.

"I believe 'twas Jane, one of Lady Barrington's maids. She delivered it to Martha very early this morning."

I see – the usual channel of communication between Number 4 and Number 1.

Edmund leapt from his bed and peered through the curtains; two shadowy figures stood on the lawn with a small dog sitting at their feet.

The sun is not even up – and yet she waits.

"Will you be going outside?" Voyle asked.

"I suppose I must."

"And what is this tangle that Mrs. Pembroke speaks of?"

"I do not believe I have mentioned a tangle."

The dishonest devil! This proves he has read the note.

"I simply meant, sir, that there must be some sort of situation if an urgent note has been sent. And I have taken the liberty of preparing these clothes."

"It does not matter what I wear," Edmund said, flinging on last night's apparel, which still lay scattered about the floor. "'Tis not a fashion parade."

"As you wish, but if you would just allow me to help you."

"Goddammit, Voyle! I am a grown man and can throw on breeches and a shirt without help."

Five minutes later, Edmund was outside on the lawn, striding towards Marianne, having grabbed the first cloak from the hall he could find on the way out.

She looked divinely pretty, as always, and was wearing a black cloak with the hood up against the chill wind, with the hint of a gray gown peeping out. Nelson was mighty pleased to see him and allowed Edmund to ruffle his coat and tickle him behind his ears.

"Jane," Marianne said, "would you mind taking Nelson for a little walk over there? Thank you. I have something particular I need to talk to Mr. Templeton about."

Jane nodded and walked the pug a few yards away.

The maid should stand at a further distance. I know she can still hear us and will enjoy reporting back to the eager pack of servants in both our households. Oh, how I long for privacy and freedom for just one day of my life.

"We do not have long," Marianne said, "for my aunt serves an early breakfast."

"Let us walk a little," Edmund suggested. As they moved well out of Jane's earshot, the wind tugged at Marianne's hood until it was half down, pulling her red curls about her face.

How I long to caress those beautiful ringlets, enfold her within my arms . . . and more – so much more.

"Edmund! I do not believe you are taking this seriously. We are in a fix – and you know it."

"Heartfelt apologies. And you are right; we cannot allow public opinion to push us towards the one thing that neither of us are interested in – the holy estate of matrimony."

"So what should we do?" Marianne said. "For if I tell my aunt she is mistaken about our romance, she will only move on to the next stage of her plan to marry me off."

"And what does Lady B have up her sleeve?"

"She will scour the entire city and present me to as many young gentlemen as she can, pushing me towards them mercilessly. I cannot express how much this fills me with horror – and I absolutely refuse to contemplate being sold off in this hideous manner."

Her resolution not to marry again is very strong – and there is some mystery about her earlier stay in Bath, too. She seemed quite overcome with emotion yesterday when her aunt referred to her visit to her old school friend. There is much I do not know about Marianne. And much I would like to discover.

"I have deep sympathy for your plight," Edmund said. "I know that one day I must marry, but I am fully determined not to be shackled too soon by those who think they know better. I am but five and twenty and have years of the single life ahead of me to enjoy."

"'Tis different for me," Marianne said. "I have been married – and will never marry again."

How her eyes flash when she is roused! And now I think I know why she is determined not to marry again. She must have been encouraged into matrimony the first time around and found it not to her liking.

Edmund felt a sudden pang.

I pray to God no one was unkind to her. I could not bear that.

He wanted to sweep Marianne up in his cloak – and never let her go.

She is right not to marry again if she has been hurt in the past. Unless she were to marry someone who could love and protect her. Someone like me.

Edmund shook his head. What in God's name was he thinking?

I will not give up my single life for any woman. Not for many years, at any rate. I will hold out against the evils of marriage for as long as possible – perhaps well into my forties?

Edmund did a quick calculation – if he and Marianne married when he was in his forties, there would be but a slim chance of children – little, sweet red-headed children with blue Templeton eyes. Would that not be a shame?

No sooner did the thought arrive, than it was crushed. Edmund would stick to his plan and marry for duty in later life – much, much later life.

Besides, what is the point of setting my heart on perhaps the only single woman in Bath who would never accept me? Why make life difficult?

"Edmund! You must concentrate! What are we to do?" Marianne demanded.

Edmund walked her further away from Jane again, for the maid seemed intent on diminishing the distance between them.

"I know not," he said, "but we need to think of something, for in a few hours, you and I are to be paraded in the Pump Room, with everyone there assuming we are courting."

They walked on in silence for a few moments, then Edmund said, "What if we do nothing?"

"Do nothing? How is that a solution? You might be used to doing nothing, Mr. Templeton; however, I am a person of resolve."

Ah! Her use of 'Mr. Templeton' cuts me to the quick; she is angry with me.

"We should have a plan," Marianne continued. "We must fight."

"Hear me out. What if doing nothing *is* the plan? You have said you do not want to be endlessly paraded to potential suitors. I feel the same. I no more want to be scrutinized at every social event I go to than I want to fly to the moon. I have had years of this – of fortune hunters trying to ingratiate themselves with me."

"I have never thought of it from your perspective. It must be hard, not knowing whom to trust."

"It is," Edmund said, "and so I trust no one – apart from my band of friends. And yes, we end up doing some rather juvenile things, and I busy myself with cards and gambling and going to private gatherings – because if I parade round the fashionable streets of Bath in daylight, mince around the Pump Room, and attend concerts and balls, then I am prey to all sorts of ambitious people. I am never valued for what I am – only for what I can do for people, most often in monetary terms."

"Edmund!" Marianne said in the softest voice imaginable. Ye gods! She even had moist eyes. "I am so sorry for this."

Edmund scuffed his heels. "I do not want you to feel sorry for me. But I will tell you something to make you laugh. I was referring to my juvenile behavior with my friends – well, last night, instead of going to bed at a sensible time like normal people, we got it into our minds that the most hilarious thing we could do would be to go down to the river near the weir. We were in our cups, which I believe is some excuse for the poor judgement, but I was dared to jump into the water there."

Marianne took a sharp intake of breath. "But I have seen the weir when I have been near Pulteney Bridge. 'Tis a very dangerous spot. My aunt told me that an escaped convict fell into the river there last summer and was drowned."

"Ah yes, Lord Steyne – though his body was never found."

"Nevertheless, you should not have been anywhere near such a perilous place in the dead of night – and after drinking."

"That is more or less what Carter said when he came across us – although he expressed the sentiment in somewhat more colorful language. He was particularly angry with me and said I was the most irresponsible brat he had ever had the misfortune to come across and that I should think of the effect my death would have on my devoted mama."

"The loss of a child is one of the greatest pains a woman can suffer," Marianne whispered. "Or so I have heard."

"Anyhow, now you know what sort of a scatter-witted nincompoop I really am, no doubt you will not want to be friends with me. And to think – you would never have known about my poor behavior if I had not confessed it to you."

"I might have guessed that you had been on some sort of adventure from your clothes."

"My clothes? How?"

"Take a look at yourself!"

Edmund cast his eyes down; his breeches were covered in mud and had strands of river weed on the shins.

"In my defense, I had to throw on last night's clothes, such was my hurry to obey your summons to the lawn."

"And I do believe you are wearing a lady's cloak," Marianne said. "Does it belong to someone you met last night?"

"What? Merciful heavens!"

Edmund gazed at the heavy – and familiar – velvet cloak in wonder. "I must have picked up Mama's favorite cloak from the hall in my haste. She wears this when she visits the theatre. She will kill me if she finds out I have borrowed it!"

I love to see Marianne laughing. Has she had enough joy in her life of late, I wonder?

"So," Marianne said, "you think we should do nothing and let everyone think we are interested in each other – for then they will stop pushing us towards others."

"Yes! Obviously this will only work in the short term, for after a while they will be nagging us to start planning our wedding celebrations."

"And at that point, we can think of another plan. Perhaps we will find we have irreconcilable differences – or maybe I shall discover that you have a mistress with five children? Or several mistresses?"

Edmund gave a great bellow of laughter. "I do assure you there is nothing like that in my life. Nor am I a libertine – in case you were wondering."

"I, I was not wondering anything of the sort."

How enchanting she looks when she blushes.

"Oh, Edmund, pray do not look at me like that. You are completely impossible!" Marianne gave Edmund a little push on his shoulder.

"And now I see you are intent on attacking me. And so the irreconcilable differences begin."

"We are agreed, then. We will do nothing to quash the rumors, but on the contrary, we will take pleasure in playing up to them."

"Yes!" Edmund said. "But without actually saying that we are intended for one another."

"We may even have to indulge in slightly flirtatious behavior when we are in public – strictly for the sake of appearances."

"Should I take you in my arms right now and kiss you, for the benefit of anyone watching?"

"You will do nothing of the sort," Marianne said. "That would go far beyond a mere flirtation. Besides, neither of us would want that – added to which, there is no one around at this hour. Apart from Jane. We have been very careful to keep out of her earshot, but I think she would notice if we embraced, do you not?"

"Perchance she could add it to her report?"

And you may not want to kiss me, dearest Marianne, but how I long to press my lips against yours.

"'Tis time I went back to the house," Marianne said.

"Yes, and I must go home and change into whatever Voyle has decided I should wear to the Pump Room today."

"Hopefully 'tis something more presentable than those breeches."

"Indeed!" Edmund said. "And look; the sun is nearly up at last. These winter days are so short."

They both looked towards the horizon to see a solitary sunbeam trying to make its presence felt. Edmund turned back to face the Crescent. What was that glinting at an upstairs window of Number 4? Something was catching the light.

"Would you believe it?" Marianne said. "My aunt has opened

her chamber window and is looking at us through a telescope."

"I admire Lady B's spirit," Edmund said. "Let us wave to her!"

They did – and she waved back.

"You do know," Edmund said, "that if we send each other messages, they will probably be read by all the servants – and the contents passed on to my mama and Lady B?"

"I had suspected that might be the case, which was why my note to you this morning was both formal, and lacking in specific information."

"How very clever," Edmund said. "And it gives me an idea – a way we can use the situation to our advantage."

"How so?"

"Think how useful a note might be if we wished people to know something – without actually telling them. We could merely write a note with the information, and the servants would pass on the information for us."

"Why yes, I see what you mean," Marianne said. "But I fear all would rapidly become too complicated. And it does seem a trifle deceitful."

"I suppose you are right," Edmund said. "But we need a private and secure method of communication between us – perhaps even a place we can meet up without detection."

"How would that be possible?"

"Leave it with me. I will talk to my sister and ask for her help. By the way – do you have a head for heights?"

Marianne

"GOOD MORNING, MARIANNE!" Lady Barrington swept into the entrance hall as Marianne was unfastening her cloak and handing it to Jane.

Nelson ran to his mistress to be petted.

"I need not ask if you had a good walk on the lawn," Lady Barrington continued, "for I can see from your pink cheeks and general demeanor that you have had a pleasant time. Ah, if Nelson could but talk and tell me all."

There is not the slightest hint of embarrassment from my aunt that she was caught out watching us. Instead, I must endure this absurd charade, complete with knowing glances. How Edmund will laugh when I relay this to him.

"Pray join me for breakfast," Lady Barrington said. "The postman has been, and we have letters. You have two – one from your mama and another from a mysterious sender whose handwriting I do not recognize. I will be interested to hear about the contents of both."

Lady Barrington and Marianne walked into the parlor.

"I see you also have letters," Marianne said.

"Oh, yes. One from Augusta and one from Amabella. Letters from Aurelia and Alicia arrived yesterday. 'Tis my girls' habit to write to me frequently and tell me everything in their lives. Truth be told, I insist on it. No detail is too small to interest me."

The two ladies read in silence while they sipped their coffee. Suddenly, Lady Barrington trembled and clutched at her throat. "I cannot believe it! Can you believe it, Marianne?"

"Believe what? You have not yet told me what has happened. My dear aunt – are you unwell?"

"Here! Look at the second sheet. You must read for yourself the joyful news, for I find I cannot control my emotions." Lady Barrington produced a large, snowy white lace handkerchief from about her person and applied it vigorously to her eyes while Marianne read Augusta's words:

I know you will be enraptured to hear my news – I am to be a mother before the year is out! The doctor says I am in astounding health.

"I am so pleased that my dear cousin Augusta and her husband are to be so blessed," Marianne said. "What wonderful news!"

"'Tis too, too thrilling!" Lady Barrington blew her nose noisily. "Such is my ecstasy that I cannot read any more from Augusta at present, but will see what Amabella has to say in her letter."

"And I will read my letter from Mama," Marianne said, pressing her fingers to her temples with a sigh. She genuinely felt joy at her cousin's good fortune – and yet hearing of burgeoning new life, especially within the family, was re-kindling the grief for her own lost child once more.

My dear Marianne,

We miss you so very much, and Papa and I send you, and my dear sister, all our love and affection. How are you enjoying your stay in Bath? Have you been out and about in the city yet?

Do not forget that this is the year you can discard your widow's weeds and begin looking in earnest for a new life. I know you said you would be happy to be a governess, but are you sure this would be the best way for you to achieve lasting happiness?

"Are they well?" Lady Barrington said.

"They send you their warmest wishes – but have not mentioned their own health yet. They ask how I like Bath."

But Lady Barrington was not listening – she was clutching at her throat again. Nelson gave a short, sharp series of yaps and clawed at his mistress's skirt.

"Shall I ring for help? You are not yourself, Aunt. Pray tell me what is distressing you."

"I am not distressed! I am overjoyed – again! Listen – this is from Amabella."

My dear mama, I am to be blessed before the year is out.

"Good heavens!" Marianne said. "Both of them?"

Her dearest wish to become a grandmother will be coming true – twice in the same year.

"I must go to them at once," Lady Barrington said. "They must be desperate for my help. Luckily, they live very near each other, and so I could easily stay with them alternately until the babies are safely delivered – and maybe for some years afterwards. I must write back directly."

"Are you sure? Would it not be better to see how everything progresses and maybe visit later?"

"Oh, I do not know! I feel in such a tizzy – my world has been turned upside down, and I cannot think what is for the best. But perhaps you are right, Marianne, and it would be prudent to stay here a while and wait. When I think back to before my own dear children were born, why, 'twas a special time for your uncle and I – the lull before the storm. And besides, I have you to think of. 'Tis my duty to help you make a fine match without delay – for then I will be able to visit my daughters with a clear conscience, knowing I have enriched your life."

Nelson pawed at Lady Barrington's skirt.

"What is it, my dearest? A little piece of toastie for my special one? Look, Marianne! See how excited Nelson is to learn I am to be a grandmother." A fleeting shadow passed across her face. "Oh, but how my dear husband would have loved this."

"'Tis a shame he was taken from you before this joyous news."

"Indeed, it is; but I have no right to complain, for I had many, many years with your dear uncle, whereas you have suffered under such sad circumstances."

If only my Richard had lived. If only our sweet babe had been born.

Marianne then tortured herself with a vision of her lost child learning to walk as she held one tiny hand with Richard holding the other. For by now, the infant would have been one year old.

And in time, we might have been blessed again . . .

"Ah, dear Marianne, how I feel for your plight." Lady Barrington briefly patted Marianne's hand, before saying briskly, "Now, chin up! My word! We will soon have to get ready to go to the Pump Room – and I am sorry to say that you will have to wear your blue dress."

Marianne buried her grief once more and gabbled a somewhat brittle reply. "Why are you sorry? I love the dress and am inordinately grateful to you for purchasing it. I felt like a princess yesterday swishing about the withdrawing room. 'Tis a long time since I have worn such a beautiful blue, and I have rarely possessed a garment of such quality and style."

"I meant that 'tis your only new dress at the moment, as we are still waiting for Madame Dubonnet and her seamstresses to send all the others," Lady Barrington said. "She assures me that they are working as fast as they can, but they cannot achieve miracles; therefore you will have to make do with wearing the very same dress that Edmund saw you in yesterday."

"Heavens, Aunt, I am not so shallow that I must wear a new dress every day."

"Nevertheless, 'twould be far better if you had something new for this most important occasion at the Pump Room. But you will be able to give your new ermine tippet its first outing, as the weather is chilly."

I have to admit I am looking forward to wearing the wondrously soft tippet.

"Now, Marianne, who is your second letter from?"

"'Tis from my old school friend, Charlotte. She writes to me regularly."

How comforting her presence was when I stayed in her parents' house in Laura Place after Richard died – and her brother, too, showed me much kindness.

When Marianne opened the letter and began perusing the contents, Lady Barrington held her quizzing glass to her eye and tried to read over her niece's shoulder.

"Do you not wish to finish Amabella and Augusta's letters?" Marianne said.

"Ah, yes! I will enjoy hearing where they have been, with whom they have socialized, and what they have eaten – the minutiae of their lives. I positively thrive on knowledge."

The two ladies read in silence again.

My dear Marianne, the letter from Charlotte said, *I trust this finds you well. I have been thinking of you lately, and of dear Richard too.*

. . . and I have a very special question to ask, which I long for you to accept with all my heart. When our baby is born in the spring, would you do us the very great honor of being their godmother? I can think of no sweeter or kinder person to play this role in our child's life than you, dearest friend. If this is in any way the wrong thing to ask – too soon, or not what you desire – then I will of course understand, but we both sincerely hope you will accept and also that ere long you will be able to come and visit with us. The Lake District is a most beautiful place, and I know you would enjoy walking here, especially when the weather is better. Please know that you are welcome in our house at any time.

Marianne's heart fluttered with joy. She was to be a godmother! She would be a part of Charlotte's family forever. And perhaps she would find a way to go to the Lake District – for her stay in Bath would come to a natural end once Lady Barrington realized she had no serious intention of marrying anyone.

I can return to my parents for a while, but then I am determined to strike out and earn my own living. Would it not be convenient if Charlotte knew a family near her in the Lakes who were looking for a governess? Would that not make for a pleasant life?

"Augusta has had plenty of trips to the theatre recently," Lady Barrington remarked.

"How lovely," Marianne answered automatically, her head far away.

"And Amabella has ordered a new red silk evening gown; 'tis apparently such a clever design, it will fit her for many months to come, possibly till the very last weeks."

"Fascinating," Marianne murmured.

Lady Barrington folded both her letters and put them flat on the table. "That is all my dear ones' news for now. I will write to them this evening; they will be thrilled to hear from me." Then she stood behind Marianne. "I see your friend is inviting you to the Lake District. What a shame, for that would have been an interesting trip, but you will be far too busy here with Edmund, planning and so forth."

"Planning what?" Marianne said innocently.

"Marianne! I know exactly what is blossoming between the pair of you. I know the truth."

You certainly do not! At least I hope that is the case.

"I will finish reading my letter on another occasion," Marianne said, "for I need to get ready for our trip to the Pump Room."

"Of course, my dear. Tis important to look your absolute best for Edmund – and for the *ton*, who will be out in force once the word gets round."

A FEW MINUTES later, in the privacy of her chamber, Marianne found an opportunity to finish Charlotte's letter.

> *. . . now you are in Bath again, I do hope that you will find time to visit my parents in Laura Place. As it happens, my brother Frederick is on leave from his regiment and is staying with them for a time – he is very fond of you and often asks after your health.*
>
> *Yours affectionately,*
> *Charlotte*

CHAPTER FOUR

Edmund

"WHAT! THE WHOLE Templeton clan? Mama, have you taken leave of your senses?"

"Yes, they will all be here; I have arranged it," Lady Templeton said to Edmund. "And I do not think it is particularly helpful for you to question my sanity."

Edmund and his mother were standing outside the Pump Room, waiting for the rest of the family to arrive.

"Your father has an appointment in the city – I do hope he will not be late," Lady Templeton said. "Ah! Here are Selina and George now – and Henry, Kitty and little Isabella. How thoughtful you all are to come to support Edmund."

Edmund scowled at his nearest and dearest. "Once Papa arrives, we can go in, I suppose? And I can be the center of extremely unwelcome attention."

"Try to sound more cheerful," Lady Templeton said. "You must surely be looking forward to seeing Mrs. Pembroke?"

"I am, Mama," Edmund replied. "But I fail to see why every person in Bath I am related to needs to accompany me."

"Family unity is important at significant times," Lady Templeton said. "And 'tis not every single person you are related to, is it?"

"You mean Carter?" Edmund said. "How I wish he were

here, for he has a sensible word to say on every occasion."

"Dear Carter," Kitty said. "We so enjoy having him reside with us."

"I did try to persuade him to come," Lady Templeton said, "but he thought his presence would prove a distraction."

"Even if Carter had accepted your invitation," Henry said, "he would have had to cancel, for he travelled to Bristol very early this morning. There was a troublesome situation there that required his presence – he would give no further details."

"His government work takes precedence over everything else," Lady Templeton said.

"But Henry," Edmund said, "it must be damned awkward sometimes when you require his services as your manservant, only to find that he is gallivanting round the country on other urgent business. I cannot imagine how I would manage without Voyle; who would look after my wardrobe and tidy my room? Who would dress me and arrange my hair? Admittedly I find him aggravating at times and oft wish he would leave me be, but dammit, I rely on the man's assistance every day."

Henry smiled. "I am more self-sufficient since my time in the army and can look after myself."

"Not everyone is as spoilt as you are, Edmund," Selina said.

Why must she always ram the point home so forcefully? Edmund opened his mouth to protest then snapped it shut again, for there was perchance a grain of truth in what his sister had said – and he was only just beginning to realize it.

I feel like an entitled cod's head. And I expect this is what Marianne thinks of me – not that I care one single jot.

"Would you like to say hello to Isabella, Edmund?" Kitty asked.

Bless Kitty for trying to distract everyone from my shortcomings – she is a kind and thoughtful sister-in-law.

Edmund tickled the baby under her chin, making her squeal with laughter.

"Are you not a bonny girl?" he said to Isabella. "Your parents are very lucky."

"Indeed, they are," Lady Templeton said, "but remember, Edmund, a child is a blessing that can be visited upon other family members too."

I know I can have children if I marry, Mama – thank you for reminding me.

Then, was it Edmund's imagination, or did Selina and George exchange wistful glances?

I do believe my sister Selina and her husband George are longing for offspring. I wish them well and hope they achieve their heart's desire ere long, for they will both of them be fine parents.

"There you are!" Lady Templeton said to her husband as he rushed towards them, a little out of breath.

"I offer humble apologies, my dear. I was held up in my business meeting." Lord Templeton shot a meaningful look at Edmund. "'Tis almost as if I need more help – there is so much to do. And on top of everything else, Mr. Grant, my steward at Templeton Park, is ill."

But Edmund had stopped listening.

Are my family going to take it in turns this morning to point out my shortcomings? Of course they are – for this is their daily sport.

"We are due to meet Lady Barrington and Mrs. Pembroke inside," Lady Templeton said. "Come along, now!"

The Templetons processed into the bustling, noisy Pump Room. But where was Marianne? Could she be behind one of the Corinthian columns? Edmund's eyes flickered over the crowds, searching for her flame-colored hair, while Lady Templeton said something quite indistinguishable.

"What was that, my dear?" Lord Templeton shouted. "The band is very loud."

"I said, if we promenade around the room, we are sure to come across them soon."

Then Edmund's heart lurched. Marianne was standing right in front of him, her sweet visage framed with tumbling curls, a triple string of milky pearls adorning her delicate neck, and her eyes glittering more prettily than the crystal chandelier high above.

She is even more alluring than I had remembered.

Introductions were made, and then Marianne, Selina, and Kitty formed a little group with baby Isabella.

"What a poppet!" Marianne said.

"Would you like to hold her?" Kitty asked.

"I am not much practiced at holding infants; perhaps I had better not," Marianne replied.

"As you wish," Kitty said, "but look; she is reaching out to you."

Isabella's plump starfish hands extended towards Marianne; she relented and took the tiny girl into her embrace.

"You are a natural," Lady Templeton said.

How delicately Marianne holds little Isabella, as if she were a fragile and rare piece of porcelain.

Then Isabella started pulling one of the pretty ringlets framing Marianne's face.

"Careful, Isabella!" Kitty said. "Do not spoil Mrs. Pembroke's arrangement."

Then, unaccountably, the three young women all started talking about hairstyles – how their maids helped them perfect their ringlets, what their favorite hairpins were, and so forth. After a while, they moved onto prison reform – always a favorite subject of Selina's.

Meanwhile, Henry and George conversed about the law and medicine – their respective professions.

And Mama and Papa are discussing estate business with Lady Barrington – something about a house in the Crescent.

Which conversation was Edmund meant to gravitate towards? Or, as usual, was he there merely for appearances' sake, so that people could point to him and boast that they had seen the heir to the Templeton estate?

And now Selina was explaining to Marianne how she had given up sugar for a while last year to further the cause of abolition – inspired by the Anti-Saccharites.

"Lord, Selina!" Edmund said. "Next you will be boring Marianne about your educational ideas; you are a true expert now you have been working with the local children."

Marianne seemed puzzled, Selina looked affronted, and Kitty showed signs of embarrassment. Only Isabella carried on gurgling and cooing as if no crime had been committed.

Dammit! What an oaf I am! That came out all wrong.

"Education is an important subject," Selina said. "I have to do something to try and make a difference. Just because *you* have no purpose in your life, Edmund, does not mean that others do not. 'Tis time you resolved to stop being such a gadabout."

"Selina!" Lady Templeton hissed. "For goodness' sake! We are in public; this is no time for your teasing."

Edmund felt a pang of guilt, for there was a grain of truth in what Selina had said. What did he ever do to try and improve things for anyone?

"Edmund," Lord Templeton said, "why do you not take Mrs. Pembroke over to the fountain? Perhaps she would care to taste the waters?"

"I would like that," Marianne said, "for their fame is widespread."

Edmund needed no further encouragement but swept Marianne away to the other side of the room. As they walked, he was conscious of the many eyes upon them.

"I am not at all sure," he growled, "that 'twas a good idea to appear together in the Pump Room, for we are being relentlessly scrutinized."

"I agree," Marianne said. "Now I know what 'tis like to be an animal in a zoo."

Edmund secured a glass of water for Marianne from the fountain, and they stood at the window overlooking the King's Bath.

"How extraordinary!" Marianne said as they looked down to see clothed figures below bobbing up and down in the steamy water. "I know you like swimming in the river, Edmund – but have you ever been in the baths here?"

"I have once or twice, but I find it far too hot – and 'tis impossible to swim freely with so many bodies around you."

But how I would love to be in the waters standing close to you, Marianne – or, better still, swim with you in the river.

Marianne took a sip from her glass and then made a grimace.

"Ah, yes!" Edmund chuckled. "'Tis an acquired taste. I believe I did warn you when talking of my tenth birthday party yesterday. Please feel under no obligation to finish the glass."

Marianne lowered her voice. "Have you found a way we can communicate in writing without our notes being intercepted by Jane and Martha yet?"

"I have not, for whichever way I approach the problem, I see the maids will outwit us."

"And you had another scheme – you asked if I had a head for heights?"

"Pray forget that," Edmund said. "I ran my idea past Selina, and she said I was a numbskull to think of doing anything so unwise."

"What had you intended?"

"You will find this hard to believe, but I had thought it might be a good idea to leave Number 1 through a servant's attic window, then walk behind the parapet to Number 4 where I would meet you on the roof."

"Whatever put that notion into your head?" Marianne asked.

"Selina herself – for she has oft had rooftop adventures. But she has never travelled between houses as I had planned to do – she always thought it would be far too dangerous. Nor did she think it at all sensible for you to climb onto the roof of Number 4."

"I am relieved to hear it, for I admit I am nervous in high places."

"Luckily, Selina has a much more practical solution – and one that I am sure will meet with your full approval," Edmund said. "There will be frequent invitations for you to visit her home –

and I will also attend, but discreetly, via the back door. My sister will chaperone us at all times, and she will ensure our meetings are not disturbed by family members or servants, for we need time to formulate a plan to defeat our enemies."

"Our enemies?"

"In a manner of speaking – I am referring to those who would marry us off."

"This sounds a reasonable plan," Marianne said, "but what if her servants see you entering the house?"

"Perhaps I should arrive in disguise?"

"Be serious!"

"There are a few details to iron out," Edmund said, "but 'tis worth a try."

Marianne giggled. "This sounds a mighty complicated way for us to have private discussions about the progress of our plan *not* to be married to each other."

"Indeed! Ah! What is that I see?"

There were advantages to being tall when in the Pump Room; Edmund was able to look across the crowds to see his family and Lady Barrington making their way over.

"Wait – 'tis not all of them. Henry, Kitty, and little Isabella are leaving. I do not blame them – 'tis very noisy for a babe in here. But here come all the others."

"And what did you think of the waters, Mrs. Pembroke?" Lady Templeton asked.

"The taste is both highly unusual and very interesting." Marianne put her nearly full glass down. "But I find I am not particularly thirsty this morning."

"I think we should take a turn around the baths themselves now," Lady Barrington suggested.

"I am not quite sure I wish to bathe," Marianne said.

"Oh no, my dear," Lady Barrington said. "That was not my intention. We shall walk around the edge of the baths. You can see so much more of the Roman heritage from the lower level. Come – follow me, everyone."

"I think George and I might return home at this point," Selina said. "But Marianne, I hope you will call on me soon – we have much to talk about."

"How about tomorrow?" Marianne said. "In the morning?"

"Excellent." Selina clapped her hands and winked at Edmund. *Excellent, indeed! Our first meeting has been planned.*

"And I must return to my business in the city," Lord Templeton said, "but this has been a most pleasant interlude."

Lady Barrington, Lady Templeton, Edmund and Marianne then went down the stairs to start their tour.

"There is a strange smell coming from the water," Marianne said.

"Yes," Edmund said. "It reminds one of eggs boiling on the stove."

Marianne raised an eyebrow. "Have you spent much time in the kitchen?"

"Edmund was an unusual child," Lady Templeton said. "If he disappeared, I always knew where to find him – down in the kitchen with Cook. She showed him how to make all sorts of dishes."

I had forgotten that. I used to love all the weighing and mixing that goes on below stairs – and tasting the results.

"There is another smell too," Marianne said. "'Tis very sweet."

"Yes," Lady Barrington said. "You see the little floating dishes? They contain fragrant oils and pomanders."

"Doubtless to mask the smell of boiling eggs," Edmund said.

They walked carefully around the paths at the side of the baths, past the colonnades of pillars, and across the uneven flagstones.

"'Tis very close down here," Lady Templeton said.

"My word, yes," Lady Barrington agreed. "'Tis almost stifling. Is it time to go back?"

As they reached the Pump Room again, Marianne commented, "What a beautiful piece of Mozart."

"Do you like music, Mrs. Pembroke?" Lady Templeton asked.

"Oh, yes! I adore it."

"Edmund and I are due to attend a concert tomorrow night in the city." Lady Templeton beamed at her son.

"We are?" Edmund said.

"What a coincidence!" Lady Barrington cried. "Marianne and I are attending that concert as well."

Marianne looked startled to hear this.

"Lady Templeton," Lady Barrington said, "if you would be so kind as to remind me where this concert is?"

Then Marianne looked very much as if she wanted to giggle.

Oh, how captivating she is!

"'Tis in the Guildhall," Lady Templeton said.

"Ah, yes! And doubtless there are many more concerts in the city," Lady Barrington said.

"There are – and balls, too," Lady Templeton added.

Lady Barrington smiled. "And I have heard there is to be a very special guest visiting the city soon. What a thrill 'twould be to see him! Of course, the rumor might not be true."

"We can but hope," Lady Templeton said. "But even if he does not appear, there are countless social occasions where young men and women can mingle – and get to know one another."

"Shall we leave all the planning of our romance to them?" Edmund whispered in Marianne's ear. "For it seems that neither of us is to have a say."

"Absolutely! I consider it best to submit," Marianne whispered back. "'Tis less trouble in the long run."

"As long as we stick to our agreement and remember that all this is to save us from being pushed towards others."

What fun this is all proving to be! Marianne is such a good sport that I almost regret not wanting to marry her.

Marianne

EARLY THE NEXT day, there was a further delivery from Madame Dubonnet's emporium.

"How wonderful!" Lady Barrington cried. "She is getting through the list at great speed. Look, Marianne! Let us unpack them right here in the parlor."

Marianne looked in wonder at the gorgeous gowns. "Are these really all for me?"

I cannot think what I have done to deserve such generosity.

"They are indeed all for you," Lady Barrington said. "Now, which would you care to wear today? We shall inspect each in turn. How splendid the amber silk looks fashioned into evening wear – the frills! The detailing! You will look simply stunning at the next ball. And here is a pretty primrose gown that will be ideal for this morning, and this more decorated crimson frock will suit for the concert tonight. Perfect! I am glad you agree with me."

I am beginning to feel like a favorite doll that Lady Barrington takes pleasure in dressing. Still, they are all beautiful clothes, and 'twould be churlish of me to be ungrateful.

"I believe you are visiting Selina soon?" Lady Barrington said.

"Yes – that is, unless there is anything else you would like me to do?"

"No, no; you should see her, for you cannot meet up with Edmund every minute of the day. Would you mind taking Nelson with you? He could do with another walk, even if 'tis only next door – and he does enjoy social occasions."

Nelson evidently heard the word *walk* and began charging at full tilt around the room.

"How excited he is!" Lady Barrington said. "He is very fond of visiting Selina, as her cook always saves savory tidbits for him."

I am excited to go to Selina's house too – but not for the reason that my aunt thinks. Unless Edmund might be considered a "tidbit?" Oh, my!

"You must hasten upstairs to change into the primrose

gown," Lady Barrington said. "And when you leave, take Jane with you, for you need a chaperone in the street."

"Aunt! What do you think is going to happen to me, merely stepping next door?"

"You cannot be too careful – I insist you are accompanied by Jane."

THE AIR WAS chilly and the sun weak when Marianne and Jane finally left the house.

"Come along Nelson," Marianne said. "'Tis this way."

But Nelson was having none of it and pulled Marianne off the pavement and over the cobbles to the railings, while Jane hurried after them.

"Oh, all right, little one," Marianne said. "A few minutes will not hurt. Now, what is it you have found?"

The pug sniffed a dry leaf, then pinned it to the ground with his paw to stop it fluttering in the wind.

"'Tis not a mouse, or anything interesting, Nelson. 'Tis merely a leaf. Come with us now, back onto the pavement. We cannot have you run over by a carriage, can we?"

Marianne turned back to the Crescent and saw a military man walking briskly at the far end, outside Number 30. The breath was all but knocked from her and she feared she would faint. 'Twas Richard, surely – in his scarlet jacket?

I must be hallucinating! For he lies cold in his grave.

The figure drew nearer. "Mrs. Pembroke!" a deep voice said. "I am so glad to see you; Charlotte has told me you are in Bath."

"Why, Captain Wyndham! How delightful to see you."

'Tis not my dear Richard – but Charlotte's brother, Frederick, enjoying a stroll around the city.

"How are your parents?" Marianne said.

"Very well, thank you. And yours? And Lady Barrington?"

"All well. And I wanted to thank you," Marianne said.

"Thank me? Whatever for?"

"For your very great kindness. I know I was a very wretched

houseguest when I stayed with your family after Richard died – but you, Charlotte, and your parents were so kind at a most difficult period in my life, and I have never thanked you properly."

"There is no need," Captain Wyndham said in a gruff voice. "We were all pleased to help, and 'tis heartwarming to see you so restored."

Nelson started pulling fiercely at his leash, perhaps desperate to go into Selina's house for the promised tidbits.

"Ah!" Captain Wyndham said. "I see this little chap is eager to move on."

"Nelson is a determined creature."

"Nelson, eh? 'Tis an unusual name for a dog, I must say."

"As an army man, you would perhaps have preferred to hear that he was called Wellington?" Marianne teased.

"Very possibly," Captain Wyndham said with a smile, "but Nelson was a great hero too. Does Lady Barrington have seafaring connections?"

"Yes. Her dear departed husband had two brothers who were in the Royal Navy – and one of them served at the Battle of Trafalgar with Nelson."

"How fascinating!" Captain Wyndham bent down to pat Nelson. "Your namesake was a distinguished Englishman – never forget that. And now, Mrs. Pembroke, I must take my leave."

"It has been a pleasure to see you again."

The captain's cheeks warmed. "Would it be acceptable for me to call on you while you are here? And I know my parents would be overjoyed to receive you in Laura Place."

"Both of those suggestions are very welcome."

"Until we meet again." Captain Wyndham gave Marianne a small bow – and an exceedingly friendly smile.

Marianne knocked at the door of Number 3, which after a few moments was flung open to reveal a smiling Selina.

She does not seem to realize that one is supposed to let one's servants open the front door – either that or, more likely, she simply does not care a fig.

"And now you may return to Lady Barrington," Marianne said to Jane.

"I believe Lady Barrington thought I might stay with you – that you might need my services," Jane replied.

"How very considerate of her," Marianne said, "but I do not believe 'twill be necessary. Thank you, Jane. You may go."

My aunt misses no opportunities in her quest for information – but this time she is out of luck.

"Edmund has told me all about Jane," Selina said once they were inside.

"I thought he might have."

"Perchance she is even now on her way to visit her sister Martha," Selina suggested, her eyes shining with merriment. "She might be telling her that you have just been talking to a handsome young officer in the street. Who is he, by the way?"

"The brother of an old friend of mine. But Selina, please tell me that you are not also spying on me?"

"How could I not see the encounter? For I have been standing at the window of my withdrawing room this good half hour waiting for you to arrive." Then Selina lowered her voice. "And Edmund is already here – he slipped in through the back door when no one was around. I have told my servants that I need nothing more this morning and that you and I need no refreshment, nor are we to be disturbed. Let us hasten to him."

Edmund's first words to Marianne were: "Who the devil were you talking to out in the street?"

Where has this come from? 'Tis almost as if Edmund has forgotten that we are only pretending to be attached to one another. Perhaps he was out on the town last night and has a sore head?

"Why, good morning, Edmund," Marianne said. "I hope 'twas not too painful for you to rise before noon."

"Touché!" Edmund said with a laugh. "A very good morning to you too – and no, 'twas not too bad dragging my weary body from slumber this morning. But had I known I was to be thus tormented, perchance I would have stayed abed."

"I will leave you two to chat," Selina said. "Or should I say, to spar? If you want me, I shall be in the far corner – reading."

"Thank you," Edmund said.

"Yes," Marianne said. "We do appreciate you coming to our rescue like this."

"Think nothing of it," Selina said. "When Edmund explained the pressure Mama and Papa are putting him under to marry, why it brought it all back to me; I used to feel as if I were in a gilded cage sometimes. 'Tis not that I did not appreciate all that my parents did for me – but how I longed to break free."

"And now you are married to George, the perfect foil for your rebellious nature," Edmund said.

"Indeed," Selina said. "And he has made me very happy. Now, pray waste no time talking to me."

She ran to the other side of the room, slipped off her shoes, flung herself into a chair and buried her nose in a book.

"Well, Marianne," Edmund said, "it would appear that you and I are going to the same concert this evening."

"And when we are there, you must try to behave yourself and give the impression that we are fond of each other – but not yet engaged."

'Twill not be hard for me to give the impression I am fond of Edmund – for he is a dear character once one gets to know him.

"Do you mean I should look at you like this?" Edmund opened his eyes very wide and gave a small gasp of astonishment.

"Please do no such thing! You look as if you have had a terrible shock – and have perchance seen a ghostly specter."

"I will have you know that I was attempting to look overwhelmed by the vibrance of your beauty. I am sorry my acting was not up to scratch." Edmund affected a disgruntled look, allowing his lower lip to jut forward.

Marianne laughed. "And now you look like a petulant child. Nelson agrees with me – see how he is gnashing his teeth?"

"Perchance I should practice the compliments I might pay

you in public?" Edmund said.

"Are compliments strictly necessary?"

"Yes, I believe they are essential. I might compare your eyes to the deep Atlantic Ocean off the west coast of Ireland – a clear, brilliant, emerald green."

"Ha! At school, a friend once told me my eyes were the color of boiled gooseberries."

"She was jealous," Edmund murmured. "Your eyes are quite exceptionally lovely."

How tender Edmund is being – is he acting now?

"And I might compare your hair to a flaming wildfire, with its amazing orange and red hues." Edmund stretched out his fingers to caress a curl. "Nature at its very best."

Oh my! My insides are turning to liquid at his touch.

"Well again, 'twould be an improvement on what people called me as a child," Marianne said.

"Tell me! What did they call you?"

"Carrot head!"

"I might have guessed," Edmund said with a chuckle.

"And what did your friends call you in your youth?"

"Mostly 'beanpole,'" Edmund admitted, "for I grew very tall quite early on."

"You are very tall."

And handsome.

"You looked like a weedy sapling," Selina said, "until you grew into your height."

"Selina!" Edmund said. "I thought you were reading."

"I was – for a while. But then I started listening – and realized that you two need to be alone. The situation is not quite as I had been led to believe."

With that, Selina put her shoes back on and marched out of the room grinning broadly, pausing only to say:

"I will be back in ten minutes – not a moment sooner."

"What the devil?" Edmund said. "My sister is a terrible tease. Can you understand the meaning behind her enigmatic comments?"

"I cannot!"

Unless she somehow senses that I have a growing affection for her brother? That I am beginning to enjoy his company more than I ever thought I would? Oh! I am feeling a trifle muddled.

"We, we are supposed to be planning how we are to behave in public," Marianne said.

How I am struggling to remember the true purpose of this meeting!

"I would rather plan how we behave in private," Edmund said softly, drawing Marianne towards him as they moved closer and closer on the sofa.

My heart is beating faster with every passing second!

"Marianne!" Edmund's voice was hoarse. "What if we have got this all wrong? What if . . ."

Ah! The feel of his arms around me!

Marianne lifted her face to Edmund's and felt long-buried desire burn within her as he slowly lowered his lips to hers and they shared a sweet and gentle kiss.

I wish this could go on forever! Perhaps, as Edmund suggested, we have got this all wrong. What if . . .

"I, I am sorry." Edmund stood up abruptly. "I forgot myself in the heat of the moment and got carried away by the strength of my own acting. I offer you a thousand apologies."

"No, the fault was mine." Marianne moved to the far end of the sofa. "We should not have been talking in the way we were; 'twas bound to lead to confusion."

He kissed me! My lips are still aflame with the beauty and emotion – oh! Can he not feel it? Is he in truth nothing but a shallow rake? Oh, how I regret betraying my Richard.

"I must return home," Edmund said. "Until this evening, then."

"This evening? Ah, yes. The concert."

Thus it was that when Selina returned to the withdrawing room, she found Marianne alone – and in tears.

Edmund

HOW COULD I have been such a dunderhead?

Edmund strode along the Royal Crescent and briefly hesitated before the door of Number 1; but he could not go home yet, for he was both incandescent with rage and burning with unspoken words of love. He had to go on a walk – the longer the better.

What in God's name is the matter with me? I have ruined everything!

Edmund continued through The Circus and across to Belvedere, then up the hill until he reached Lansdown Crescent. 'Twas a steep climb, but one he was pleased to make, as the necessary exertion diverted his mind from his former shameful conduct.

Once in the middle of Lansdown Crescent, Edmund gazed out at the glorious view across the city and tried to take stock of what had just happened in Selina's withdrawing room. He had been getting on so well with Marianne – dash it all, they had been teasing each other, perhaps flirting, and he had truly felt a close intimacy combined with friendship that he had never before encountered with any woman.

And the exquisite kiss! I could have stayed like that forever – in perfect Elysian bliss.

Edmund shivered as the memory of the sensation streamed through his body, like the aftershock of a mighty volcano. Then he sobered up.

'Twas the kiss that ruined everything.

He had apologized as best he could and moved away quickly, but dammit! Was not that Marianne's chance to say that the kiss had been just what she wanted? That the tide of their friendship was changing – to something entirely different? Had Edmund not said to her earlier, "What if we have got this all wrong?" She could have answered in the affirmative, agreeing that yes, they had both made a huge mistake in not understanding the true situation – and then told him that she loved him, just as he loved her.

Do I love her? Oh, all is confusion!

But no, Marianne had said nothing of the sort; instead she had moved to the far end of the sofa and said they should not have been talking in the way they had, for 'twas bound to lead to confusion.

Is a kiss really best described as "confusion?" Did the kiss not signify friendship moving naturally to love?

The sheep on the lawn in front of the crescent carried on grazing. The sweet creatures had nothing much to concern them in their day-to-day lives, save chomping through acres of grass.

How I wish I could lead such a simple life, with so little to trouble me.

Then Edmund smiled ruefully, seeing the absurdity of wishing to live an ovine existence instead of being heir to the Templeton fortune. And he resolved to attempt to accept Marianne's rejection with better grace, for he would never want to force unwelcome attention onto a woman.

Now, more than ever, I am determined to continue with our plan. We can be useful to one another, Marianne and I, as we share a common aim – and one I must try very hard to remember – the wish to remain unwed.

Edmund began a rapid descent down the hill, past Camden Place, on and on, until he was in the very middle of Bath, mixing with throngs of high society personages. And where to next? Should he perchance visit the Pump Room?

No! For 'tis too full of sweet memories of Marianne.

He would walk across Pulteney Bridge, down Great Pulteney Street, and thence to Sydney Gardens where he could walk off the remainder of his dark mood.

Many were the times Edmund and his friends had gamboled about in the Labyrinth, running hither and thither in their attempt to reach the center and take a ride on Merlin's Swing. Edmund blushed as he remembered that sometimes they had visited at night, when they were foxed. It was a different sort of society there, after dark.

Edmund quickened his pace as he marched through the Labyrinth, taking a few wrong turns as his concentration was not at its best.

Where am I? Curses! This is not the usual way.

There were few people about, so Edmund sat down on the path to regroup and allow his sense of direction to return. And his sense of proportion too – for he was still battling to accept his lot in life.

I have missed my chance with Marianne – and yet I must accept the necessity of continuing with the farce of pretending that we are intended for each other, however confusing and painful – ludicrous even – it seems.

Edmund stood up and adjusted his jacket. 'Twas time to be positive – and make the best of a tricky situation.

I do not intend to marry for many years, if at all; therefore this pretense with Marianne is a good thing, surely? 'Tis key to the preservation of my unwed state. And while I remain unwed, I am free to live a normal life, keeping whatever hours I wish, seeing who I choose, and going wherever I want.

Just then, Edmund heard voices on the other side of the hedge; he peeped through a tiny gap to see the scarlet coats of two army officers. Good Lord! They were discussing their plans to go to a concert that evening – the very same recital that he and Marianne were attending at the Guildhall.

"I have heard there are many attractive women in Bath for the season," one officer said.

"Yes," his companion replied. "I am on the lookout for a flirtation."

"You had better be careful," the first cautioned, "for 'tis dangerous sport to dally with young ladies in Bath, for they are generally seeking marriage."

"Unless you happen to find a willing widow or married lady," the other said, "for sometimes they are after the same sport we are."

Frustratingly, the men's voices then disappeared – they must have taken a different turning – and Edmund could no longer hear what they were saying.

Yet I have heard enough. My blood is boiling to think of the way these fellows are talking.

And yet, in all honesty, did these sentiments not sound a little like the opinions bandied about by some of Edmund's bolder friends, when they were the worse for wear? And did not Edmund himself enjoy flirting?

But what if they pursue Marianne at the concert?

Then another thought struck Edmund like a thunderbolt. What if one of these young officers was the repugnant captain he had seen greeting Marianne that very morning, yards from Selina's house?

I say "repugnant," because although the man seemed more than unusually blessed with good looks, I could easily judge how unpleasant his character was straight away. For what right had he to brazenly accost a lady in the street like that?

Edmund bit his lip; perchance he was not being entirely rational. Marianne had said she knew the gentleman in question, so it was not such a departure from civilized behavior for the captain to say good morning to her in the street. In reality, 'twas quite the reverse – a fine example of good breeding and gentlemanly manners.

Nevertheless, Edmund determined that he would follow the men to the center of the Labyrinth, for he felt increasingly sure that one of them must be Marianne's acquaintance, Captain Wyndham. His memory of the geography of the Labyrinth came flooding back, and Edmund raced through the last few twists and turns and catapulted himself out into the middle where he saw the two officers standing on the other side of Merlin's Swing.

I will challenge Captain Wyndham concerning his disrespectful comments – perhaps to a duel?

Edmund ran over to the pair and yelled, "How dare you!"

His anger soon changed to acute embarrassment as he realized that neither officer looked remotely familiar. Overcome with mortification, Edmund then muttered, "I beg pardon – 'twas my mistake. I thought you were someone else," before plunging back into the Labyrinth with such force that the hedge scratched his boots quite horribly.

At least 'tis not that accursed Nelson ruining my footwear this time.

Edmund marched home full of resolve that tonight at the concert he would do his very best to protect Marianne from unwelcome advances – especially from members of His Majesty's Armed Forces. But if he and Marianne happened to find themselves alone together this evening, he would hold her at arm's length, for he no longer trusted himself – or his tender feelings.

And perhaps there is no real need for us to meet privately at Selina's again. For I have no wish to offend her with another kiss.

And so it was that by the time Edmund met Marianne at the concert in the Guildhall, he had his feelings totally under control and had made a firm pledge to act his part to the very best of his ability.

"May I say, Mrs. Pembroke," Edmund said in a loud voice, "how ravishingly beautiful you look this evening." He bowed and kissed her hand, giving every appearance of a gentleman greeting his intended.

Whereas the truth is that I have hardened my heart towards Marianne. I was compelled to do so – 'twas a matter of self-preservation.

"Why, good evening Mr. Templeton," Marianne said.

"Shall we take our seats?" Lady Barrington said. "'Twill not be long before the concert starts."

"Yes! Oh, how frightfully exciting!" Lady Templeton said.

"Let us sit here," Lady Barrington said. "Marianne, you sit on my right, and Mr. Templeton, if you would care to sit next to Marianne?"

Edmund found it torturous to sit in such close proximity to Marianne after the embarrassing misunderstanding of the afternoon.

I must pull my leg away from hers, in case I inadvertently touch her thigh – and endeavor to lean away from her so that my shoulder does not caress hers. Oh, why are these chairs so small? And so close together? Ah, me! I need to exercise every ounce of self control I possess, for how I long to take her into my arms and enjoy another sweet kiss.

"Do you like Mozart, Mr. Templeton?" Marianne asked.

"I do," Edmund said. "I am not as knowledgeable about music as the rest of my family, but I find it strangely moving. Selina oft sings Mozart arias."

"Oh yes," Lady Templeton said. "And her performance of one of her favorites played a special part in George's courtship of her – did you not think so, Edmund?"

"I think 'tis very possible, Mama," Edmund said, "for music has magical powers."

Just then, a group of army officers entered the room, including the two Edmund had seen in Sydney Gardens earlier.

"I had heard there were military men in the city," Lady Templeton said. "These here will set hearts aflutter."

"And I have heard, my dear Marianne," Lady Barrington said, "that you yourself had a conversation this morning with a dashing young officer."

Lord! Jane has informed on Marianne. For once, I thoroughly approve of her loose talk, for 'tis quite right that Lady Barrington should know about this matter.

"Yes. That was Captain Wyndham," Marianne said. "He is my friend Charlotte's brother."

Lady Barrington pursed her lips. "You have not mentioned a brother before."

"I did not think I needed to."

Marianne stayed with his family, did she not, after her husband died? I hope Captain Wyndham did not try to take advantage in any way. You cannot always trust a military man – or so I have heard.

"Ah!" Lady Templeton said as the musicians trooped in. "The music is about to begin."

Whatever piece was played next, whether Mozart or not, Edmund had absolutely no idea, for his whole mind was eaten up with jealous imaginings of Captain Wyndham and Marianne.

When he saw the audience clapping at the end, he belatedly joined in.

"What are your thoughts about the piece?" Marianne said to Edmund.

"'Twas quite delightful," Edmund mumbled.

Marianne smiled – and Edmund was relieved to find he had managed to make the correct response.

During the interval, the party went into the next-door room for refreshments, and soon everyone was furnished with cool glasses of lemonade.

How I wish for something stronger – yet I must keep my wits about me in this unfamiliar situation.

"Mrs. Pembroke! What a joy to see you twice in one day."

Confound it! Captain Wyndham stood before them. Why must the man be so well turned out? Edmund stood up as straight as he could, attempting to match the confident bearing of the officer.

"And you remember my parents, of course." Captain Wyndham indicated the couple beside him who were responsible for producing this paragon of all the virtues.

Introductions were made amongst the whole party, and warm greetings exchanged. Then Lady Barrington and Lady Templeton gravitated towards Mr. and Mrs. Wyndham, while Marianne, Edmund, and Captain Wyndham were left to converse amongst themselves.

"The music is very beautiful, do you not think?" Marianne said.

"I do indeed." Captain Wyndham beamed with pleasure. "In my humble opinion, Mozart is the greatest composer who ever lived, surpassing even the mighty Bach himself. I doubt we shall ever see his like again." Captain Wyndham's eyes creased at the corners in a slightly repulsive fashion – like a lizard, perchance? – then his voice dropped to a sickening, conspiratorial whisper that Edmund found decidedly irritating. "Marianne, pray do call me Frederick, for if all goes well, I believe we will be family soon.

After all, I know a certain question has been asked of you."

What is the man talking about? And Marianne is simpering and blushing. Ye gods! Could it be possible? Does Captain Wyndham intend to make Marianne his bride?

"I thought Charlotte would have confided in you," Marianne said, "and this reminds me that I must write to her directly to accept. She and her husband do me a great honor by asking me to be godmother to their child."

I see 'tis not quite as bad as I had feared – and yet I am not sure I altogether approve of the easy familiarity this connection will bring. And the invitation to use Captain Wyndham's first name is presumptuous – added to which, Frederick is the sort of name for a hero in a romance novel. How I wish he had been called something far uglier and more suited to what I think his true nature must be. Perhaps Adolphus – or Cecil?

Captain Wyndham then held forth at length about the many pieces of Mozart he had heard recently – the list seemed positively endless. Marianne took this all remarkably well, smiling and occasionally murmuring her agreement, while Edmund was forced to remain silent until the end of the interval.

Surely his name is Captain Windbag, not Captain Wyndham? I can scarce believe Marianne enjoys listening to the tripe he is spouting.

At least *Captain Windbag* had to leave them when the second half of the concert began, as he and his parents had seats on the other side of the room – which meant Edmund no longer had to endure his noble countenance and pretentious prose.

As the music recommenced, so did Edmund's exquisite torture, for he was once again seated next to Marianne.

She is perfection! Ah! She dreams deep in the music, her complexion glowing, pearls nestling in the hollow of her adorable neck, her crimson dress enhancing her divine form. How I long to embrace her! But sadly, she wants to have nothing to do with me.

And yet, she kissed me! Oh, if only all had turned out differently.

Edmund clenched his teeth and endeavored to concentrate on something other than the incomparable beauty beside him. But what could he do – ah yes! What about scrutinizing every aspect of the grand room he found himself in? His governess used to advise him to do just that when a small fidgety boy, and it oft helped keep him in his chair when all he really wanted to do was run.

Edmund started by allowing his eyes to rove over the highly decorated ceiling, inspecting the delicate molding and plaster work as if he were the famous architect Robert Adam himself. And then he counted the elegant pillars topped with decorative carvings – and checked they were arranged symmetrically around the room.

Though what I am to do about it if I find they are randomly scattered, I have not the slightest idea.

Next, Edmund studied the oil paintings. The bewigged man high on the left wall looked rather haughty and conceited – but his horse was a prime beast.

I would be happy to place a bet on that fine black bay.

Ah! There was a portrait of a lady next.

Damn and blast! 'Tis a Titian, and the lady therein looks so like Marianne, with her smooth complexion, copper red locks, and enigmatic smile that I find I am quite undone.

Somehow, Edmund survived the rest of the concert, before stumbling disconsolately towards the Templeton carriage.

"Did you enjoy the evening?" Lady Templeton asked on the journey home.

"Tolerably well."

"Is that all you have to say? I thought 'twas very interesting to meet Captain Wyndham. He is unmarried, you know."

"Why would that be of interest to me?" Edmund grunted.

"Why, it signifies that if you intend to make an offer for Mrs. Pembroke, you should not delay."

Edmund stared out into the darkness. Would his mother ever leave him alone?

Lady Templeton tapped Edmund on his knee with her fan. "I am sure Mrs. Pembroke is just the sort of young woman that Captain Wyndham might wish to make his wife – as a matter of fact, his mother confided to me that one of his purposes in visiting in Bath is to find a bride. His career has been going well, the war is long over, and he now feels his position is secure enough to contemplate entering the bonds of matrimony."

Well, good for him! He can contemplate away to his heart's content, and enter the bonds of matrimony with whomsoever he likes –just as long as it is not with Marianne.

"I cannot believe Captain Wyndham and Marianne are suited," Edmund said through gritted teeth.

"Why ever not? They seemed to get on remarkably well this evening and share a common interest in music. Moreover, he is the brother of one of her dearest friends. If you are serious about her yourself, Edmund – which we all believe you are, for your obvious partiality is hard to ignore – then I would advise you in the strongest possible terms to secure her affections while you can."

Edmund flung himself back in his seat and said precisely nothing during the rest of the short carriage ride back to Number 1. Once home, Lady Templeton retired to her chamber pleading an "overwhelming fatigue – exacerbated by my elder son's refusal to take life seriously," leaving Edmund to help himself to a stiff drink from the tantalus in the dining room. One brandy was not enough to fully drown his sorrows – nor two – and as he was taking his third through to the parlor, he spotted Martha coming into the hall, twisting her hands in her apron.

"Is everything all right?" Edmund said. "You look a smidgeon worried."

"I have some news," Martha replied, "and need to talk to Lord and Lady Templeton."

"Lord Templeton is still out at his club, and I am reluctant to disturb my mother, as she has already retired for the night. Could it wait till the morning?"

"I, I am not sure."

"Why do you not tell me what the problem is? You look as if you need to unburden yourself, and who knows, I might even be able to help."

"Very well, sir. It's just that there is something very wrong at Number 4. An urgent message arrived earlier in the evening from Clifton, and now Lady Barrington and Mrs. Pembroke have returned, the house is at sixes and sevens."

"Why, exactly?"

"Mrs. Pembroke's mother has been taken ill very suddenly, and her father has requested Mrs. Pembroke's presence as soon as possible."

"Is she gravely ill?" Edmund asked.

"I believe so, although I do not know what is wrong," Martha said. "The doctor has advised that the family should gather – and prepare for the worst."

"Have plans been made for Mrs. Pembroke's return to Clifton?"

"The intention is there, but no one is quite sure what has been arranged. Mrs. Pembroke is crying and trying to pack some clothes; she says she is determined to travel as soon as possible – while Lady Barrington is not taking it well, no, not at all. In short, it would seem they need help."

"I thank you for telling me, Martha; I will take it from here. And there is no need to wake Lady Templeton, for I will go round to Number 4 directly to see what can be done. Now, you should retire, for 'tis way past your bedtime."

Martha scurried away with a relieved expression on her face, and Edmund downed his drink and made for the front door. If there was any service Marianne required him to perform at this time of crisis, he would gladly undertake it.

Perchance I could escort her to Clifton? It matters not that I had planned to spend the day with Lymington and Forbes, for my social life is nothing compared with Marianne's predicament. Papa's carriage could be commandeered, although the fastest way would be on horseback. I wonder how accustomed Marianne is to riding? She might be better off on my horse – with me.

A captivating vision of Marianne nestling against him while

his horse galloped along, the wind pulling at her fiery curls, appeared in Edmund's brandy-fueled mind.

She is so tiny and delicate, 'twould hardly be any extra weight — and she would have my strong arms around her, to steady her. Ah! How I long to protect her from all that is harmful in this life.

CHAPTER FIVE

Marianne

"MARIANNE! LOOK WHO is here!" Lady Barrington called up the stairs.

Marianne left her packing and ran to the entrance hall. "Edmund! I am afraid you find us in chaos."

"I heard of your predicament," he said, "and came to ask if you would like me to accompany you to Clifton. 'Tis not a journey for a young lady to make on her own, especially as you have to pass through Bristol. I am ready to leave whenever you want. We could go on horseback."

Horseback! What a wild idea. Dear Edmund!

"That is very thoughtful," Marianne said, "but there is no need."

"She will not be travelling alone," Lady Barrington said, "for I will be going with her in my carriage – but I am concerned about highway men."

"Highway men?" Edmund said. "I think that danger has now passed."

"You cannot be too careful," Lady Barrington insisted.

"Indeed," Edmund said. "And I can offer my protection to both of you during your journey– if you would like it."

"I think we would feel more confident on the road with a man with us." Suddenly, Lady Barrington swayed on her feet.

"Please, Aunt, come back into the parlor and sit down," Marianne said, offering an arm for her to lean on. "It has been such a shock."

Edmund followed the ladies into the parlor.

"My poor, dear sister," Lady Barrington said. "Why, I remember how I used to look after her when she was tiny. I taught her to read, you know. And now, to think that she is so gravely ill – I cannot take it in."

"Here, Aunt." Marianne passed Lady Barrington her vinaigrette. "Perhaps a little sniff?"

Lady Barrington bent her head and inhaled deeply – then burst into tears. "'Tis not working! I am still worried to death about my poor sister. Oh dear! I did not mean to mention the word *death*."

"I think you should sit down as well, Marianne," Edmund said. "You look exhausted. Please, allow me to help. What if I run to the stables now and ask the men to have the carriage and horses ready a good half hour before first light tomorrow?"

"But we should leave now!" Lady Barrington said. "Time is of the essence."

"'Tis too dark a night for the carriage." Marianne stroked her aunt's hand.

"Ah, yes," Lady Barrington said. "I scarce know what time of day 'tis. Thank the Lord, Marianne, for your common sense and steady temperament. And thank you, Mr. Templeton, for your offer of assistance."

If only my aunt knew how wildly my heart is beating, and how violently myriad dark fears are gripping my soul!

"I am going to the stable now and will return to you directly," Edmund said.

"And as for you, dear Aunt," Marianne said, "let me take you upstairs."

"I fear I am too weak!" Lady Barrington moaned. "My knee hurts, too, and I cannot put my weight upon it."

"We will rest awhile here in the parlor, then," Marianne said.

After some time, she tried again. "Shall we make our way upstairs, dearest Aunt? Jane has already packed a few things for you in case you need to stay overnight."

"What about your packing?" Lady Barrington said.

"Jane is busy helping with my trunk."

"Your trunk?"

"Yes. I anticipate my stay will be for quite a few weeks – whatever happens."

Perhaps I will not return to Bath and will never see Edmund again! Oh, how can I even think about him when Mama is so gravely ill?

Edmund reappeared just as Marianne had managed to help Lady Barrington to reach the foot of the stairs.

"All is settled," he said, "and I will be here well before first light, ready to go with you to Clifton."

"I thank you," Marianne said. "Until tomorrow, then."

Edmund is warm-hearted – how many others would have offered to help in this way?

Marianne managed to support Lady Barrington up to her bedroom. Another application from the vinaigrette was needed before Lady Barrington's maid was allowed to help her undress, then Marianne went to her own chamber where Jane was closing the lid of her trunk.

"You have everything you need now, Madam."

"Thank you. Did you pack my mourning dresses? I will have little need for my newer, more colorful ones."

"I remembered," Jane said, "and packed your toiletries too. Oh, and I took the liberty of adding a few extra items to your luggage – nothing of much importance."

"Thank you, Jane." Marianne stifled a yawn. "I am sure I have forgotten half the things I should have put aside, therefore I am grateful for your additions – whatever they are."

I expect I have forgotten some undergarments or personal items that Jane is too shy to mention.

"Will there be anything else?" Jane said. "Should I help you undress?"

"I can manage by myself, but thank you. You have been a great help; now, please take some well-earned rest."

"Thank you, Mrs. Pembroke. And good night."

Marianne got ready for bed and lay under the thick covers, grateful that Jane had prepared the sheets with a warming pan. She did not anticipate that she would get much sleep; her heart was pounding relentlessly as her mind became increasingly unsettled by the knowledge that her dear mama was dangerously ill. How could this have happened so quickly?

Mama has often suffered from various minor ailments – and has been a little frail in the past year or so – but I never expected anything like this. Not a sudden, dangerous condition, whose nature is as yet unknown.

Tears started to pour down Marianne's cheeks, the floodgates opening at last. Until now, it had not been possible to give way to her emotions, so busy had she been planning for her trip and trying to cope with Lady Barrington. But now she could vent her feelings without the fear of letting anyone down.

After the storm of weeping had subsided, Marianne got out of her bed and knelt to say a fervent prayer, begging that her mama's life might be spared.

"I will do anything you want," Marianne promised her creator, "anything at all, if you will only restore Mama to health. I promise to put aside all selfish thoughts in return for your mercy. Tell me the nature of the sacrifice you wish me to make."

As Marianne climbed back into bed, she wondered whether her determination to remain unwed could be considered a selfish thought, since it went directly against the advice of both her parents and Lady Barrington. Perhaps she should give up her ambition to become a governess and marry instead? Would a second marriage be a suitable sacrifice?

Would it be a sacrifice to marry Edmund? Marianne recollected the exquisite kiss they had shared; it had promised so much, and yet he had immediately said he had been acting. Ah, now she knew the answer to this last question; yes, it would be a very great sacrifice to marry Edmund, for marrying a man who did not love her would make her life a living hell. Especially after she had been married, however briefly, to a man who had fully reciprocated her love.

Perchance my logic is a little twisted – Mama says I have a tendency to over examine, thus making a situation more knotted than it need be. Oh, Mama! Will I ever hear your voice again?

Marianne then fell into a fitful sleep disturbed by bleak thoughts of loss.

AN HOUR BEFORE dawn, Jane knocked gently at her door, but when she came into the chamber, Marianne was already dressed in a gray gown, putting the finishing touches to a simple hairstyle.

"I have bought you some tea, Madam – and a slice of bread and butter."

"Thank you," Marianne said automatically.

Although I do not think I could eat a thing.

"Lady Barrington asked me to tell you she will see you down-stairs directly."

Suddenly, the door swung open and Nelson bounded into the room. Marianne buried her face in his neck to hide her tears.

"I am going to miss you, little one. Look after him, will you not, Jane?"

Jane nodded. "Do not worry. Nelson will be having tidbits morning, noon, and night from Cook, and I will make sure he has plenty of walks. And we all hope that your mother . . . that is, I mean, we trust that things are not as bad as you think." Tears filled the maid's eyes.

Marianne touched Jane gently on her shoulder. "Thank you. Your words are treasured."

"There you are," Lady Barrington said as Marianne came downstairs. "The carriage is waiting, and we can leave forthwith. I have already seen Mr. Templeton out of the parlor window; he is waiting on the pavement."

"'Tis very kind of him to accompany us," Marianne said.

'Tis particularly thoughtful – heroic, even – when everyone knows he is not a natural early riser.

Before long the carriage was travelling along the Crescent pulled by six horses, with Marianne sitting next to her aunt and Edmund facing them. His expression was that of warm compassion and sympathy.

How I wish there was no need for him to look at me like that – and that my mother were not in this dangerous situation. However, since this is what we have to deal with – the real world – then I am grateful for his reassuring presence.

They followed a route through the city, with streetlamps lighting the roads. Then they crossed the river and took the Bristol Road through the countryside.

"Perfect timing," Edmund said, "for dawn is breaking just as we require illumination."

Lady Barrington had already closed her eyes, and Marianne too felt drowsy with the rhythm of the carriage. Perhaps ten minutes of sleep would not hurt? As she drifted off, she was conscious of her fingers loosening their grip on her reticule, which then slid gently to the floor, scattering its contents.

"Allow me." Edmund bent down to pick up the various items that were rolling around haphazardly, replaced them in the reticule, and returned it to Marianne with a smile.

"Thank you," she said sleepily and tucked her bag under her skirt for safety. "I would not wish to lose my possessions, for one in particular is very precious."

Her dreams were vivid – her mother playing with her as a small child, her father swinging her round in a circle and making her squeal for joy, meeting Richard for the first time at a ball when she was Miss Marianne Oakley – and laughing with Edmund at the first line of *Pride and Prejudice*.

There came a gentle tap on her shoulder – and she awoke in an instant. It was full daylight and they were in the city of Bristol. How had she slept for so long?

"We are nearly in Clifton," Lady Barrington said, "and I pray

God we are not too late."

Marianne retrieved her reticule from under her skirt and clung to it as if her life depended on it. She was conscious of Edmund's scrutiny. Had he been watching her the whole time she slept? How embarrassing that would be. She looked up – and their eyes locked together. For a brief moment, she felt she could transfer all her anxiety and worry to him – he would shoulder her burden.

For his manly shoulders are surely wide enough; oh, how I wish he had not been acting when we kissed.

"Thank you for accompanying us here," Marianne said. "I hope we have not disturbed your plans for the day too much."

"Yes, we are very grateful, Mr. Templeton," Lady Barrington said. "And you say you are happy to return by stagecoach if I wish to stay on in Clifton?"

"I am," Edmund said. "'Twill be no bother at all. I will rather enjoy travelling by coach."

I cannot believe Edmund has ever been on a public coach before. I hope he is not in for too much of a shock.

"You must come into the house first for refreshment," Lady Barrington said.

The carriage was now weaving through residential streets and soon stopped outside a terraced house on Sion Hill near the river.

As soon as she was able, Marianne leapt from the carriage and rushed up the path, then knocked furiously on the door of her family home.

"Mama!" she whispered. "Mama! I love you so much."

The door opened and there was her papa. Marianne flung herself into his arms.

"Come inside!" he said. "We must go upstairs – at once."

Papa has tears in his eyes – and he looks completely exhausted.

Edmund

LADY BARRINGTON HOBBLED up the path behind Marianne, muttering about her back aching after the tedious journey, while Edmund stood by the carriage, reluctant to go into the house yet.

"Should I take the luggage in, sir?" the driver asked.

"I think 'twill just be Mrs. Pembroke's for now, for we do not yet know whether Lady Barrington will be staying overnight."

Should I go into the house too? I do not wish to intrude upon a family matter, especially if the news is dire, and yet how I long to fold Marianne in my arms and take away her pain – and if the news is of the worst kind, to help mend her broken heart. She has already had to cope with unendurable loss not so long ago. How cruel life can be.

Then Edmund took Marianne's trunk from the driver and insisted upon carrying it in himself. 'Twas the least he could do – and it meant he did not feel quite so awkward entering the house.

Once inside, he heard murmuring from upstairs.

And is someone crying?

"Pray, sit down in the parlor, sir." A maid indicated the room on the left of the entrance hall. "I will take the luggage."

"I thank you – but are you sure you can manage?"

"I can, sir."

"And pray, what is your name?"

"Betsy."

"Have you been with the Oakleys long?"

"I have been with the family since I was little more than a girl – and Miss Marianne was but a babe in arms."

A loyal servant, indeed.

"Will you be requiring refreshment, sir?"

Edmund shook his head. "No, nothing, thank you. I will wait here till Lady Barrington and Mrs. Pembroke come downstairs."

"Very good, sir."

The parlor was charmingly yet modestly furnished; Edmund sat alone, listening to the quiet tick tock of the mantlepiece clock.

So this was Marianne's childhood home – and the house she re-

turned to after losing her husband.

An image of the contents of Marianne's reticule scattered about the floor of the carriage appeared in Edmund's mind. He had tried not to scrutinize the objects as he had been retrieving them, for Selina had always impressed upon him that the contents of a lady's bag were highly personal – and yet his attention had been riveted by a miniature of a very young, red headed infant. He looked about the room. Were there any family portraits here that might give a clue as to the identity of the child? Perchance Marianne was an aunt – did she have a brother or sister? Wait! She had already told him that she was an only child. So was the tiny painting a representation of Marianne herself in her younger years?

But would it not be odd to carry a self-portrait about with one? Ah, what a strange line of thought I am pursuing. My concern should be for the poor lady lying gravely ill upstairs – or has she already departed this life?

Ten minutes went past, then fifteen. Edmund drummed his fingers on his knees before walking around the room, staring at the ceiling. Just as he was deciding a brisk march outside was in order, the door to the parlor opened and Marianne appeared, with her father and Lady Barrington.

And Marianne is smiling!

Then Edmund frowned, noticing the tears in her eyes. Had it been her sobs he had heard?

"Mama is recovering!" Marianne said. "She turned a corner in her illness as we were travelling here. The doctor is with her now and says we may go to see her again in a little while. The important thing is, she is out of danger."

"How relieved I am to hear this," Edmund said.

And how I long to kiss away your tears.

Marianne then made all necessary introductions and invited everyone to sit.

"Now the crisis is over," Marianne's father, Mr. Oakley, said, "I do not mind saying that 'twas touch and go in the night."

Lady Barrington whipped out her lace handkerchief and applied it to her eyes.

"My poor sister! She looks so frail."

"She will do for some time, according to the doctor," Mr. Oakley said, "but the fever has broken and she will recover a little more every day."

"'Tis her determined spirit that has helped her," Lady Barrington said. "She gets that from our blood."

Marianne squeezed her father's hand. "Your devoted nursing has been invaluable."

"The doctor's skill saved her," Mr. Oakley said. "The illness came upon her rapidly, like an enemy attack. For a few days, 'twas merely a sore throat, then suddenly, in the early morning of yesterday, she was fighting for breath, with every joint in her body aching painfully. The doctor was very concerned about her heart and lungs, and diagnosed rheumatic fever."

"I have had similar symptoms myself, many times," Lady Barrington said. "Only last week I was struck down with a mysterious affliction. 'Twas was like a bolt of lightning from a clear blue sky – extremely dangerous, and very unexpected. But you will be pleased to learn I made a rapid recovery, such is the strength of my constitution."

Ah! Marianne has told me of Lady Barrington's famous affliction – hypochondria. I believe 'tis a persistent disease and one often detected at highly inappropriate moments when others are ill and thus have attention on them.

"How terrible," Edmund murmured, while Marianne and her father exchanged glances whose meaning could only be guessed at.

"And now I must apologize," Mr. Oakley said, "because I feel I have dragged you all here under false pretenses, yet the doctor's advice yesterday was clear – the family had to be alerted, as the situation was dire and could have gone either way."

"Do not worry, Papa," Marianne said. "I am happy to be in attendance, and anxious to help nurse Mama back to full health."

"You cannot know how grateful I am for this," Mr. Oakley said, "for your mama will be weak for some time and your presence in the house will help her immeasurably."

"I fear I will not be much good at helping," Lady Barrington said. "I suppose I should book myself into a hotel and see to the driver outside. He will be wondering what our plans are. Mr. Templeton – might you be able to assist me?"

"Certainly," Edmund said. "I will do whatever you want."

"There is no need for you to stay in a hotel, Aunt," Marianne said. "You must stay here with us."

"Absolutely not!" Lady Barrington said. "I can see you will have enough on your plate nursing an invalid in a tiny house with only one servant who is no longer in the first flush of youth. I will stay in a hotel nearby for two or three weeks – and visit for the whole of every day."

Marianne looked a trifle dismayed to hear this news.

Lady Barrington intends to be helpful, but perchance looking after the sick is not what she is best at. I will make a suggestion.

"Lady Barrington, if I might be so bold," Edmund began, "I wondered if you would like me to escort you back to Bath this very afternoon? I can sort everything out with the driver, and there will be plenty of time for you to sit with your beloved sister for a while. If we left in the early afternoon, we would be home within daylight. What do you think?"

"Well – I would not wish to let anyone down."

"You would not be letting anyone down," Marianne said quickly. "'Tis fitting that you came here with me, but we have found that things are different from our darkest fears and for this we thank God. Mama mostly needs to sleep and rest."

"Yes," Marianne's father said, "and once she is recovered, we could perchance travel over to Bath and bring Marianne back to you."

Lady Barrington tilted her head to one side. "I suppose 'tis an interesting and sensible possibility – and would mean I would get back to Nelson this evening. Also, I do find your stairs rather steep and narrow, which is a little trying on my knee – and oft on my back. And, of course, I do not wish to be a burden to anyone."

"That is settled, then," Edmund said. "You and I will travel back this afternoon."

"And I will go to the kitchen and ask Betsy to prepare some refreshments," Marianne said. "You must be tired after the journey."

"I am incredibly weary," Lady Barrington said. "I hardly had any sleep last night, consumed as I was with worry for my dear sister. I had to wake Jane many times in the night to help me find my smelling salts, and after that, I suffered the most ghastly palpitations."

The corners of Edmund's mouth twitched, and he could see a faint smile on Marianne's face as she left the room.

"I will let the driver know what is to happen," Edmund said, "and ask him to make the necessary arrangements for our return journey."

"I will come with you," Mr. Oakley said. "I can direct him to stables nearby where there will be everything he needs."

Lady Barrington stood up. "I should come outside with you – however, I fear the chill wind will do my lumbago no good at all."

"You must rest, then," Mr. Oakley said, and the two men walked out of the house together.

Once they had sorted the necessary arrangements, Mr. Oakley said to Edmund, "I must thank you again for your very great kindness in acting as an escort. Thank God the situation was not as grave as I had feared yesterday when I sent the note, but I know now, even on a short acquaintance, that whatever you had found here this morning, you would have been able to offer Marianne the support she needed. In short, you are a young gentleman who can be relied on."

I do not believe anyone has ever expressed this sentiment to me before.

"'Twas no trouble, sir," Edmund said. "Your daughter and I

have become firm friends in the short time she has been in Bath – and friends always make themselves available to help each other."

I will not talk of what it is that Marianne and I have in common – namely, our mutual wish to remain unwed. This is neither the time nor the place.

"I must also thank you for offering to escort Lady Barrington home," Mr. Oakley said. "'Twas right and proper that she attended her sister's bedside; however, I would not wish to put her to any inconvenience."

"I understand completely," Edmund replied. "And I would not dream of letting her make the journey back alone, for apart from it not being seemly, she is scared of highway men."

"She still talks of highway men? There are none in this neighborhood now, although when I was young, the roads between Bristol and Bath could be dangerous places."

"So I have heard. 'Twas another world entirely."

"Well, things do sometimes change for the better."

"Yes," Edmund said. "For instance, I know we are all pleased the Napoleonic Wars are over."

Mr. Oakley bit his lip.

"I do beg your pardon," Edmund said. "I know the distress Waterloo brought to your family."

"'Twas not only the loss of Marianne's dear husband, but also the loss of her hopes for the future. She took it very badly – and is still recovering."

I feel mortified at my blunder. How can the thought of the Wars be anything but horrific to this poor family?

Just then, two women walked past on the other side of Sion Hill.

Edmund frowned.

One of them looks familiar. Where have I seen her before?

He shook his head.

I cannot quite place her – for I had only a fleeting glance of her face – and yet for some peculiar reason, I feel uneasy.

Marianne

THE FOLLOWING AFTERNOON, Marianne sat by her mother's bedside holding her hand.

"I still cannot believe you are here, my dear," Mrs. Oakley said.

"Well, I am – and I do not intend to leave till you are fully restored to health."

Mrs. Oakley smiled. "It might take many months. I sincerely hope you will be back in Bath before then."

"We will see."

And maybe once Mama is well enough for me to leave, I shall not return to Bath, but will take a post as a governess.

"Now, my dear, you must tell me more about how you have been getting on with my sister."

"'Twas quite a change at first, getting used to her many social engagements and to the luxuriousness of her lifestyle. And I must say, Nelson is quite a handful; he is so fond of running off when I take him for a walk. I fear he is a little indulged."

"Your fear is justified; my sister spoils that dog as if he were a sickly child. Does he still sit on a silken cushion in front of the fire?"

"He does," Marianne said. "And mostly he is very well behaved when Lady Barrington is around, although a few days ago he attacked Edmund's evening shoes and scratched them quite badly."

"I see 'tis *Edmund* now, not Mr. Templeton."

Marianne flushed. "We are friends. That is all."

"He is an exceedingly good friend to have escorted you here," Mrs. Oakley said. "How glad I am that I was able to meet him before he left yesterday."

Before Edmund had taken his leave to escort Lady Barrington back to Bath, Mr. Oakley had taken him up to the doorway of his wife's chamber – at her insistence.

"Here he is, my dear," Mr. Oakley had said. "Here is the fine young gentleman who has been so kind to Marianne and your dear sister, offering them his support and protection. He is to make the return journey very soon."

"I am delighted to make your acquaintance, Mrs. Oakley," Edmund had said, "and I wish you a very speedy recovery."

The whole encounter was over in seconds, for the doctor's instructions were clear; there was to be no overexcitement. But no one wanted to deny Mrs. Oakley her wish to meet Edmund.

"He seems an admirable man," Mrs. Oakley said, "and very dashing, too. Fancy! He lives only a few houses away from you."

"'Tis almost as if the two households are connected," Marianne said, "for the maids communicate on a daily basis. Nothing is private."

"This is what 'tis like in the grander houses. I believe the more servants you have, the less privacy you enjoy. Thank goodness we only have one. Betsy would never talk about our family business to those outside."

"I wish you and Papa could afford more help, as you used to."

If I married, then I could help Mama and Papa with their finances, for sadly their investments have not proven to be as secure as they thought. Could it therefore be considered my duty to marry – and marry well?

"However," Marianne continued, "now I am here, I will be able to do so much to help in the house."

"Ah, but I do not want you to spend your days doing chores," Mrs. Oakley said.

"I am happy to, Mama."

"You are indeed a kind and thoughtful daughter. Now, please tell me more about your Edmund."

"There is nothing else to say, save that I am good friends with his sister Selina. And he is not my Edmund!"

"He seems an eligible young man," Mrs. Oakley persisted.

"There is more to life than getting married, Mama."

"Maybe, but I do worry about what you will do when we are gone. You know there will not be much left to pass on to you. How I wish that we had been able to have more children, for if you had been blessed with brothers, then I could die happy, knowing I was leaving you under their protection. But that is not the situation we find ourselves in. I know you do not like me talking of this, but your best option is to marry well."

Marianne closed her eyes.

"You know this is partly why we sent you to Bath, and that your aunt is in full agreement with us."

"I could still become a governess," Marianne whispered.

Why must the plan of my life be decided by others? I will not be married just for the sake of it, as a business deal, in order to avoid a life in which I might only have one servant, or perhaps none.

Marianne shifted in her chair. How could she explain her feelings to her mother, especially at a time like this when she was so frail?

"I will not press you on this," Mrs. Oakley said, "for I see you are upset and I am sorry for it. But believe me when I say that I have your best interests at heart. Now, tell me more about your stay in Bath. Have you perchance visited Charlotte's parents?"

"Not yet, but I have spoken to her brother, Captain Wyndham. Oh, Mama! Please do not look at me like that. I have no intention of marrying Frederick, any more than Edmund."

Mrs. Oakley clasped Marianne's hand. "You will find it passes, my dear."

"What passes?"

"Your sorrow at losing your husband and unborn child. There will be another future for you – I know it. Are you worried that you will feel as if you are betraying Richard if you marry again?"

"Not exactly. I will always love Richard, until the day I die, but I fully understand that he is gone. 'Tis more that I find it hard to think of loving another, when I know the pain love has brought me. I do not have the necessary courage."

And I am afraid that my heart bears so many scars, I will not be able to truly love another man – or babe – again.

Marianne cleared her throat. "Besides, I am very interested in helping young children to learn. Selina has asked me if I would like to assist her with the work she does with the local boys and girls, and I think this would help prepare me for life as a governess."

"But how would you find a post?" Mrs. Oakley said. "And how could you be sure you were going to a good family?"

"I am going to write to Charlotte. She might know a neighboring family looking for someone now she is settled in the Lake District."

"The Lake District? Heavens! That is so far away. We would hardly ever see you." A tear trickled down Mrs. Oakley's cheek. "I had hoped you might settle nearer us. Would it not be better if you married a man who lived in Bath – or one whose family oft goes there for the season?"

"I long to be near you and Papa, with all my heart, yet you know I must make my way in the world as best I can, considering my circumstances and opportunities. But Mama, we can talk of this another time, for I see that I, in my turn, have upset you, and for this I apologize. Now, let me rearrange your pillows to make you more comfortable as you recline in bed. Or would you care to sleep a little?"

"I have slept too much recently. Maybe you could read to me?"

"Gladly! What about *Pride and Prejudice?* Aunt was kind enough to buy this for me, and 'tis so amusing. I know you will enjoy it."

Mrs. Oakley nodded. But before Marianne had read more than a couple of pages, her mama was fast asleep.

OVER THE NEXT few weeks, Mrs. Oakley slowly regained her color and strength, until one day she actually left her bed and walked to the withdrawing room. Then the next, she managed to go downstairs to the parlor for breakfast.

"This is tremendous, my dear," Mr. Oakley said. "You are returning to us! 'Twill not be long ere you can walk outside again."

"I look forward to that greatly," Mrs. Oakley said. "I have missed my morning walks along the Avon Gorge."

"But you must not venture outside till the doctor gives his blessing," Marianne said.

"You are sounding like the mother – with me the child," her mama said.

"Well, the doctor did say that rheumatic fever is usually a disease of childhood," Mr. Oakley said. "'Tis unusual that you were afflicted in this way."

"Indeed," his wife replied. "I had thought I was far too old."

"It must be your youthful spirit that caused it, my dear," Mr. Oakley said gallantly.

"The post has arrived." Betsy placed a large bundle of letters upon the table.

"Good heavens!" Mrs. Oakley said. "Thank you, Betsy." She opened the top one. "Ah! 'Tis from my sister. She says she hopes I am recovering well, for she longs for you to return to Bath, Marianne. Apparently Nelson misses you quite dreadfully. And listen to this!

I must get Marianne engaged by the spring and then married before the summer is out, for I will be very busy with my grandchildren later in the year."

"Your sister was never one to hold back from expressing her opinions," Mr. Oakley remarked. "She likes the world to dance to her tune."

And she is not the only one! For Mama will not stop fretting till I am married again.

"A letter for you, my dear," Mrs. Oakley said to her husband. "Here."

"Thank you." He perused the contents. "Ah! I have here an invitation for you, Marianne, from our good friends and neighbors Mr. and Mrs. Radcliffe. They would be honored if you could join them at a ball in Bristol tomorrow evening, and they propose to collect and return you in their carriage. They apologize for the very short notice, but they have heard that your mama is on the mend and thought you might enjoy an evening out."

"Oh!" Mrs. Oakley clapped her hands. "How kind of the Radcliffes. They are a thoughtful couple – and truly Christian; I have never heard them speak ill of anyone."

"I am not convinced I should go," Marianne said. "How can I leave you on your own, Mama?"

"I will be here to look after Mama," Mr. Oakley said, "and 'tis high time you had some fun, my dear."

"Well, maybe it would be possible, Papa, if you are quite sure? And you, Mama?"

After many assurances from her parents, Marianne was at last satisfied that the world would not come to an end if she went out for the evening.

"But I beg you to send a message straight away if Mama is taken ill again," Marianne said to her father.

"I promise," Mr. Oakley replied.

Mrs. Oakley shuffled the pile of letters in front of her. "How thoughtful all my friends are. I have already received quantities of good wishes in past days, and doubtless these missives contain more. Oh, and here amongst them are two for you, Marianne."

"The first is from Charlotte," Marianne said.

"Another piece of toast, dearest?" Mr. Oakley asked his wife.

"Do you know what, I think I will indulge. Thank you."

"What a joy 'tis to see your appetite returning," Mr. Oakley said, his eyes quite moist with emotion.

Marianne's father went in search of Betsy to ask her to pre-pare another slice of toast, Mrs. Oakley read further messages from her many well-wishers, and Marianne started to read Charlotte's words.

My dear Marianne,

I do hope all is well with you and your dear mama.

Frederick remains in Bath, and I know he hopes very much that you will be back soon. He told me, and not for the first time, how overjoyed he was to have seen you shortly before you left for Clifton.

My time is soon, and I am looking forward so much to the arrival of my baby – your godchild.

Marianne decided to read the rest of Charlotte's letter later, for she could see the next letter was from Selina, who had been a frequent and cheerful correspondent since Marianne's arrival in Clifton. She soon became absorbed in the tales of goings on in the heart of Bath, seen through the amusing lens of Selina's unique perception of the world – and started giggling.

"I am guessing that one is from Selina," Mrs. Oakley said.

"It is. She has been telling me about Nelson's antics and says that he has taken against Edmund again. The other day on the Crescent Fields, the little pug jumped up and covered Edmund's cream pantaloons with mud. He was not best pleased."

"I can imagine! Why my sister must allow that dog to be so wild, I do not know."

Marianne continued reading.

...and so I must away, Marianne, for I am due to visit Kitty and play with little Isabella. But there is someone here who wishes to pen a line to you and I have said he can write it here at the end of my letter, seal it and then give to the servants to send.

Yours affectionately,
Selina.

The next section was written in a different hand entirely.

I hope 'twill not be long before you return. If you want me to collect you, I will be happy to do so. You only have to say the word.

Yours,

Edmund.

PS Know that you are missed.

Mr. Oakley came back into the room with fresh toast.

"Wait," Mrs. Oakley said. "There is another letter here for you, Marianne. It was hidden, right at the bottom of the pile. I wonder who this is from?"

"Perhaps you have an admirer we have not yet heard about?" Mr. Oakley said, a twinkle in his eye.

Marianne opened the letter and looked at the end. "Why, 'tis from Charlotte's brother."

How unexpected!

"Charlotte is such a special friend of yours," Mrs. Oakley said, "and I will always be grateful to her family for having you to stay after dear Richard . . ."

But Marianne did not listen to the end of her mother's sentence; instead, she forced herself to concentrate on her letter.

My dear Marianne,

I trust this finds you well.

Please forgive my boldness in writing to you, but there is something I must address urgently. I know that my sister Charlotte has mentioned a certain possibility to you; in short, that she thinks we would be a good match.

Marianne put the letter down with a gasp of astonishment. She would never have expected to be addressed thus.

"Is everything all right," Mrs. Oakley said.

"I, I think so." Marianne continued reading. "Ah! Yes. I see how things are now."

Frederick finished by saying:

When we next meet again, I hope to be assured that I have not offended you by explaining my feelings in this way.

Yours affectionately,
Frederick.

Marianne sighed, folded the paper and gently tucked it under her other letters. She would not be sharing the contents with her parents yet. But she would be answering Frederick's letter tonight.

CHAPTER SIX

Edmund

"'T IS VERY KIND of you to walk with me this morning, Mr. Templeton," Lady Barrington said.

"The pleasure is all mine," Edmund replied. "I say! Steady, Nelson. If you continue pulling like that, I will topple over and get mud on my pantaloons again."

Edmund and Lady Barrington were walking on the Crescent Fields on a crisp February morning; clumps of snowdrops round the trees were waving merrily, and occasional glimpses of the tips of purple and yellow crocuses could be seen peeping through the grass to foreshadow the spring to come.

"Is there any news from Clifton?" Edmund asked.

When will Marianne come back to me?

"The last letter I had was very encouraging," Lady Barrington said. "My dear sister is making great progress. She has been tending her herb garden and was talking about walking along the Avon Gorge again. But has Marianne not been keeping you informed? I thought perhaps you two would be corresponding – for surely you have much to plan for the future?"

Edmund coughed. "We have not been corresponding."

Not unless a couple of lines penned on Selina's letter counts. Sending her a full letter would have been far too risky, with the amount of surveillance that goes on in my life.

"We are nothing more than good friends, Lady B, as you very well know. Are you teasing me?"

"Perhaps! Yet I suspect you will become much more than good friends one day. Has that thought never crossed your mind? Edmund?"

"Nelson!" Edmund shouted as the dog managed to slip from his lead and shoot off across the grass. "Excuse me, Lady B. I will fetch the wretched, erm, I will fetch Nelson. Oh, why does he keep wanting to run away from me?"

But Nelson had no intention of being caught; instead, he ran inside the overhanging branches of an enormous old yew tree, barking excitedly.

"What are you doing?" Edmund pulled the branches aside and went into the middle of the tree after the pug. "You are scrabbling at the ground like a squirrel hiding acorns. Careful! Oh, my pantaloons – not again!"

Edmund picked Nelson up and then reversed, bowing his head in a vain attempt to stop the branches shedding their needles upon his hair and jacket.

"I must apologize," Lady Barrington said when they were reunited. "I simply cannot think what has got into Nelson except that I know that he has warm feelings for Marianne and misses her very deeply."

He is not the only one! Dash it all, I miss her intensely. I may even have feelings for her – but of what nature those emotions are, I could not say.

Lady Barrington brushed a few yew needles from Edmund's shoulders, then, taking charge of Nelson's lead with one hand, she linked her other arm firmly through Edmund's and led him back to Number 4.

Once inside the hall, Jane was summoned to refresh Edmund's clothes, but he waved her away. "Do not worry; Voyle will deal with everything once I get home."

"If you are sure, sir."

"I am, thank you."

In truth, Voyle might already be waiting with a brush, such is the speed of communication between Numbers 1 and 4.

"Now Mr. Templeton – Edmund – will you join me for a coffee?" Lady Barrington said.

"Gladly."

"Let us go to the parlor. Jane! See if Cook can rustle up something special for Mr. Templeton."

"You are too good to me," Edmund said. "I have lost count of the number of times you have showered me with delicacies from your kitchen over the past few weeks. And tell me, Lady B, how are Augusta and Amabella? I trust all is well?"

"They are in superlative health, and are lucky they suffer not from the ailments I was plagued with when I was in a similar condition. The stories I could tell you!"

Edmund's attention wandered a little as Lady Barrington outlined each of her four pregnancies in an abundance of frequently rather unwelcome detail.

I wonder what my dear Marianne is doing now.

"My doctor said that with his help I would manage well, but oh! If you only knew how I suffered. And sometimes with quite rare conditions, for example I fell victim to *pica* and occasionally felt compelled to taste the ashes from the fireplace and to eat coffee grounds. Naturally, these substances did my digestion no good at all, and my poor husband was at his wits' end, until the doctor told him 'twas a sign of both a sensitive constitution and great refinement to be thus afflicted."

Edmund closed his eyes and could see the diminutive figure of Marianne, her beautiful hair blowing softly in the breeze, green eyes shining with merriment.

"But my trials ended well," Lady Barrington continued, "with four daughters, all of them beauties. Do you know, my dear husband insisted on having their portraits painted considerably larger than life – you may have noticed the masterpieces upstairs in the withdrawing room?"

How could anyone miss them? Those intense gazes linger in the mind.

"Yes. I have oft admired them," Edmund said.

She may describe them as beautiful. But neither Augusta, Amabella, Aurelia nor Alicia can hold a candle to their fair cousin, Marianne.

"I love to have family memories." Lady Barrington walked across to her desk and opened a drawer. "I have the most charming miniature of Nelson here. What do you think?"

Edmund inspected the tiny portrait of his canine friend – and sometime attacker.

Now, this is interesting! There is a mystery to unravel here.

"'Tis not done by a professional," Lady Barrington said, "but you would never know."

"I agree. 'Tis admirably executed."

"You will never guess who gave this to me," Lady Barrington said. "'Twas Captain Pembroke, Marianne's dear departed husband. He was a talented amateur painter. He only saw Nelson once when he and Marianne came to visit shortly before their wedding, but he took the trouble to make a few sketches of Nelson and then afterwards sent me this superb representation to thank me for my hospitality."

"How unusual! A military man with artistic flair."

Edmund's mind seethed with questions, for the miniature was not only of a strikingly similar style to the one Marianne carried in her reticule, but it also possessed a virtually identical frame. He would put money on the pair being by the same hand – therefore it would seem that the portrait Marianne treasured was not of her as an infant, for the timing was wrong.

But wait! Had Marianne given birth to a child after her husband's death? However, it would still have been impossible for the portrait to have been executed by Captain Pembroke in that case. And if she had given birth, where was the child? And why did no one talk about him or her?

Edmund handed the miniature back, opened his mouth to question Lady Barrington, and then closed it quickly. 'Twas none of his business. Besides, 'twould be tricky to frame a question that did not sound impertinent or prying, and yet he longed to know the truth, for whatever the answer was, 'twas part of Marianne's story.

After a pause, Edmund said, "Did Captain Pembroke paint other miniatures?"

"I believe he did a good few," Lady Barrington said. "He found painting relaxing, and something totally different from his military duties."

How strange it must be to have a profession that you need respite from. My whole life seems to be relaxation. How lucky I am!

Or am I?

"Richard painted a beautiful miniature of Marianne as she was when they were first engaged," Lady Barrington said.

Edmund nodded attentively.

"'Twas a very good likeness, although Richard was a little dissatisfied and thought it did not capture her full beauty. Be that as it may, he was very attached to the picture and kept it in his pocket constantly when away soldiering. Unfortunately, when his body was found by his commanding officer, the miniature of Marianne was not about his person."

"I wonder what happened?"

"Well, when my dear husband was alive, he once told me that after battles, soldiers are sometimes stripped of their uniforms and valuables by scavengers. Can you imagine someone unscrupulous enough to steal the scarlet jacket from the back of a fallen hero, together with his personal possessions?"

I can imagine this scenario only too well, for I have heard many shocking tales of the battlefield from my brother Henry.

"Perchance this happened to Richard," Lady Barrington continued. "His commanding officer made no mention of this in his letter of condolence to Marianne, merely saying that Richard had passed away instantly, without any pain whatsoever, and had been given a fine funeral and burial."

"'Tis possible official narratives from the battlefield are oft sanitized to spare loved ones' feelings."

"I believe you are right," Lady Barrington said, "for it serves no useful purpose to burden bereaved families with additional distressing details. Marianne suffered enough that summer, with the double loss of first her husband, and then her unborn child."

My poor, dear Marianne. She lost her Richard – but for a while at least must have been consoled with the thought of the new life growing within her. But then, how cruel to have that taken as well. My heart bleeds for her.

Does this not point the way towards understanding her solemn determination never to marry again? For she has already lived through more distress and pain than she can bear.

"But enough of sadness and the past," Lady Barrington said. "Here is Jane with fragrant coffee and a plate of deliciousness."

"Goodness! What a feast Cook has supplied for us this morning." Edmund eyed the pastries in front of him appreciatively. "I feel thoroughly spoiled. Jane, pray give my very best regards to Cook, and all the staff downstairs, for I know you all work as a team."

"I will, sir," Jane said, moving towards the door.

"And Jane," Edmund called after her, "Make sure everyone below stairs knows that I consider the domestic arrangements both in this house and in Number 1 to be equally superlative. Is that understood?"

"Yes, sir."

For I do not want it reported to our cook at Number 1 that I consider the pastries here superior – for she can be quick to take umbrage at the slightest whiff of dissatisfaction. Oh! Why cannot each household be private? This constant passing of information is beyond annoying.

"Here, Nelson," Lady Barrington said. "Taste the crust from this fruit tart." Nelson licked his lips and ran to Lady Barrington.

"I am not sure that sugary tidbits are awfully good for dogs," Edmund said, biting into a tart. "George says that dessert pastries are a little over rich, and hard for animals to digest."

"Well, much as I hesitate to criticize a medical man, I simply cannot believe that. For if sweet pastries are bad for dogs, they would also be bad for humans, would they not? And I can honestly say that I believe they are one of the best foods possible for nourishment. Would you care for another?"

Edmund held his hand up. "I am defeated, Lady B. But I thank you. And now I should be going home."

"There is no rush, is there? Look at Nelson's dear face; he is quite upset at the thought of your departure."

"He actually looks as if he wants to take a bite out of my pantaloons. Not content with covering them with mud, now he wishes to savage them. I wish I knew what I had done to disturb him. Perchance he heard me caution against too many sugary tidbits for him and is angry?"

"Edmund! How excessively amusing you are! As I said before, Nelson is upset at Marianne's absence – and perchance he realizes you are, too? He is empathizing with you."

"Can dogs empathize?"

"Of course!" Lady Barrington scooped up the pooch and held him to her bosom. "My Nelson is a sweet, sensitive soul. He and I have so much in common."

I feel laughter threatening to erupt. How I wish Marianne were here to share the jest.

Breathing heavily, Nelson glared at Edmund from Lady Barrington's lap.

"You will make Nelson very sad if you abandon us now."

"Nelson's feelings notwithstanding, I must regretfully take my leave." Edmund stood up. "My mama is expecting me home as I am accompanying her on some visits today. We are to visit various of her friends who have daughters, and then I am to be paraded through the city, perchance visiting the Pump Room and Sydney Gardens, then this evening I shall be forced to attend a ball. I am forced to become a gadabout!"

Lady Barrington frowned. "Your dear mama has no need to search for an alternative wife for you, for once Marianne returns, I feel sure all will be settled between you."

Zounds! What a tangle this is becoming.

"I thank you for your kind hospitality," Edmund said as he

left the room. "Farewell, Lady B. Until our next encounter."

Stepping out into the winter sunshine, he sniffed the fresh air appreciatively. Then he saw Kitty on the pavement outside Number 2 with her maid and little Isabella, who was well wrapped up against the cold.

"Edmund! How delightful to see you," Kitty said. "Look, Isabella. Are you not pleased to see your uncle?"

The babe cooed and gurgled.

"But what happened to your pantaloons?" Kitty said.

"A long story," Edmund said, "and one involving Nelson."

Kitty smiled. "He is such a dear. Did you perchance do something to provoke him?"

"No! We have to accept that Nelson loves everyone in the world – apart from me."

"Da! Da! Da!" Isabella said.

"Is she trying to say 'dog?'" Edmund was astonished at the precocious behavior of his niece.

"I do not think so," Kitty said. "Babies like to join in a conversation with their babbling – it does not signify anything."

"For a moment there I thought you might have to start thinking about hiring a governess to teach her to read."

Kitty shuddered. "We will delay finding anyone as long as possible, after my experiences with my former governess, Miss Steele."

"Ah! Yes, I remember the lady well, and her fall from grace – not to mention that hideous brooch she used to wear all the time. Whatever happened to her?"

"She moved to Bristol to live with her married sister," Kitty said. "If I am being honest, she was more sinned against than sinning – but she needed to leave Bath."

TEN MINUTES LATER, Edmund was in his chamber removing his pantaloons so that Voyle could deal with the mud – and the light dawned.

For the lady I saw on Sion Hill in Clifton a while ago and Kitty's

Miss Steele are one and the same. I am sure of it.

Marianne

"THE DRESS IS absolutely perfect, my dear Marianne. Amber suits your coloring so well. What do you think, Betsy?"

"Why, Miss Marianne looks as pretty as a golden sunset."

Marianne was getting ready to attend the ball, assisted by her mama and Betsy. All three were squeezed into Marianne's chamber in Clifton as she stood in front of her mirror.

How glad I am that Madame Dubonnet delivered this gown and other oddments before I had to leave Bath – and that Jane slipped the outfit into my case on that strange evening when I was packing to come home, not knowing in what state I would find Mama.

"And I have just the thing to go with it," Mrs. Oakley said. "Betsy, would you mind fetching my jewelry box?"

Betsy returned a few minutes later with a rosewood box inlaid with mother of pearl, and Mrs. Oakley pulled out a string of amber beads.

"I remember you wearing these years ago," Marianne said. "Thank you for allowing me to borrow them, Mama. I promise I will take great care of them."

"There is no need to borrow them; they are yours to keep. My mama gave them to me, and now 'tis my turn to pass them on." Mrs. Oakley stood up, still a little wobbly on her feet. "Let me fasten them for you. There we are. They are perfect!"

Marianne smiled at her reflection.

"What elegant gloves," Betsy said, unwrapping them from tissue paper. "And the shoes! So dainty, and dyed to match the dress."

"My sister has thought of everything," Mrs. Oakley declared. "And her dressmaker, Madame Dubonnet, is a genius. Look here – there is a matching silk band to tie up your hair."

"I am indeed a very fortunate recipient of my aunt's generosity," Marianne said. "And I am pleased there is something to help control my tangle of curls."

If only 'twas as easy to control the tangle inside my head!

Betsy set to work coaxing Marianne's locks into spirals, then she used two tortoiseshell combs and the silk band to secure the style.

"Thank you, Betsy," Marianne said. "I have missed your skillful fingers. Lady Barrington's maid is very capable and kind – but she is not your equal in lightness of touch and speed."

"Thank you," Betsy said softly.

Mrs. Oakley picked up the midnight blue velvet cloak lying on Marianne's bed. "Try this on, my dear. And if we add the fur tippet – that's it –you will be as warm as toast in the Radcliffe's carriage. Promise me that you will have a magnificent time and come and tell me all about it on your return."

"If I find you still up on my return from the ball," Marianne replied, "I shall be very concerned. I shall tell you all about the ball at breakfast."

"If you imagine you will feel like getting up for breakfast," Mrs. Oakley said, "you are sadly mistaken; I do not anticipate you will be home till the early hours."

Marianne laughed. "Let us agree, then, that the next time we see each other, we will dissect the ball – the music, the fashion, the food – and the gossip."

"And the eligible young men?" Mrs. Oakley added.

"Mama! I can tell you are feeling better."

As MARIANNE GOT into the Radcliffes' carriage, she felt a little nervous – for the last time she had attended a ball in Bristol Assembly Rooms had been with Richard, a memory that was both painful and exquisitely tender.

Ah! What an evening that was, dancing with my beloved spouse, his eyes sending messages of steadfast love, and our conversation full of our hopes for the future, in blissful ignorance of what fate had in store for us.

She need not have worried, however, for both Mr. and Mrs. Radcliffe took great pains to put her at her ease, chatting merrily as the carriage rattled along the cobbles on its way to Prince Street.

"We are thrilled you accepted our invitation," Mrs. Radcliffe said. "Now all our children have flown the nest and have their own families, we find we miss the company of young people. Really, you are doing us the most tremendous favor by accompanying us this evening."

As soon as she arrived at the ball, Marianne saw to her relief that she knew quite a few of the young ladies there.

"You must go and talk to your friends, my dear," Mrs. Radcliffe said. "We will sit by the side here and watch the dancing; I have no doubt you will have a great many dance partners this evening."

Marianne's friends greeted her with obvious affection.

"How wonderful to see you!"

"You are looking so well."

"What a gorgeous frock!"

"'Tis lovely to see you in brighter colors again."

"I was sorry to hear of your mother's illness – but how pleasing to know she is recovering."

"You must tell us all about your time in Bath."

"Have you met my cousin? I believe he would like to be the first to ask you to dance this evening."

"Here comes my brother – with a group of his friends."

Marianne felt exhilarated as she flew around the ballroom.

My first ball since Richard died – oh! How I have missed all this.

In the break, Marianne went to the refreshment hall with Mr. and Mrs. Radcliffe.

"Punch all round?" Mr. Radcliffe asked. "'Tis an excellent drink for a chilly night."

"And while we wait for our drinks, Marianne," Mrs. Radcliffe said, "pray look around the room. Are there any gentlemen here that you wish to be introduced to?"

'Tis a kind offer – but I cannot help feeling that the Radcliffes are in league with my mother and my aunt, and wish for nothing more than to see me paired off with someone suitable. They think this is the only way I will get over my heartbreak – and secure a sound financial future for myself.

But I cannot ever think of replacing my Richard and therefore am resolved to remain unmarried – to that end, I will seek Charlotte's help.

Marianne could imagine herself enjoying the beauties of the Lake District while introducing her charges to sketching and nature studies.

Perchance I should search for a position in other areas too, in the west of England?

What a shame little Isabella, Kitty's daughter, would not be needing a governess for many years yet – for would it not be convenient to live and work in the Royal Crescent?

If I lived with Isabella's family at Number 2, I would reside next door to Edmund, and we would be able to continue our friendship. Did he not write at the end of Selina's letter to me, "Know that you are missed?"

Mr. Radcliffe returned with drinks. "I have been talking to a gentleman of my acquaintance, Mr. Teysen, and he has expressed a wish to be introduced to you, Marianne. Would you mind? 'Tis entirely your choice."

"I have not heard you speak of Mr. Teysen before," Mrs. Radcliffe said.

"He has not been in the city long," Mr. Radcliffe replied. "I met him at my club, and he seems a decent sort of fellow – and wealthy. He has been abroad for some time."

"I can see that he is very tanned," Mrs. Radcliffe said.

"He says he has been refashioning his life. Between you and me, I think he has suffered from some sort of loss, possibly a bereavement."

How well I know how hard 'tis to recover from loss.

"I would be happy to meet any friend of yours," Marianne said.

"Ah!" Mr. Radcliffe said. "Mr. Teysen is coming over to us

now."

The gentleman approaching them was old enough to be Marianne's father. And he seemed to have an unnaturally thick and abundant thatch of hair – could it be a wig?

"Good evening, Mr. Teysen," Mr. Radcliffe said. "Might I present my wife, Mrs. Radcliffe, and our young friend, Mrs. Pembroke?"

Mr. Teysen gave a deep bow. "I am delighted to make your acquaintance. Would you honor me with a dance, Mrs. Pembroke?"

His expression was haughty – and his eyes blazed darkly.

"I thank you for the honor – and believe I do have one free. 'Tis the first dance after the refreshment break."

"In that case, would you allow me to escort you back to the ballroom? I believe the music is about to commence."

Marianne smiled tentatively, Mr. and Mrs. Radcliffe nodded their permission, and Mr. Teysen led Marianne to the dance floor.

How I wish 'twas Edmund I were about to dance with! Now that Mama is so much recovered, every day I miss him more and more. I wonder how long 'twill be before I might enjoy his dear smile – and handsome countenance – again.

The band struck up the introduction to a lively jig, and the couples took their places.

"I see you enjoy dancing," Mr. Teysen commented after a few measures.

"Yes, I do."

And Mr. Teysen is surprisingly nimble for a man of his age.

"Your face is familiar, Mrs. Pembroke. Have we met before?"

"I do not recollect having made your acquaintance."

"How strange. Perchance you have been to London? Could I have seen you at a concert or ball?"

"I did spend some time in London with my dear departed husband before he left for Waterloo."

"Ah! Was he one of the fallen at Waterloo?"

Marianne nodded.

"I am sorry for your loss, my dear. How proud you must be of your husband."

Proud? I suppose I am proud of his sacrifice – all army widows are encouraged to feel thus – but how I wish with all my heart he had not been called upon to offer up his life. In my darker moments, I fully wish he had never joined the army but had chosen quite another profession.

The rest of the dance was spent in silence, and Marianne was pleased when it was over, for she found Mr. Teysen stared at her face rather too much for her liking.

The rest of the ball passed in a happy blur of country dances and reels – and snatched conversations with her friends. Marianne made many new acquaintances too, for everyone was in the best of spirits and seemed more than happy to have fleeting conversations about the weather, the beauty of the music, and the elegance of the ballroom.

But all too soon, 'twas time to return to Clifton.

"Well, my dear," Mrs. Radcliffe said as the carriage left Prince Street, "have you had a good time?"

"I have enjoyed the evening greatly. Thank you!"

"Mr. Teysen spoke to me after your dance," Mr. Radcliffe said. "He is convinced he recognizes you from somewhere."

"Yes, he told me the same, but I am afraid I could shed no light on his recollection."

Mr. Radcliffe smiled. "I hope it would not be improper of me to say, my dear, that a beautiful lady is unforgettable. Why, the first time I saw Mrs. Radcliffe, 'twas as if her face became forever etched into my mind. And the sad thing was, I was far too shy to say anything to her for such a long time."

Mrs. Radcliffe chuckled. "In the end, I had to help him out. I may even have dropped my handkerchief for him to pick up."

How lovely it is to see a couple who married for love and who have enjoyed a fruitful and happy family life together.

Yet I am sure I will enjoy being a governess – for I hear there are great comforts to be had from teaching. The children I teach will be like my own offspring, and I will have as great a satisfaction from being a governess as if I were the mistress of a household with my own husband

and children.
Will I not?

Edmund

A FORTNIGHT LATER, Edmund was looking out of his chamber window when he saw a carriage arrive at Lady Barrington's house.

"Quick, Voyle," Edmund said. "Hurry with my jacket!"

I cannot believe how fast my heart is beating – for I have missed my dear friend Marianne so much.

Both Lady Barrington and Selina had conveyed the message to Edmund a few days ago that Marianne's return to Bath was imminent. She had been offered an opportunity to travel with the Radcliffes, who had already planned to make a trip to the city to take the waters and generally enjoy the season.

"Marianne's mama is much recovered," Selina had said to Edmund.

Lady Barrington had been more blunt. "Marianne had to be positively forced to return to Bath," she had said to Edmund. "She was enormously reluctant to leave her mother, saying that she felt it was her duty to stay longer until her parents could accompany her, but in the end 'twas decided, after a lot of discussion, that she should accept the Radcliffes' offer to escort her back here."

I would willingly have gone to collect her – as I assured her in my note so long ago.

Edmund stood transfixed at his window – for the ravishing Marianne was descending from the Radcliffes' carriage, her hair glistening in the sunlight.

Mr. and Mrs. Radcliffe look like very pleasant people. How lucky they are to have had the pleasure of Marianne's company during the journey.

Mr. and Mrs. Radcliffe stood for a while looking along the elegant terrace, then they turned and faced the lawn and fields. The Royal Crescent and surrounding greenery were always a wondrous sight, no matter if one had seen it many times before.

But the beauty of Bath has been dimmed over the past weeks, without the fair Marianne as the jewel at its center.

The door of Number 4 opened and Nelson shot out, thrilled to see Marianne again. He did not approach the Radcliffes until she bent down to stroke him and whisper in his ear. After that, the dog ran to them with an enthusiastic greeting.

Nelson can be persuaded to trust almost everyone in the world – apart from me.

Once fully dressed, Edmund left home, intending to pay a call on Lady Barrington – and Marianne. However, as he passed Number 3, Selina appeared at her front door.

"Edmund! Come in, will you not? I can ring for coffee."

"Thank you, but no. I am on my way elsewhere."

"I know exactly where you are headed, and I have to tell you that 'tis too soon. Imagine if you had been travelling from Clifton and had recently arrived travel-stained and weary."

Edmund's reply was in a somewhat indignant tone. "Marianne did not look at all travel-stained nor weary. She never looks anything but perfection."

Selina sighed. "Edmund, please! Come in for a few minutes; they will not want to see you yet."

Edmund glowered.

"Let me put it another way; they will be more pleased to see you if you wait a while and let them catch their breath."

Edmund admitted defeat and stepped into the hall.

"I only saw by chance that they had arrived," he said.

"I find that hard to believe."

"'Tis true! I happened to glance out of the window as I was dressing."

Selina burst into peals of laughter. "You were still dressing – at this hour? Edmund! You should have a proper routine to your day.”

“I do have a proper routine and generally rise much earlier than I used to, for I have been in the habit of walking with Lady Barrington and Nelson most mornings, sometimes almost before daybreak.”

“So what happened this morning that meant you were reluctant to rise at a decent time? No, do not tell me, for I already know. You were with your friends last night, carousing and drinking, and ended up with one of your famous swims in the river.”

Edmund was astonished. “How do you know this?”

“I saw Carter earlier this morning, and he reported your antics to me.”

Carter! He is always abroad in the city at night, on some special secret business or other.

“Come and sit in the parlor,” Selina said, “and try not to scowl so.”

Edmund followed Selina. “’Tis hard not to scowl when you cannot lead a private life.”

“You have great freedoms, as well you know.”

Just then, there was the sound of voices from the street, and Selina and Edmund both pressed their noses against the window.

“The Radcliffes are departing in their carriage,” Selina said. “They must be going to their lodgings.”

“Do you think now is a good time for me to go round to Lady B’s?” Edmund asked.

“I do not, for Marianne will want to change her clothes for one thing, and then have a good breakfast. Lady Barrington has told me that there were further deliveries from Madame Dubonnet when Marianne was away; perchance she might want to wear something new.”

“Why would she want to change her clothes? She looked perfectly fine in what she was wearing.”

“Oh, Edmund! You must learn to be patient – and you should admit the reason you are so anxious to see Marianne. Are you still maintaining the fiction that you are but friends?"

"We are friends – nothing more. I have no idea what might give you any other impression."

Selina raised an eyebrow. "Have you not? And I had thought you a perceptive individual."

After more of his sister's infernal teasing, Edmund settled down to read the newspaper with freshly brewed coffee beside him.

Would that Selina had offered me something stronger!

"I must go and talk to the housekeeper," Selina said. "Can you manage on your own?"

"Of course I can," Edmund snapped. "I am not a child."

At the mention of the word *child,* Selina's face fell.

"I, I am sorry if I have pained you," Edmund said. "I meant no offence."

"There was none taken. 'Tis only that I have been hoping to be blessed for some time."

Lord! What a blundering ninny hammer I am, to be sure!

Edmund stood up, crossed the room rapidly and folded his sister in his arms. "Please forgive me," he said gruffly. "I had no intention to upset you by my ill-judged remark – indeed, I had suspected previously that you and George were longing for a child. And although I know nothing of these matters, I believe all will work out in time."

"Thank you," Selina whispered. "Apparently 'tis most likely a matter of waiting – at least that is what George says."

"And after all, he is a medical man."

"Indeed."

"Now, dry your tears. Damnation! How I wish I had never visited you today, for I have distressed you greatly."

"It does not take much to set me off these days," Selina said. "I cry at the slightest thing, and my moods change with the wind. I have hoped for a child since the day George and I married last summer. When Kitty and Henry were wed, Kitty seemed to be blessed almost straight away."

"I know one thing for certain. When you do have a baby, you and George will be commendable parents. And I shall be proud to be an uncle again."

Selina managed a half smile. "You are not quite such an irritating brother as usual today."

"High praise! Might I visit Number 4 now? Do you think 'tis a good time at last?"

"I would not bother to visit Number 4," Selina said on looking out of the window again, "for I see that Marianne is now on her way out with Jane. They are taking Nelson for a walk."

Edmund shot out of Selina's house like a bullet from a gun, and then stood awkwardly in front of Marianne, twisting his hands together.

"How delightful to see you again," he mumbled.

"Edmund! The pleasure is all mine."

I had forgotten just how bewitching her eyes were.

Lady Barrington's front door opened, and she called out, "Jane! I am afraid I need you back here; 'tis a matter of some urgency as my knee is suddenly misbehaving. I need you to fetch my embroidery from the withdrawing room."

"Coming, Lady Barrington," Jane said as she went back and the door to Number 4 closed firmly.

Edmund grinned at Marianne. "It would seem Lady B is keen to leave us alone. I assume you were going for a walk – might I accompany you and Nelson?"

"You may."

They walked in silence along the Crescent until they reached the path that led down to the Crescent Fields; Nelson pulled at his leash, straining towards the open space.

"I have joined Nelson on his walks many times since you have been away," Edmund said.

"He does love to scamper about the fields."

"Nelson is definitely a nature lover. Why, only the other day he dragged me inside the branches of a large yew tree. I was covered in needles by the time I came out."

"I am sorry that Nelson has not been on his best behavior with you. I gather mud was involved, too?"

"How do you know that?" Edmund asked.

"Selina's letters have kept me informed. And I have seen the yew tree of which you speak."

"Yes, 'tis quite a landmark – I remember hiding from my governess within its leafy embrace when but a boy."

Nelson growled to hear this.

"It would seem that Nelson is on the side of the governess," Marianne said.

"He is probably right to be, for we gave her many troublesome moments."

"I hope you will not be offended to hear that I can fully believe that." Marianne cleared her throat. "Thank you for the lines you penned at the end of one of Selina's letters. 'Tis good to know I was missed."

Edmund looked at Marianne, and his heart stopped.

Ah! The luminous depths of her incomparable green eyes are drawing me inexorably closer and closer. Is she a siren? I must hold my nerve – and remember we are but friends.

"But tell me," Edmund said, "how is your mama now? I am so sorry for all she has had to endure – and 'twas not easy for you, nor your papa."

"Mama is much recovered, thank you. Her life is returning to normal; she has been going for daily walks and has resumed most of her activities. And Edmund, I hope you will accept my long overdue thanks for escorting us to Clifton at a most worrying time; I will never forget your kindness."

"I was happy to help. And how are you?"

"I am well and have been enjoying life. I even went to a ball recently. The Radcliffes were kind enough to take me."

Edmund jerked his head in surprise. A ball? Marianne attended a ball when he was not there to make sure she was properly treated?

"I hope the Radcliffes took good care of you."

"Oh, they did," Marianne said with the sort of smile that suggested she was nursing a particularly joyful memory. "I already knew quite a lot of people there, but they introduced me to their friend Mr. Teysen, and I met many other new acquaintances too."

Edmund felt a frisson of envy.

"I expect you were not short of dance partners?"

"No, I was not. I love to dance – and was on the floor for every number."

Now the frisson of envy had become a mighty torrent of jealousy surging through Edmund's arteries. Marianne had danced for the entire evening – with other gentlemen! And although Bristol was meant to be a fine place, 'twas not as elegant nor as favored with the *ton* as Bath. No doubt there were unscrupulous fellows in Bristol, the sort of lowlifes who might try their luck with a beautiful young widow like Marianne. Why, even in Bath there were undesirables like the two officers Edmund had heard talking in Sydney Gardens. Not to mention Captain Wyndham. How much more dangerous, then, was a ball in Bristol.

"I wish I had been there to protect you," Edmund said.

"Protect me?" Marianne laughed. "From what, pray? Edmund, you forget yourself. I am allowed to go to a ball and dance, am I not? Or are you saying that my duty was to stay by my mama's side every hour of the day and night?"

Marianne's eyes flashed and Edmund felt alarmed.

"I will have you know that initially I did not want to attend the ball. It took some persuasion on the part of my parents before I dropped my opposition."

"I must apologize," Edmund said. "I, I forgot myself."

"You used those very words before, when we kissed," Marianne retorted. "You must have a very poor memory."

Edmund looked down at the ground, hoping it might open and deliver him from Marianne's wrath. But no! She took another breath and continued.

"We are just friends. You have been speaking to me as if I were your intended. And another thing! When we made that silly mistake – when we embraced – you said something about acting. Are you acting now? Possibly the fool?"

I did say that, about acting. And I am a fool. Marianne thinks me shallow, as everyone does – and she thinks me an entitled hedonist. Perhaps that is the truth?

I have ruined everything. I always do.

CHAPTER SEVEN

Marianne

*E*DMUND IS INSUFFERABLE! *How dare he question me about where I have been since I last saw him?*

Marianne stood quivering in front of Edmund and Nelson growled at her feet.

How I wish Nelson would attack him! Rip his throat out – or at least scratch his shoes again.

And yet Edmund was looking rather bewildered and even apologetic. Was this all part of the acting he liked to boast about?

This is wreaking havoc with my emotions! Oh, but how I long to fling myself into his arms and have him press me against his heart and hold me there forever.

To say Marianne felt in turmoil would be an understatement. She felt positively split in twain. On the one hand, she longed for Edmund and desired him with body, mind, and heart. On the other, she was terrified by the depth of her feelings and conflicted by the ever-present thoughts of her great losses.

And I resent Edmund's patronizing attitude towards me.

But most of all, she wanted to rewind to when they had kissed so passionately on the sofa in Selina's withdrawing room.

For then I would stop his lips with mine again, to prevent him saying 'twas all an act.

"I can only apologize again, Mrs. Pembroke," Edmund said.

I see we are on formal terms again.

"I should not have spoken to you as I did," Edmund said. "'Tis not my place to interfere with what you do, nor to offer my protection as if I were a family member. I spoke out of turn and am mortified to have caused offense."

Prettily said – but does this great actor mean a word of it? However, I must be gracious. And 'tis possible that in my tiredness I am misunderstanding Mr. Templeton – a little.

"I accept your apology, Mr. Templeton. Now, perhaps we should walk, for Nelson seems keen to take his daily exercise." Marianne bent down and released the dog from his lead. "I am sorry to hear that he has not been behaving well for you. Let us see what happens today."

Nelson turned to face Edmund and growled quite horribly before uttering a series of irritable yelps and shooting off across the grass.

"Oh, my goodness!" Marianne said. "We must pursue him, for if he somehow reaches a road, he could be mowed down by carriage wheels."

"And Lady B would never forgive us! You stay here, Marianne. I will rescue him."

Is he suggesting I cannot run as fast as he can?

"I am perfectly capable of catching a dog, Mr. Templeton," Marianne said, hitching up her skirt slightly. To her horror, she then saw Nelson in the distance for a fleeting moment – before he totally disappeared.

"Ah!" Edmund said. "This is what he did the other day. He has gone right inside the mighty yew, for he enjoys scrabbling about next to the trunk. Do not worry! I will find him."

"I am coming too. You might frighten the poor dear pug."

It was dark inside the curtain of branches, but surprisingly roomy.

"'Tis a secret hideaway," Marianne said.

"Selina's husband came inside here once with his horse Trigger – but that is a story for another day."

Once both were fully inside, 'twas like a different world; they were shielded from all the other walkers out on the fields.

"But where is Nelson?" Marianne said. "I thought you said he would be by the trunk?"

"He is here somewhere, because I can hear him wheezing."

"The poor dear must be terrified. Now, let me see. I might have something in my reticule for him. Nelson! Here, my sweet. I have one of Cook's tidbits for you."

Nelson appeared, and Marianne managed to fasten the lead again.

"Well done!" Edmund said. "I see you have Nelson's measure; he loves his treats."

"He is easy to please. I cannot comprehend why you have so much trouble with him."

"That is a trifle unfair, for I believe he ran away from us both this time, did he not?"

"I suppose so, but, Mr. Templeton, pray do not rest under the illusion that you have been forgiven for your earlier comments."

Edmund took a step towards her. "I do wish you would stop calling me Mr. Templeton."

"I will, then – Edmund." Marianne's insides were full of butterflies. He had but to be near for her to forget all her previous reservations. Oh, how she longed to feel his embrace once more.

"You know what we were talking about before?" Edmund said.

"Do you mean – when we were close?"

"Yes, dash it all! I mean when we kissed on Selina's sofa."

I will never forget that.

"Mrs. Pembroke – Marianne! You said 'twas a mistake that we kissed. Did you mean it?"

"Did I say that?"

"Perhaps you did not use those exact words. I think you said we should not have been talking in that way, for it was bound to lead to confusion."

"I feel confused now," Marianne confessed. She put her hands on Edmund's shoulders. "Perhaps should we kiss again and then you could *not* say you forgot yourself and had been carried away by your acting."

"Yes, I believe that would be a good idea, and then perhaps you might *not* say 'twould all lead to confusion."

Two pairs of eyes looked together in the soft light under the tree. Two pairs of lips moved towards each other.

"You are so beautiful," Edmund murmured.

"And you are . . ." Marianne's next words were lost as their lips locked together.

I thought the first time we kissed was bliss, but ah! This is beyond everything! I have never in my life felt such passionate abandon.

Suddenly, Marianne pulled away sharply. What was she thinking? That she had never experienced this level of joy with her Richard? What nonsense! Her mind was playing tricks. And her body, too. As for Edmund – why, he was not a man one could rely on.

Marianne burst into a torrent of sobs. How could she have been so naïve? Edmund was a practiced charmer – a rake.

How many women has he kissed – maybe even inside this mighty yew tree – and no doubt deceived? He is nothing like my dear Richard, who was a sincere and upright young man. A man, moreover, who laid down his life for his country – to protest the interests of the entitled aristocracy, such as Edmund.

Marianne started to fight her way through the branches – she was desperate to escape – but Edmund, his brows knitted together, called out to her.

"Wait! Marianne! Mrs. Pembroke. This has fallen from your reticule." He held the small leather pouch that she always carried about her person. "Please, take it. I know how much this means to you."

Marianne paused, then snatched the pouch from Edmund, stuffing it back into her reticule.

"You know how much it means to me?" she spat. "What do you mean by that?"

"I, I only meant that when I took you to Bristol in Lady Barrington's carriage, I, er, I think you were half asleep when you dropped it, but I saw . . . and since then I have discovered what the picture signifies."

No one has ever seen this miniature before save Richard and myself – and he is dead.

"You had no authority!" Marianne screamed at Edmund. "You had no right to touch my private things then – and you have no right now. Nor is it your place to find out things about me that are none of your business. I never want to see you again. I hate you!"

Edmund needed no further encouragement to leave. He pushed his way through the branches while Nelson growled menacingly.

Marianne bit her lip. She had thought that she was recovering, that her heart was mending – she had thought she was ready to embark on a new life, that of a governess. But this now seemed a distant possibility, for how it would be possible to have charge of other children when she still felt the loss of her unborn babe so keenly?

If only I had not spoken out in the way I did.

If only we had been able to continue in the way that we were before, sharing friendship – a friendship more precious to me than perhaps I realized.

Her body then betrayed her as she became flooded with the sensations of the quite extraordinary kiss they had shared.

If only I had clung more persistently to Edmund – and allowed him to comfort me fully. God help me, for sometimes I wish I could forget Richard and my life with him – and start again. For I am tired of grief. And tired of being alone.

Marianne dried her eyes and came out from under the tree, putting on a cheerful smile to mask her inner turmoil. As she threaded her way across the fields back to the Royal Crescent, with Nelson tugging at his lead, a respectably dressed woman approached her.

"Begging your pardon, madam," the lady said, "but I think we have spoken before, at a ball in Bristol."

"Ah, yes," Marianne said. "I remember you. I believe we exchanged views about the weather."

"We did. Today, however, I want to talk to you about something else."

"I am not sure this is quite proper," Marianne began.

"But I must talk with you! I need to warn you against Mr. Teysen and have travelled from Bristol expressly to see you."

"Mr. Teysen? I have only met the man once and have no further plans to see him again."

"Ah, but since the ball I have come to suspect he has plans for you," the lady said. "He is not a good man and has ill-treated many people in the past."

Suddenly, Marianne lost patience. All she wanted to do was get back to Number 4, make her excuses to Lady Barrington, and retire to her chamber for a good cry.

"I know not of what you are talking," she said to the woman, "and besides, I never listen to gossip."

As Marianne walked away, the woman called after her, "Remember what I said. Oh, and please be careful!"

Marianne ran all the rest of the way across the grass and up the path. Once on the pavement, she felt she was being observed and looked up to the window of the withdrawing room of Number 1.

I thought so! 'Tis Edmund. He thinks he is king of the Royal Crescent. How dare he stand there all day long spying on passersby? Has he nothing better to do?

Marianne reflected that the answer to that was no, Edmund did not have anything better to do, for he spent his life in idleness and luxury – possibly in debauchery as well. Had she been the victim of a libertine? Were his kisses that depraved and dangerous?

And yet he was a dear friend of mine at one point. How did everything go so wrong? Oh, how ashamed I am to have spoken to him with such venom!

When Marianne reached Number 4, she opened her mouth to make her excuses, but Lady Barrington pre-empted her.

"Marianne! You are going straight to your room."

Ah, so the cheerful expression I have plastered onto my face is not convincing my aunt.

"I will instruct Jane to light a fire and bring tea and toast immediately. You are positively worn out from looking after your dear mama and from your long journey today. I can see that you have a megrim brewing, for I know a fellow sufferer when I see one. Why, the pain I have endured over the years with aches in my head – you would not believe it."

A little while later, Marianne found herself sitting on her bed sipping tea, with a comforting fire burning merrily in the grate. In her hand she held the tiny portrait of the future that never came.

I must think of Richard and what he would want for me – and I must pray to God for the strength to make a new life.

She kissed the miniature tenderly and put in back into its leather pouch then hopped off the bed and placed it in her top drawer with her trinkets.

I have carried my grief around for too long. 'Tis time I put it aside – not to forget, for I will never forget – but so that I can have a new future.

I will have a sleep as my aunt suggests, and then maybe later today I should write my long-delayed letter to Charlotte and entreat her to find me a family who have need of my services.

Edmund

EDMUND STOOD STEADFAST at the window of Number 1's withdrawing room to ensure Marianne's safety, only turning away when he was quite sure she had reached Lady Barrington's house without mishap.

I am fairly sure she noticed me, and doubtless thought I was spying, but I care not, for 'twas my duty as a gentleman to make sure she arrived home in one piece – and that little Nelson did too, bless his canine soul. Unseen dangers can lurk in the most unlikely places – who knows when and where a stranger might take advantage of an unaccompanied young woman in this city of ours?

My, but Marianne had been volatile that morning. She had positively exploded with anger when launching into her catalogue of Edmund's wrongdoings.

'Tis all to do with her loss, both of Richard and her unborn child. Even I am sensitive enough to realize that – and to know she was in the grip of such high emotion that she scarce knew what she was saying – nor the effect it might have. For truth to tell, 'tis not possible that she hates me.

Is it?

But from whom could Edmund seek advice? There was no point in talking to his mother, for she would merely redouble her efforts to find Edmund another suitable bride. And Selina had enough heartache in her own life at the moment. His friends would not be interested – and besides, they usually met in a large group, which did not leave much opportunity for personal debate. And most of them, as Selina was very fond of pointing out, were just as immature and wooden-headed as Edmund himself was.

Edmund began to pace the room in an attempt to restore his equanimity.

I am not used to this; people find me irritating, people ignore me, and some are envious of my circumstances – but hate?

He reflected that the only person who had ever truly seemed to hate their family had been the infamous Lord Steyne.

Just then the door to the withdrawing room opened and Carter appeared. He was a frequent visitor to Number 1 and came and went as he pleased, visiting both the family and the servants' quarters.

"Hello, Edmund. I am looking for your parents."

"They are out and will not be back for some time."

"That is a shame." Carter's face clouded over. "I had something quite particular to say to them."

"Will I do?" Edmund said. "I am happy to listen to important matters."

"Do not trouble yourself," Carter said. "Now that Mrs. Pembroke is back in Bath, your calendar must be full of social engagements."

"'Tis funny you should mention that; she is not too happy with me at the moment and wishes never to see me again."

"Is there perchance conflict in paradise?"

"Look here, Carter, I do not appreciate your tone. I have had a very trying time already today and 'tis taking all my self-control and maturity to calm my mind."

Carter opened his mouth and looked very much as if he were about to make another quip, possibly something about the paucity of self-control and maturity Edmund possessed, but then he closed his mouth again and his eyes softened.

"You look as if you could do with a drink, lad."

"How well you know me."

"Come on," Carter said. "We are going downstairs. I find on a chilly day like this, especially when affairs of the heart are concerned, a strong coffee with a nip of brandy is efficacious."

"Only a nip?"

"Perchance a slug!"

The two men left the withdrawing room.

"I will fetch coffee from below stairs," Carter said. "You go and sit in the parlor."

"My preference is to come with you," Edmund said. "I enjoy going to the kitchen – or used to."

"I had forgotten that. Cook was only saying the other day what a very practical interest you took in making scones when you were but a boy."

Edmund grinned. "My early childhood days were the happiest of my life. Once we had done our lessons, we were essentially allowed free rein – and I oft found tasks to occupy me in the kitchen."

Carter shook his head. "You need to find something to occupy yourself now, Edmund. There is plenty to do in this world of ours."

The two men went down the narrow back stairs to the basement kitchen.

"Carter! And why, as I live and breathe, 'tis Mr. Templeton." Cook said. "You have not been down here for years."

"I miss the old times," Edmund said. "Ah! I see you are making one of your delicious chocolate puddings."

"I am, sir. And might I be so bold as to request your assistance?"

"Try and stop me!" Edmund peeled the blue paper from a sugar cone and started to use the nippers to break off lumps.

Cook smiled broadly. "I knew you would not forget all that I had taught you."

I am thoroughly enjoying this. Domestic tasks allow the mind to quieten and rebalance – how could I have forgotten this?

Meanwhile, Carter busied himself making a pot of coffee.

When all was ready, the pair took the tray to the dining room and poured liberal amounts of brandy from the tantalus. They then repaired to the parlor and topped up their brandies with a small amount of coffee.

"Now then," Carter said, stretching his legs out in front of the fire. "Tell me all about you and your Marianne."

And so Edmund did. He started at the very beginning and continued with an account of all their time together since – save any mention of the two kisses, and their recent argument, for those occasions were too personal. And none of Carter's business.

"But our friendship has fractured, now," Edmund said, "and Marianne says she hates me. Moreover, I find my own emotions are perplexingly jumbled."

"Balderdash! You obviously love the woman and want to marry her – so declare yourself."

A further long monologue from Edmund followed, outlining the many reasons why this was not straightforward. Even Nelson's dislike of Edmund was offered as a reason for any romance to be doomed before it began.

"Well, there are obstacles aplenty, that is for sure," Carter agreed. "But you can forget the one about the pug – for that is plain ridiculous."

"You do not know Nelson as I do," Edmund said darkly. "He does not approve of me."

"He is but a dog."

"Allegedly. Anyhow, today, I have made everything worse. The trouble started when I became insanely jealous upon hearing that Marianne had recently attended a ball, socializing with both old friends and new acquaintances."

"Where was the ball?"

"Clifton. No, wait. 'Twas in the Assembly Rooms in Bristol."

Carter's back became ramrod straight.

"Whom did she meet amongst these new acquaintances?"

"She only mentioned one by name – a Mr. Teysen – and Mr. Radcliffe, a friend of Marianne's father, vouched for him."

Carter slumped down in his chair again. "I have never heard of Mr. Teysen. But I have heard good accounts of Mr. Radcliffe."

"You are always on the lookout for trouble."

"'Tis the nature of my work to be suspicious, for there are oft plots afoot where you least expect them. I had occasion to visit Bristol early last month after a tip off, but the trail went cold. And my purpose in coming here today was to inform your parents of a report, as yet unverified, about – oh, no matter. I am sure all will be well."

"'Tis only by the covert actions of heroic people like you that the public are kept safe."

Carter laughed. "Flattery? If you are fishing for details, I am afraid you are out of luck."

"Fair enough! But would you like some more coffee?"

"Not particularly. But I would not say no to another brandy."

Edmund stood up. "Wait here! I will bring the whole bottle this time."

After a few more drinks and much merriment, Edmund felt

considerably better.

Then Martha put her head round the door. "Begging your pardon, but Cook was wondering if you would like some sandwiches sent up."

"I wonder what makes her think we need feeding," Edmund said.

"I would not like to say, sir."

Carter slapped his thigh and shook with mirth. "I know why! Cook can hear us enjoying ourselves and thinks it might be wise to soak up the alcohol before Lord and Lady Templeton return. Am I right?"

Martha giggled, then nodded.

"In that case, some sandwiches would be very welcome," Edmund said. "Thank you."

While waiting for the food, Edmund's eyes lit upon the mahogany box of alphabet letters on the desk. "How about a few games?"

Carter nodded his agreement.

Edmund spread the letters over the table. "We used these as children to spell our names backwards."

"For what purpose?"

"Fun! It can be very amusing. For example, my name backwards is *Notelpmet Dnumde*. I recall saying to our governess I could no longer answer to the name Edmund Templeton, as I had changed my name to *Notelpmet Dnumde*. She said in that case, I could have no food or water that day, but must only eat *Doof* and drink *Retaw* – which prompted me to change my name back very quickly."

"She sounds a sensible woman," Carter said.

"Anagrams can be fun too." Edmund moved some of the ivory letters around. "I can make Templeton into *pelt me not*."

"Not bad," Carter said. "And what about this? I have made Barrington into *bring art on*."

"Ah!" Edmund said, picking out some more letters. "I will try your name. Excellent! Carter becomes *Crater*."

But Carter did not seem to be listening. "There must be something I can make from this," he muttered, as he stared at the word in front of him, then shuffled the letters this way and that.

Edmund decided to try another name while Carter's attention was elsewhere.

What about Marianne Templeton? Oh, how annoying! I cannot find a word or phrase that uses all the letters, but the word 'temperamental' is in there – well, they say redheads are fiery, and she is no exception. Despite her oft rather shy demeanor, she is a woman of strong passions – as I know only too well.

Suddenly, Carter banged his fist on the table. "Eureka! I might have guessed as much! Excuse me, Edmund – but I must be going, for there is danger emerging."

And with that, Carter rushed from the room.

What on earth was going on? Edmund moved to Carter's chair and looked at the last word Carter had formed: *Steyne.*

Edmund started rearranging the letters. If one put the first here, and moved the others thus, what new word could be created?

My God!

Edmund stared at the table in horror. For he had managed to change *Steyne* back into *Teysen.*

Marianne

"Mr. Teysen! I had not expected to see you in Bath."

"The pleasure is all mine, I do assure you."

Marianne was on a walk with Nelson and Jane that same afternoon. She had enjoyed a refreshing sleep and was now keen to inhale fresh air before she tackled writing her letter to Charlotte.

"I have but lately arrived from Bristol," Mr. Teysen said.

What a coincidence! Perchance I would do well to heed the mysteri-

ous lady's warning?

"Mrs. Pembroke, I have thought of you many times since I met you at the ball."

Ah, I feel a little alarmed to hear this. There is something quite strange about Mr. Teysen.

His thick thatch of hair had looked unusual at the ball, but now that it sported a large hat, the effect was bizarre in the extreme.

I am being unkind. One should not judge by appearances. And I have no grounds for being suspicious, for did not the Radcliffes introduce me to Mr. Teysen? Mr. Radcliffe said he was a personal friend. No, wait! Perchance he said he was a new acquaintance? Oh dear!

"I must return home," Marianne said. "'Twas very pleasant to meet you here on the Crescent Fields, but now I must bid you farewell."

"Please stay a while," Mr. Teysen said, "for I have come to tell you I have remembered where I saw you."

"You saw me at the ball in Bristol."

"I have seen you before – many times."

Mr. Teysen uttered no further words, because a tall burly figure appeared as if from nowhere and knocked him to the ground – then another man sat upon him.

What is happening?

"Oh, good heavens, Carter! 'Tis you!" Marianne said. "And Edmund! I mean, Mr. Templeton. Why are you treating Mr. Teysen thus?"

"His name is not Mr. Teysen," Edmund said.

"No," Carter said. "He is Lord Steyne – the infamous villain who has plagued the residents of Bath too many times."

"Lord Steyne?" Marianne said. "But he drowned in the river, did he not?"

"It would appear not," Carter said. He pulled the hat from Lord Steyne's head – and the wig came with it.

"You are looking more like yourself now," Edmund said, "and the sooner you return to gaol, the better."

"I do not understand what is going on," Marianne said.

Edmund launched into a puzzling tale about coffee with brandy, alphabet letters – and managing to catch up with Carter after he had run from the house.

"And Carter had received news of a possible sighting of Lord Steyne in Bath and tried to warn my parents this very morning," Edmund said. "And back in January, when we were in the Pump Room, Carter was in Bristol following a reported sighting in the Assembly Rooms."

"Stop!" Carter shouted. "There will be time for full explanations later. Our mission now is to send for a constable to arrest this man."

"But I have not done anything wrong," Lord Steyne said. "Well, not recently."

"I think you were about to," Carter snarled. "I know what you are like!"

"You shall not arrest me! I will find Lord Templeton and explain all to him. He will listen." Lord Steyne wriggled free, leapt to his feet and ran as fast as he could across the grass towards the Crescent.

"You will not get away that easily," Edmund said as he chased after him, with Carter but a yard behind.

"Stay there, Marianne," Edmund yelled over his shoulder. "I would not have you in any danger from this villain."

Is not a woman capable of facing peril as well as any man?

Marianne hesitated, for she knew in her heart 'twould be unwise to run after the men, but then Nelson made the decision easy by slipping his leash and chasing after Carter.

"Hasten back to the house," Marianne said to Jane, "and tell Lady Barrington to send for a constable."

She then headed off after Nelson, but by the time she reached the cobbles, she had lost sight of him. Wandering across the road, Marianne noticed that the door to the servants' entrance of Number 1 was open.

Perchance they have all gone in this door, for did Lord Steyne not say he wished to find Lord Templeton?

Once inside the servants' quarters, all was chaos.

"Have you seen Carter and Mr. Templeton – and Nelson?" Marianne said.

"They have just gone upstairs," Cook said.

"Yes," Martha said. "Lord Steyne came in first, demanding to see the master – but he is not at home."

"Then the rascal fled up the back stairs, pursued by all," Cook said. "But madam, you should stay down here with us. The man is an escaped convict!"

"What if Lord Steyne has a pistol?" Martha said.

"Oh, what is to become of us?" Cook wailed.

Marianne heard Nelson yelping upstairs.

If Lord Steyne has harmed a hair on the body of that sweet pug, I will not be answerable for the consequences.

She climbed the four flights of narrow stairs, right to the servants' attic chambers, and found Carter and Edmund cornering Lord Steyne in the end room. Nelson, to his credit, was uttering a series of menacing growls.

Marianne scooped the dog into her arms. "There, there, my dear. You are safe now. I will take you back to Lady Barrington."

"But I need to talk to you, Mrs. Pembroke," Lord Steyne pleaded. "You do not understand; I am a changed man. I am no longer the villain you think."

"Just because you have dressed yourself up and changed your name to Mr. Teysen means nothing," Carter said.

"It means everything," Lord Steyne said. "When I nearly died falling into the weir, my entire life paraded before me in grotesque detail, and I truly repented of all my wickedness. Why do you not believe me? Why will you not give me another chance?"

"Because we do not trust you," Carter roared. "Now, surrender yourself. There is no escape from this room."

"Oh yes, there is!" Lord Steyne flung open the sash and climbed outside.

"Good God, man!" Edmund said. You are surely not going to go out there?"

Heavens! Selina is wont to climb onto the rooftop, but I cannot believe 'tis safe for anyone unfamiliar with the layout.

"I must give Mrs. Pembroke something first," Lord Steyne said. "I need to tell her about seeing her sweet face before."

"How dare you say her face is sweet?" Edmund shouted. "You have no right because she is . . ." He stopped abruptly.

What was Edmund going to say about me? I thought I had made it abundantly clear that I have no need of his protection.

When Marianne next looked at the window, Lord Steyne had disappeared.

"I will go after him," Edmund said, "along the ledge."

"You will not," Carter said. "Leave it to me."

But Edmund had already gone.

Marianne ran to the window, holding Nelson firmly in her arms. Outside, Lord Steyne was walking along the narrow gulley behind the parapet, clinging to roof tiles and stones for support, pursued by Edmund.

Oh my goodness! Now they are climbing over the ledge to the next house. This is too much!

Marianne could no longer bear to watch and fled from the room.

I will stand underneath and attempt to break Edmund's descent if he slips and falls – and I care not if I die in the attempt.

By the time she was at ground level, the word had spread, and throngs of people stood on the cobbles, necks tilted back, to see Edmund pursuing Lord Steyne across the rooftops.

I pray God Edmund takes care! I could not bear it if anything were to happen to him – even though I am still furious with him.

Marianne turned her conflicting feelings over and over in her mind – and her anger evaporated as her courage increased.

I love him! Oh, my heart is beating so wildly!

Lady Barrington rushed to Marianne's side. "My dear! This is frightfully thrilling, is it not?"

"No! 'Tis absolutely terrifying. I cannot believe that one or other of them will not fall to their doom."

"Well, as long as 'tis not Mr. Templeton, it does not matter, does it? Lord Steyne has a terrible reputation in Bath."

"He was trying to say that he had changed; he said he recognized me from somewhere. And pray tell me what has he done that is so bad?"

Lady Barrington kept her eyes firmly on the parapet above them while she outlined Lord Steyne's hideous deeds.

"He is an out and out scoundrel," Lady Barrington declared at the end of her rant. "I am surprised he has not tried to kidnap my Nelson before now, for he is capable of the most heinous skullduggery."

"Ah! I begin to understand why everyone is so perturbed about his re-emergence," Marianne said.

But sometimes people change – do they not?

Suddenly there was a massive intake of breath from the crowd. Lord Steyne and Edmund had reached the opposite end of the Crescent – the roof of Number 30 – and there was nowhere left to go. All the while, Edmund seemed to be arguing with Lord Steyne.

"And now Lord Steyne has passed a small item to Mr. Templeton," Lady Barrington shouted to the growing crowd, observing the action through her telescope. "And Mr. Templeton is nodding."

A small attic window in the roof of Number 30 opened behind the men.

"Carter is there!" Lady Barrington yelled.

He must have slipped round the backs of the houses. Oh! I do hope Edmund is being careful up there.

"And the Constable is with him," Lady Barrington said. "We are safe!"

MUCH LATER, WHEN they were all sitting in Lady Barrington's withdrawing room, many explanations were made, and many mysteries solved.

"The Constable has taken Lord Steyne back into custody," Carter said. "He went as meekly as a lamb this time."

"I think the man has changed," Edmund said.

"You believe him?" Lady Barrington asked.

She sounds a little disappointed at his reformation.

"I do," Edmund said.

"And I," Carter added. "He said he has had much time to reflect and no longer wants to be Lord Steyne. He is happy to be Mr. Teysen."

Marianne frowned. "And you say this Miss Steele – the lady I met at the ball in Bristol and here on the fields – has in the past been both an ally and a victim of Lord Steyne's? And you saw her in Clifton?"

"Yes," Edmund said. "I saw her right outside your parents' house. She was enjoying a stroll near the Avon Gorge, and would have had no idea at that time of your existence. Then, at the ball in Bristol, she must have seen through Mr. Teysen's disguise, but chosen not to reveal his identity to anyone out of a misguided sense of loyalty. We presume she observed his keen interest in you later that same evening, and then some while afterwards reflected upon the situation and became concerned for your welfare."

"She seemed so convinced he was a danger to me," Marianne said. "Fancy travelling fifteen miles to warn someone you scarcely knew."

"Yes, she was brave to do so," Edmund said, "and very resourceful to have tracked you down to Bath. Would that there were a way to thank her. But in actuality, Lord Steyne was not a danger to you. He wished to give you something."

Edmund reached into his pocket and handed Marianne a small leather pouch.

"Be brave, Marianne," Lady Barrington said, "for Edmund has already told me what lies therein. You may find it distressing – but also comforting – to be reunited."

Marianne opened the pouch and pulled out a tiny likeness of

herself. 'Twas the portrait Richard had painted when they had become engaged – the portrait he had taken with him to Waterloo.

"But how can this be?" she said.

"Lord Steyne was at Waterloo in the aftermath of the battle," Carter said. "There is no need to dwell on what evil deeds he committed there concerning Henry – God knows we have all tried hard enough to forget them. But we know that many scavengers took items from fallen soldiers and shockingly, this is how Lord Steyne acquired not only this miniature, but many other mementos from the fallen of both sides."

"When he met you by chance in Bristol," Edmund said, "he thought he recognized you, but could not remember from whence. Then, later, he realized you were the lady in the picture. His conscience had been plaguing him for some time since becoming Mr. Teysen, and although there were many past misdemeanors he could not change, returning this picture to its rightful owner was a step he could take. Put simply, he wished to right a wrong. And I for one cannot blame him for that."

ALONE IN HER chamber that night, Marianne studied the portrait. The young woman there was but a girl, whose eyes were full of happiness – and hope.

And now Marianne was a woman. She had loved. And lost.

She put the miniature with the one of their child painted by Richard and closed the drawer firmly. If a character like Lord Steyne could start again, then so could she.

Sitting at the desk, Marianne took a piece of paper and began writing.

My dearest Charlotte,

I have a favor to ask, for I am determined to begin my life as a governess as soon as reasonably possible.

CHAPTER EIGHT
Edmund

Edmund woke exceptionally early the next day and leapt out of bed. What an adventure they had all had yesterday! He looked out of his window. Would he see Marianne walking Nelson on the lawn, perchance with Lady Barrington? If so, he would dress quickly and hurry down to join them. But no! 'Twas still dark and there was no one around.

At least we do not have to worry about Lord Steyne anymore. In point of fact, we know we need not have worried about him for some time, ever since he became Mr. Teysen.

Edmund wondered what would happen to the man now he had been returned to prison, for when he had escaped last summer, he had been awaiting trial for threatening behavior.

That will be up to the courts, but whatever his sentence is, I do not believe it will be long, for whether he is Lord Steyne or Mr. Teysen, he has wealth.

"Ah! You are up, sir." Voyle was at the door. "I thought I heard movement from your room."

Voyle must have the ears of a bat.

"Why are you up and dressed at this hour, Voyle?"

"I always rise at this time. Those in the kitchen rise even earlier."

"What? You mean Cook and all the others? Every day?"

"Of course, sir." Voyle seemed a trifle impatient. "How else do you think...?" He stopped abruptly and looked down. Perchance he felt he was being too bold?

"Pray continue," Edmund said. "I will take no offense."

"Well, I was only going to say that by the time the family rises, fires are already burning in the grates, are they not? Rolls and pastries have been baked, and coffee has been ground."

Now Edmund understood. The vast machinery of the house sprang into action long before he and his parents arose.

Voyle smiled. "I will bring you some hot water, sir – and will be back directly."

Edmund felt a little ashamed that he had never quite appreciated the strange hours the servants needed to keep. And yet he had sometimes been aware of slight sounds on the stairs and muffled voices in the distance in the early morning.

I should have pieced all together, should I not?

There were other things he should have worked out, too; he should have anticipated how he would grow to feel about Marianne long before he made his stupid vow about not wanting to marry for years and years, if ever.

I wonder what she is doing now.

Edmund lay down on the bed again.

She must still be asleep, for she endured such a long day yesterday with the carriage ride from Bristol followed by dramas of every variety.

He closed his eyes and imagined Marianne lying beside him in his bed, her red hair spread out across the pillows like the rays of a brilliant sun somewhere hot. Egypt, perchance?

Edmund stretched out his hand and imagined touching the soft white muslin of her nightdress – then he turned onto his side and whispered in her ear, "I love you, I love you, I love you."

Then he ran his hand over the contours of her body, lowered his face to hers and trailed kisses down her sweet neck. Dare he undo the ties of her robe?

"Is anything the matter, sir? If you are tired, I can come back later."

Damnation! For there was Voyle standing before him.

"No, no, I am not tired. Please leave the water there, Voyle. I will wash myself this morning. You may go."

"But sir, should I come back to help you dress? Your cravat can be tricky."

"I will deal with it myself!"

Dawn was breaking by the time Edmund was fully dressed. The dratted cravat had taken longer to tie than he had thought. He had never paid much attention to how many times Voyle usually wrapped the cloth around his neck, and at first attempt the whole thing just lay in a puddle of crushed linen about his collarbone. The second attempt was not much better, for he felt he was being slowly strangled, such was the tightness of the knot.

The third attempt was more comfortable – although when Edmund looked in the mirror, he had to admit that the effect was not of his usual sartorial elegance. 'Twas more reminiscent of a child's first attempt to dress themselves.

Ah! But I cannot wait to see Marianne.

Edmund sent a silent prayer heavenwards. How he hoped that the dramatic episode when he had chased Mr. Teysen along the roof yesterday would have finally driven from Marianne's mind her unjustified hatred of him.

In truth, there were times last night at Lady Barrington's when I felt her looking at me with a great deal of tenderness; she thanked me many times for making such a brave attempt to keep her from harm. Admittedly, she included Carter in these thanks as well, but I like to think she addressed me particularly fervently.

Edmund hummed to himself as he ran his fingers through his hair, attempting the artfully tousled look that Voyle was expert in creating.

I will use the lemon pomade, for just as the potion holds my hair in place, maybe 'twill help to secure Marianne's affections. Lord! I wonder if that is too much?

Now, what could Edmund do to pass the time until it would be proper to call at Number 4? He stood in the corridor outside his chamber. The house was extraordinarily quiet, and 'twas evident that his parents were still abed.

I had such a good time helping Cook measure the sugar yesterday. Perchance I might help with the preparation of food again this morning? I am sure the kitchen staff would be glad of an extra pair of hands.

Edmund skipped down the stairs, not quite full of the joys of spring, for 'twas only February, but certainly with the sort of bounce in his step that he had not felt for a long time.

Would today perhaps be the day that he might finally be able to untangle his perplexing feelings for Marianne? He already recognized the friendship that lay within his heart, but there was a transformation in progress. Friendship was rapidly moving towards another feeling.

Edmund hesitated in the hall. Was it quite proper that he should use the servants' staircase and descend to their quarters? If the servants wandered up through the main house at will, would they not be rebuked and reminded of their place?

And yet, Voyle comes into my room at the most inappropriate times. I have no privacy.

Edmund decided his intrusion below stairs would be acceptable if he was discreet. Creeping down, he heard the back door opening, whereupon he concealed himself in a shadowy alcove till he could ascertain who had entered.

"Ah, Jane! 'Tis you," a voice said.

"Dearest Martha," Jane said. "I know I said I would come round later, but sometimes news cannot wait."

I have caught them in the act! I am witness to the secret channel of communication that goes backwards and forwards between Number 1 and Number 4.

"Come and sit down in the kitchen," Martha said to her sister. "There is a pot of tea on the table, and you can rest your feet and tell us all your news."

Edmund was very disappointed to hear this – for he could scarce follow the maids and sit listening openly with the other servants.

"No, not today," Jane said. "What I have to say is for your ears only."

Thank the Lord! Oh! I cannot wait to hear what gossip Jane has brought with her from Lady B's house.

"Well, be quick," Martha said, "for the others will be wondering where I have gone."

"Wait! Can you smell lemons?" Jane said.

Edmund smoothed his hair down and pressed himself further back into the recess.

"Maybe," Martha said. "Cook must be cutting up fruit. But tell me – what is your news?"

"'Tis to do with a letter," Jane said.

"A letter?"

"Yes, Mrs. Pembroke was writing a letter very late last night in her chamber."

Was she writing to me?

"I went in to ask if she needed help undressing," Jane said, "but she said there was nothing I could do for her, and then it was I noticed a tear in her eye."

"Oh no," Martha said. "As if she has not suffered enough."

I agree wholeheartedly with that sentiment.

"Exactly," Jane said, "so I stayed with her a while. I even put my arm on her shoulder, and she did not seem to mind."

How I wish I had been the one to comfort her.

"And then she told me that she was intending to start again, to make a new life for herself."

This sounds promising.

"What does she want to do?" Martha said.

"She intends to become a governess," Jane said. "She has written to her friend Charlotte to ask for help finding a suitable family in the Lake District."

What?

"Oh dear," Martha said. "She will not like being a governess."

"No! And I told her how lonely she would be, for the governess is neither above stairs nor below."

"But why would she want to do that, when she could marry any of the eligible young men in Bath? There are many would be pleased to ask her."

She could marry me!

"That is what I told her," Jane said, "but she said she did not wish to marry."

"There has been talk," Martha said, "of how she might marry Mr. Templeton."

Both the maids started giggling. Whether 'twas the thought of marriage itself, or the thought of Marianne marrying Edmund, 'twould be hard to say.

Then Cook's voice was heard. "Martha! What are you doing out there? 'Tis nearly time for you to take tea to Lady Templeton."

"Coming," Martha said.

"I can see how busy you are," Jane said, "but I was bursting to tell you this news. I will come by again later and we will talk some more and have that cup of tea you promised."

"I look forward to it. And bring some news you can share, for you know everyone here lives for your daily account of the goings on at Number 4."

If I ever have my own household, I will make quite sure that I only employ maids who are not sisters of Jane or Martha – and, moreover, are preferably mute.

Edmund waited till Jane had left and Martha had gone upstairs with his mama's tea, then he entered the kitchen.

"Good morning, Cook. How are you?"

"Good morning, Mr. Templeton. How might I help you this morning?"

"I wondered if I might help you," Edmund said. "I so enjoyed coming to the kitchen yesterday with Carter. Perchance you and I could make some scones, as we used to years ago."

Cook seemed rather flustered today, and not quite as friendly as she had been the day before.

"'Tis not right that you are down here, Mr. Templeton, especially when we are rushed off our . . . er, I mean, you are a gentleman and belong upstairs."

What a mistake I have made! She had been about to say, "especially when we are rushed off our feet." Who do I think I am? I am making Cook's already busy life much more difficult, merely to indulge my childish desire to play at cooking.

"My mistake, Cook. I apologize." Edmund backed out of the kitchen.

"No, wait," Cook said. "Mr. Templeton, pray forgive me if you think I am speaking out of turn – after all, I have known you since you were a tiny babe – but I can see that something is troubling you today."

"There is nothing amiss," Edmund said. "In fact, I am on my way to the city to take the air."

"This early?"

"I believe I must."

"But you have not yet had your breakfast. Here, take this with you."

Cook bundled together a few pastries and some cuts of meat left over from last night, and tied them up in a napkin.

"These are for you, sir. You enjoy these tidbits and maybe have a good walk to clear your head."

Edmund nodded his thanks; he did not trust himself to speak.

I have tidbits now from Cook. I am treated as Nelson is. And yet that is unfair, for Cook is a kind woman; she senses something is wrong and is offering her support in the way she used to when I was a child – by feeding me.

Edmund went up onto the street and then ran along Brock Street and through The Circus, running and running as fast as he could until he reached the very center of the city, the mighty Abbey. There he sat on a bench and wolfed down Cook's tidbits.

My Marianne intends to leave Bath! And I feel as if my heart is breaking in two.

Marianne

"MARIANNE! THE CARRIAGE will be ready to take us to Laura Place soon."

"Thank you, Aunt. I am all but ready. I just need a minute in my chamber."

Marianne ran up the stairs. She and Lady Barrington were due at the Wyndhams' house this morning to pay a call. She still felt a little tired after all the excitement and drama with Mr. Teysen yesterday, but knew she would particularly enjoy the visit.

But first I need to re-read Frederick's letter – the one he sent me in Clifton.

Opening the top drawer of her chest of drawers, she looked briefly at the two leather pouches containing the miniatures – her past – but her heart maintained a steady, sensible rhythm. Then she picked out Frederick's letter from a neat pile.

I do not mind admitting that at first I was extremely surprised to receive this letter from Frederick, for he has never written to me before.

Her eyes ran over the letter once more.

My dear Marianne,

I trust this finds you well.

Please forgive my boldness in writing to you, but there is something I must address urgently. I know that my sister Charlotte has mentioned a certain possibility to you, in short, that she thinks we would be a good match.

Marianne felt amused as she remembered the absolute consternation these opening words had caused in her heart when first she had read them – but her anxiety had soon been set aside, for the letter continued thus:

This has led me to write to you, for although I love you as a brother loves a sister, I want there to be no misunderstanding – for my heart is engaged elsewhere. I have recently met a young

*lady that I feel could well be the person I wish to spend the rest
of my life with. I intend to ask her to be my bride, and if she
accepts, we will be married before I return to my post.*

*My dear Marianne, forgive me if I have ever given the im-
pression that what I felt for you was any more than fraternal
love. Perhaps my sister Charlotte, in her eagerness to see us both
married, has tried to push us together, thinking us well suited?
How I hope this is the explanation for this predicament, for I
would not wish to be the cause of further heartbreak for you.*

*When we next meet again, I hope to be assured that I have
not offended you by explaining my feelings in this way.*

Yours affectionately,
Frederick

As soon as she had received the letter in Clifton, Marianne
had written back to Frederick saying that she had never thought
of him as a future husband, but as a very dear friend who had
helped her when she was in despair; she wished him every
happiness with the young lady who had been fortunate enough to
win his heart.

*And now I am to find my happiness as a governess – pray God this
is the right choice.*

Marianne was looking forward to seeing Captain Wyndham
again this morning.

*For we will be able to laugh at the misunderstanding that Char-
lotte's match making has provoked – and I hope to hear that he is now
engaged to the lady he truly loves.*

"Marianne! The carriage!" Lady Barrington's voice could be
clearly heard even though the chamber door was closed.

"Coming, Aunt."

As Marianne, Lady Barrington, and Nelson traveled through
the streets, they saw invalids in sedan chairs on their way to the
Mineral Water Hospital. Lady Barrington winced and clutched
her back.

"I must book treatments soon, for I am a martyr to my lumbago."

Marianne made sympathetic noises, and Nelson gave a wheezy sigh. Then they spotted Edmund lounging on a street corner.

"He is looking a little disheveled this morning," Lady Barrington said.

And he is pulling at his cravat in the strangest way. Oh! Now 'tis unraveling, and he is trying to re-tie it.

Marianne waved to Edmund, and he waved back – but with such a sorrowful look.

He must be worn out after his rooftop escapade – unless something else is amiss?

Very soon they reached Laura Place and entered the Wyndhams' home. Marianne looked around her in wonder. She had not been there since she had been in the throes of her bereavement.

Now I find I can look back upon the terrible time after Richard's death without fear; for a new chapter as a governess is about to unfold, far away from Bath. This is what I long for with heart and soul. Is it not?

At first the conversation was general; the weather, the state of the streets, and whether the river would flood again that year. But ere long, there was a chance for Marianne and Frederick to talk privately.

"How happy I was," Frederick said, "to receive your letter from Clifton and know that I had not offended you."

"Dear Frederick, you could never offend me, and I am so glad you wrote, for 'tis important to clear up misunderstandings before they become too big to deal with."

I blush to say this, for the whole of my stay in Bath so far seems to have been nothing but a series of misunderstandings which I have strived quite desperately – and unsuccessfully – to negotiate.

"And might I ask," Marianne said, "what the young lady said?"

Frederick's eyes twinkled and he smiled most engagingly. "She said yes! Both sets of parents are delighted, the engagement will be in the paper soon, and a special license has been obtained.

We will be married in London before I return to my regiment."

"Warmest congratulations!" Marianne glanced over her shoulder "Ah! I do believe your parents are conveying the same news to Lady Barrington as we speak."

"Is it not wonderful, Marianne?" Lady Barrington said. "Captain Wyndham is engaged to be married. Ah! I feel spring is coming. There is love in the air." Then she winked at Marianne.

How my aunt never loses a chance to remind me that she has set her heart on my marriage. Well, she is going to be sadly disappointed. I do hope Charlotte replies to me soon.

"Do we both agree," Frederick asked, "that my sister Charlotte tried to interfere a little between us?"

"We do! For she told me you were very fond of me and often asked after my health."

"And she told me," Frederick said, "that she suspected you nursed secret romantic feelings for me."

"Marianne! What are you two laughing about? I must know!" Lady Barrington said.

"'Twas just something amusing that Charlotte said in her letters, Aunt," Marianne replied.

Then she turned back to Frederick. "Thank God the country is no longer at war and you and your new wife will be able to enjoy much time together."

"Thank you," Frederick said. "That is exceedingly generous of you to say that, my dear." He coughed. "Under the circumstances."

"Do not worry that I am about to dissolve into tears. That time has passed. In point of fact, I wrote to Charlotte last night about my future plans."

"And what are they, pray?"

"I intend to become a governess."

Frederick's smile drooped a little. "Is this what you want?"

"It is."

"I would hate to feel that you are being pushed into this because of your circumstances. If there is ever anything I can do to assist you, please do not hesitate to ask."

"I admit that it is a necessary and prudent path for me, financially speaking," Marianne said, "but that does not mean I will not find fulfilment in the vocation of teaching."

Does it?

"I wish you well, then," Frederick said, "but you must know there are many eligible men who would regard it as an honor were you to accept their proposals."

"Please do not make the mistake Charlotte made and try to steer my life. I must be allowed to decide my own destiny."

"I apologize. But might I at least caution you not to make any sudden decision? There is no terrible rush, is there?"

"I am resolved to leave Bath as soon as I can," Marianne said.

How can I explain to Frederick that I am in love with Edmund but that he has resolved to embrace the single life as long as he can? I will not stay in this city and chance seeing him again – for how could I bear it? He is the only man alive I wish to be joined with, and if I cannot have him, then I will turn my back on the whole business of matrimony and family.

Edmund

I wonder how long Marianne is going to spend visiting this house? How I long to see her beauteous face again – and attempt to dissuade her from becoming a governess. Perchance if I stand here awhile, I can address her as she exits and ask if she might like to stroll round the city with me – we might visit the Pump Room again. I must be patient.

Edmund was standing in Laura Place opposite a row of golden Bath stone town houses. It had been quite an effort to track Lady Barrington's carriage, especially when he was both exhausted and despondent, yet he had managed to keep it within sight.

Suddenly, his attention was caught by faces at an upper window. 'Twas Marianne! How darling she looked. Next to her was Lady Barrington, cradling Nelson. And then there was someone rather less welcome.

No! 'Tis Captain Windbag! This must be his family home. Why in God's name would Marianne want to visit him?

Edmund shivered. He was feeling hungry, too, for Cook's tidbits seemed a long time ago. Just then, he saw a couple of army officers swaggering along the pavement.

"Do we not know you?" one of them said.

"Yes," said the other. "You attended the same concert as we did, back in January."

"And you were in the Labyrinth at Sydney Gardens," the first said with a rather unpleasant laugh.

"Yes," the second said, "until you disappeared!"

How mortifying that they remember my humiliation – when I had mistakenly thought one of them was Captain Windbag.

Edmund looked into their smug faces then shrugged his shoulders. "I do not recollect meeting you."

"Suit yourself," the first one said.

"I shall," Edmund replied.

And then, maybe because he was cold, or maybe because he was still reeling from the shock of finding out that Marianne was visiting Captain Windbag, Edmund followed the officers along Great Pulteney Street.

"In actual fact, I do remember you," he said as he caught up with them.

"I thought you did," the first man said. "I am Captain Hasket, and this is my friend Captain Hardy."

"Edmund Templeton, at your service."

"Templeton, eh? A name well known in Bath," Captain Hasket said. "Your father is a very rich man."

"You live up in the Royal Crescent, do you not?" Captain Hardy said.

"Guilty as charged," Edmund said. "And where might you be staying?"

I will be friendly towards these two – and hope to find out more about Captain Windbag, for I do not fully trust the man, nor his intentions towards Marianne.

"Our lodgings are in the lower part of the city," Captain Hasket said. "We are here for the season, to see what sport there is before we must rejoin our regiment."

"There are plenty of card games in the Upper Rooms," Edmund said. "And dice as well. But if you want to place a wager on some races, I can give you advice, for I know where the best horses are bred."

"That is not the only sport we are looking for," Captain Hasket said.

"Yes! We seek the fairer sex," Captain Hardy said.

The two men laughed – in a most disagreeable way.

Women are not sport! These men are dangerous: I must warn Marianne.

"I have met another from your regiment," Edmund said. "Captain Wyndham."

"Oh, yes," Captain Hasket said. "I saw you talking to him at the concert."

I was listening to him, not conversing – I was scarcely allowed to utter a single word.

"I believe there is a rumor flying around that he is recently engaged," Captain Hardy said, "but I cannot vouch for its veracity."

Engaged? Surely he cannot be engaged to my Marianne?

Edmund's heart beat wildly, until he remembered that Marianne was intending to leave Bath at her earliest convenience and become a governess. This is no way indicated that she had recently given her heart away.

"To whom is Captain Windbag engaged?" Edmund said.

"Captain Windbag?" Hasket frowned deeply. "Be careful what you say, sir. You go too far. Captain Wyndham is a distinguished officer."

"Even if he is indeed intoxicated with the exuberance of his own verbosity," Captain Hardy sniggered.

"I ask you to withdraw your comments, Mr. Templeton, for I am not as forgiving as my friend Hardy here." Captain Hasket stood to attention. "Otherwise, I will be forced to challenge you to a duel. 'Twill be pistols – or perchance swords – at dawn. Verily, I will hesitate no longer. We will fight! Consider yourself well and truly challenged."

Edmund felt sick to the pit of his stomach. What in God's name had he provoked with his ill-judged jibe?

Hasket affected a pugilistic pose, with fists clenched, legs braced and nostrils flared most unattractively – before bellowing with raucous mirth for a full ten seconds. Then he punched Edmund lightly on his shoulder. "Mr. Templeton – your face! 'Tis quite the picture of terror."

"Yes, dearie me," Hardy said. "I think I might split my sides with laughing."

"You must know," Hasket said, "that I would never challenge you to a duel."

"You did not mean it?" Edmund said. "Thank the Lord! I suppose 'twould not be wise, for you could be in trouble with your regiment."

"That would only be if they found out," Hasket said. "But that is not the real reason I would not challenge you."

"What is?"

"You are but a namby-pamby weakling."

"Indeed," Hardy said, "Hasket would make mincemeat of you."

"Remember," Hasket said, "that we have been trained in the use of firearms. I do not believe you have."

"I have not; that has been beyond the scope of my education," Edmund said, "but it does not mean I am not brave and would not fight for a just cause."

Hardy gave a pitying smile. "Brave men die every day from lack of training."

"Yes," Hasket said, "and if you think I would fight to the

death merely because someone called my friend *windbag*, then you are even more of a muttonhead than you look."

By now the men had reached Sydney Gardens. Edmund did not much like these two characters, nor did he appreciate being the butt of their jokes – but he decided he would be wise to refrain from replying to Hasket's last comment, for whatever he said could lead to more unwelcome jests. Or possibly something far worse.

Edmund also decided 'twas time to part from the two captains – for now – but he would instead follow them at a discreet distance, hoping to overhear further revelations about Captain Windbag. For Edmund was still not entirely convinced that the loquacious Captain Wyndham did not have designs upon the fair Marianne.

The two officers walked ahead into the Labyrinth, still snorting with laughter, and Edmund hung back for a few minutes. 'Twould not do for them to realize he was following them – but 'twas relatively easy to work out which way they went, such was the volume of their conversation.

They must have developed these excessively loud voices by shouting commands on distant battlefields.

After a decent interval, Edmund crept into the Labyrinth, taking care to stay concealed. It was a while before he managed to locate a convenient hedge behind which to listen to their inane conversation in more detail.

"Should we tell Wyndham about this fellow who is so rude?" Hardy said.

"'Tis not worth spending another second on that bonehead," Hasket replied.

"Fair enough. And if truth be told, 'twas quite funny to call Wyndham *windbag,* was it not?"

"It certainly was! I must say I felt jealous of Wyndham at the concert, though, talking to that shapely redhead. What was her name?"

"Mrs. Pembroke," Hardy said. "A widow, I do believe."

Hasket gave a disrespectful cackle. "She is a very tasty morsel. Ah! What I would not give to have a woman like that in my bed."

Edmund let out a scream of rage.

"What was that?" Hardy said.

"I have no idea," Hasket replied. "Maybe 'tis someone who is as lost as we are in the Labyrinth. It can be mighty frustrating wandering around here. Do you think this path is the way to the center?"

Edmund ran on to where he knew there was a shady section of the hedge with sparse branches. As boys, he and Henry used to leap through this shortcut sometimes if they were having trouble negotiating the maze. And if Edmund wanted to, he could squeeze through there right now, confront these damnable fellows, and reprimand them for the disgusting way they were talking about his beloved.

Edmund leaped into the hedge enthusiastically – before he remembered that when he and Henry used to do this in years past, they were both much smaller. And so, perhaps, were the plants.

This is scratchier and more constraining than I could ever have imagined.

With some wriggling and pulling – and a deep laceration to the sleeve of his jacket – Edmund managed to struggle through until he stood in front of the astonished officers.

"You!" Hasket said.

"Hell's teeth!" Hardy's eyes were near popping out of his head.

Hasket regarded Edmund closely. "What have you done to yourself, man? And why are you here?"

"Are you following us?" Hardy said. "Do not think we have forgotten your strange behavior the last time we encountered you in the maze."

"How dare you disrespect Marianne? I mean, Mrs. Pembroke," Edmund shouted. "You are loathsome!"

"Marianne, is it?" Hasket sneered. "First name terms, eh?"

"I challenge you," Edmund said.

"You challenge me?" Hasket laughed. "What on earth could you challenge me to?"

"I will fight you!" Edmund held up his fists.

"A fist fight is not what decent gentlemen do," Hardy said. "That is definitely for the lower orders."

"You are not decent gentlemen," Edmund said. "If you were, you would not speak of Mrs. Pembroke – or any woman – in that way."

"Look here, Templeton," Hasket said, "you are seriously beginning to annoy me."

He walked towards Edmund and pushed him to the ground.

Edmund leaped to his feet. "If you will not indulge in a fist fight with me, I have only one option."

"You have no options," Hasket said. "Be away with you before I really lose my temper and run you through with my sword."

"I challenge you to a duel," Edmund said.

"Do not be ridiculous!" Hardy said. "Captain Hasket is trained to fight; you could not win against him."

"We shall see!" Edmund said, catching Hasket unawares and flinging him against the prickliest part of the hedge, then kicking him in the shins for good measure and boxing his ears. "You will withdraw your comments about Mrs. Pembroke, sir – or I will have satisfaction – at dawn, tomorrow."

Hasket then went for Edmund with a roar.

"Let go of my throat," Edmund croaked.

"I accept your challenge, you measly worm!" Hasket yelled. "Hardy will be my second. And dawn tomorrow it is – on the far western area above the Crescent Fields, for there will be no one around at that time."

"Do not be late," Hardy said as the two soldiers disappeared down a path.

Edmund clutched his neck.

They mean it this time! Oh, what have I done?

The day was going from bad to worse.

Was I supposed to ask him whether 'twas pistols or swords? Should I take both? And where will I get them from? Oh, why could I not have held my tongue?

Edmund grimaced. He was a gentleman and knew he could not have kept silent, for the man had insulted Marianne. And that was unforgivable.

For I know now that I love her, with all my heart, body, and soul.

CHAPTER NINE

Marianne

"WAKE UP! OH, please, madam; wake up!"

"I am awake. What is it? Is Lady Barrington unwell?"

Jane shook her head. "No. And we must keep our voices down. 'Tis a situation – or will be soon."

"But 'tis not yet light."

"That is the point of dueling at dawn," Jane said. "You have to be ready far before first light."

Marianne gasped. "A duel? Who is involved?"

"Mr. Templeton."

"Mr. Edmund Templeton?"

Jane nodded.

Marianne started dressing rapidly in the most practical clothes she could find. "Tell me all you know, Jane. Quickly! There is not a moment to lose."

Jane explained to Marianne that Edmund had come back home yesterday in a terrible state and gone straight to his room. Cook had asked if he wanted sandwiches sent up, or a drink perhaps, but he had said no, for he could not stomach anything – he just wanted his valet. Voyle had stayed in Edmund's room for a long time, and then left the house with a grim face. He would not say where he was going, only that Mr. Templeton had sent him out to procure a very important item and that Voyle was to be Edmund's second in a duel.

"And what did Mr. Templeton ask Voyle to get for him?" Marianne asked.

"A pistol," Jane said. "There is already a sword at Number 1 he can use, although Voyle thinks it might be rather blunt, for no one can quite remember when 'twas last used."

"But whom is Mr. Templeton to fight – and where?"

"A certain Captain Hasket – they are to meet beyond the Crescent Fields to the west. His second is his friend, Captain Hardy."

"Do you know why?" Marianne said.

"I do not. They say some soldiers pick fights deliberately."

"And is anyone else in Number 1 aware of this?"

"The news has spread, but only below stairs."

Marianne sighed. "Now, listen carefully, Jane. You are to go to Number 2, find Carter, and ask for his help. And then go to Number 3." Marianne gave a small sob before she could continue. "There, you should ask Doctor Fitzgerald to attend – as a precaution, in case any person is injured."

Or worse!

"Then you must go back to the house, Jane, to await my return. And keep your own counsel. I mean it!"

"What will you do, madam?"

Marianne swept her long hair away from her eyes and snatched up a ribbon to tie it back. "I intend on helping Mr. Templeton out of his predicament. Pray God I am not too late!"

Courage roared through her body as she ran from the house.

"No, Nelson," she whispered as the dog slipped out of the door behind her. "You must stay inside. 'Tis not safe!"

But Nelson scampered merrily ahead across the cobbles.

Oh, I should take you back – yet time is of the essence.

Marianne soon caught up with the pug. "You must be a good dog, then, and make no sound. Come! Follow me."

How could this situation have happened? Marianne fled past

the yew tree where she and Edmund had embraced so recently.

His sweet lips! If anyone harms him, I will challenge them to a duel myself.

She ran and ran across the fields, then veered to the right, to a wild, hilly stretch – 'twas an area she had never been to before.

I will conceal myself behind this tree, for I can see shadowy figures over there, in the mist.

"Nelson! Nelson! Come here, my little one," she whispered.

The pug ran to her and cowered by her ankles; could he sense something was gravely amiss? Marianne bent down to caress his damp coat, and as she did so, her hair escaped its hastily tied ribbon and her curls cascaded over her shoulders. Flinging them back impatiently, she bit her lip.

What should I do now? Call out to the men, and tell them to desist? Or await help?

'Twould not be long before the arrival of Carter's reassuring presence, surely? But what if a passerby saw and went to fetch a constable? Oh, then there would be trouble.

As the mist lifted slightly, Marianne could see the two officers in their uniforms.

And there is Edmund! The other figure must be Voyle.

Marianne was too far away to see Edmund's countenance, but she could imagine the fear and panic that was sweeping through his mind. She lifted Nelson into her arms and decided to risk moving a little closer.

For how will I be able to intervene if I am at this far distance?

Very soon she stood but yards away from the men, concealed behind another tree. The four men were talking to each other, with Voyle holding both a pistol and a sword, which the officers seemed to find very droll.

I want to run forward and hold the sword to the first officer's throat, and threaten the other with the pistol! How dare they have involved Edmund in this farce?

Very soon Edmund and one of the officers – it must have been Hasket – stood back-to-back, each holding a pistol. They were walking away from each other and the sound of counting could be heard, when suddenly, Marianne could bear the tension no longer. Flinging Nelson from her arms, she ran between the men.

"No!" she cried. "You cannot do this! 'Tis against the law, and I will not allow it."

Marianne heard the sound of shouting, and then Carter appeared, snatched Hasket's pistol, and tackled him to the ground, while George pulled Hardy's hands behind his back, forcing him to lie face down in the mud.

"Edmund, my darling!" Marianne screamed, running towards him. "You are safe! Oh, thank the Lord!"

But Edmund did not look pleased. "You put yourself in danger, Marianne. And you should not have stopped the duel. I was defending your honor."

"My honor? There is no need! Who cares if these vile officers said anything untoward? I only care that you are safe. I cannot believe these villains forced you into a duel."

"They did not force me. 'Twas my idea."

"*Your* idea?" Marianne flinched and took a step back. "How could you be so half-witted as to endanger your life? Did you not consider all the people who love you? What about your parents, your sister and brother? And what about – everyone else who holds you dear?"

I love him too! But I am not about to tell him now, for I am furious that he has risked everything. How could he be so selfish?

Hasket and Hardy were on their feet now, both liberally smeared with mud, and Carter was giving them a lecture. The gist was that if they breathed a word of this – ever, to anyone – he would report them to their commanding officer and ensure they were dishonorably discharged.

"But 'twas not our idea," Hasket said.

"Exactly," Hardy agreed. "The man made an idiotic challenge."

"You took advantage of a young man who knew no better," Carter roared. "You are in His Majesty's Armed Forces and have a duty to the crown to behave in a responsible way. Now, begone!"

Hasket and Hardy needed no further invitation to slink away.

How magnificent Carter is! I knew he would get this dangerous situation under control. Why, if Edmund possessed but an ounce of Carter's sound sense, how different his life might be. And mine, too.

"Marianne," Edmund said. "I am sorry."

"'Tis too late for apologies," she said. "You have behaved disgracefully. Why do you never consider the consequences of your actions?"

Why am I saying this? Edmund came close to losing his life this morning. Ah! Think what a dark world 'twould be without his unique spirit.

"Lord Templeton will have to be told of this," Carter said, "for the news will be spreading amongst the servants as we speak."

"No!" Edmund said. "Not Papa, I entreat you. He thinks little enough of me as it is. I will perchance now sink so low in his estimation as to be unwelcome in his house."

Oh, poor, poor Edmund! His face is a picture of abject misery. But he should have thought of what Lord Templeton might say before he made his rash challenge.

"We should disperse," Carter said. "'Tis fast becoming light, and discovery is unthinkable. George, could you make sure Marianne and Nelson get home safely to Lady Barrington's? The rest of us will follow on separately to lessen the danger of discovery."

With Nelson scampering at her feet, Marianne walked back with George across the fields.

"I do hope we do not meet anyone on the way back," Marianne said. "I will not know what to say."

"We might have to concoct a story, if challenged," George said. "Perhaps Nelson was keen to leave the house for reasons of nature? You opened the door for him and waited, but he would not come back to you, and so you had to chase after him through the fields. I might have been out on a walk and come across you, and offered to escort you home."

"That sounds a little unbelievable."

George grinned. "I am sorry! I am not much used to lying."

"We are only put in this position because of Edmund's mis-judgment," Marianne said.

She stumbled slightly on a tuft of grass and George lent her his arm for support.

"I do not condone Edmund's behavior," George said, "and yet he thought he was taking an honorable path – the route many in our present society think is a good solution to a perceived insult."

Perhaps he acted no worse than any other hot-blooded young man in a privileged position. I have been very hard on him.

Once back at the Crescent, George escorted Marianne to the servants' entrance at the back of Number 4, where Jane was waiting.

"I leave Mrs. Pembroke in your capable hands, Jane," George said. "She has had a tiring – and shocking – morning, and I am sure you will do your best to look after her."

"Of course, sir."

"I prescribe sweet tea, a breakfast tray in her room, and a morning of rest with little exertion and no excitement."

"We had best move quickly then, sir, for if Lady Barrington becomes aware of this . . . ." Jane quickly covered her mouth with her hand.

George laughed. "I see what you were about to say, Jane. Once Lady Barrington knows what has been going on, there will be little rest in the house and a considerable amount of excite-ment. Am I right?"

Jane's face became quite pink. "I could not possibly say, sir."

"Quite right," George said with a broad grin. "And now I must go home."

"Not without my heartfelt thanks," Marianne said. "You have been so kind, Doctor Fitzgerald."

"Please, call me George. There is no need for formality, especially after all we have experienced. Now, 'twill be nigh impossible for me to keep certain events secret from my wife, so what say you – shall I send Selina over to keep you company for a while this morning? Will that suit?"

"I would like that very much," Marianne said.

As luck would have it, Marianne managed to get upstairs without encountering Lady Barrington, who, unusually for her, was still fast asleep. Shortly after that, Jane brought up a tray.

"There is everything the doctor ordered here, madam; you enjoy a good breakfast, and I will fetch hot water."

"Thank you, Jane," Marianne said gratefully. "And I will require your help combing out these tangles too."

She smiled ruefully as she looked in the mirror. Her hair streamed exuberantly down her back; 'twas entirely wild after the early morning mist had wreaked its own peculiar havoc.

LATER, SELINA ARRIVED and sat with Marianne in the withdrawing room of Number 4.

"Is Lady Barrington out?" Selina asked.

"Yes – she is making a few calls this morning but will be back soon. I said I felt a little fatigued and would prefer to stay at home."

"Did she not ask the reason?"

"No. I think she assumed 'twas a womanly complaint."

"I have been quite fatigued of late," Selina said. "And 'tis definitely a womanly complaint. I have only had confirmation of what it means very recently – yesterday, in fact."

"You mean?"

Is Selina expecting a baby? She has looked slightly wan since my return from Clifton. Oh, how I hope I am proved correct!

"I mean," Selina said, "that there is to be a blessed event!"

Marianne embraced her friend warmly, offering hearty congratulations. "I could not be more pleased!"

And how thrilled I am to realize that I can now rejoice in another's good fortune without the deep pain of my loss gnawing uncontrollably at my heart.

"George says 'twill be before the end of the year, in the autumn," Selina said. "We wish this to be kept private from the wider world for now, for 'tis early days, but I wanted to tell you, dearest Marianne."

"What is to be kept private?" Lady Barrington stood before them with an extremely inquisitive look on her face.

She makes so little noise on entering a room; 'tis quite extraordinary.

"Oh, nothing," Selina and Marianne both said at precisely the same time.

"Well, no matter, for I have some news – 'tis all over the city – and it concerns Edmund. He is to be sent away to Templeton Park for a while so that he can 'come to his senses.' Is that not strange? What could he have done wrong?"

Edmund

EDMUND SAT IN his chamber that afternoon, staring at the trunk on the floor which had already been packed by Voyle.

I have been lectured by Carter, and reprimanded by Papa; Mama has given me hurt looks and retired to her bed with a megrim, and Marianne is not pleased with me. Is there anyone I have not disappointed today?

He looked at the blank paper in front of him and picked up his quill pen.

My dear Marianne,

I must see you before I leave. I have much to apologize for.

Then he screwed the letter into a ball and threw it into the fire. Despair swept over him like the dark clouds that presage thunder.

'Tis very hard to put one's soul on a piece of paper – but I am to be sent away tomorrow at first light for God knows how long and must communicate with my darling.

What was it his papa had said when he had returned in disgrace from the failed duel?

"You will stay working on the estate for as long as it takes you to grow up."

Growing up sounded rather a lengthy process, perhaps months or years – and Edmund could not bear to be parted from Marianne for hours or even minutes.

He tried again.

My dear Marianne,

I love you and respect you. Perhaps in the years to come, if I decide to marry, I might want to marry you. What do you think?

That was truly appalling and went the way of the first attempt. Ah, well! They said the third is sometimes the best, did they not?

My dear Marianne,

I long to see you before I leave for Templeton Park.

With all my love forever,

Edmund.
PS Will you do me the honor of becoming my wife?

"Is it all right if I come in, sir?" Voyle was at the door. "I have a few extra items to place in your trunk."

"Do whatever you want, Voyle. I have no say in my life anymore."

"Very good, sir. I will tidy your room a little as well."

Edmund flung himself onto the bed and pretended to read a book while Voyle busied himself for quite a while.

"I have finished now, sir."

"Thank you, Voyle. I hope you will be ready early tomorrow, for we must make off at first light."

Voyle twitched his nose. "I am sorry to say that Lord Templeton's instructions to me are that I am to stay here."

"What!" Edmund was aghast. "But how will I manage without you?"

"I believe Lord Templeton expressed an opinion on that – but 'tis not one that I am at liberty to repeat."

"I bet he did," Edmund said bitterly. "I will wager he said that I would have to manage on my own for once and stop expecting to be mollycoddled."

Voyle looked at the ceiling and Edmund knew he had guessed correctly.

"Will that be all for now, sir?"

"Yes, thank you. You may go."

Now, where was I?

Edmund sat down and read through his third attempt at a love letter again.

This is completely unsatisfactory. 'Tis too direct – for there are bridges to build between the two of us before I can get anywhere near declaring myself. It also reads like the ravings of a lovesick milksop.

Edmund crumpled up his third letter to Marianne and tossed it into the flames, to join the others.

He knew there was precious little point in writing to her anyway, whether or not it read like the ramblings of a jingle brained young whippersnapper – for he had no means of having the note delivered that would save it from being scrutinized by servants, with the contents then being relayed to other interested parties such as his mama and Lady Barrington.

Edmund ran down to the front door. He would ask his sister if she could help him have a private meeting with Marianne before he left for the country.

"And where do you think you are going, Edmund?" Lord Templeton was sitting in the parlor with the door open.

"I am going to see Selina," Edmund said, "to bid her farewell."

"I think that is acceptable," his papa said, "but pray proceed straight to Number 3 – do not linger in the street – for there is plentiful gossip abroad concerning you. We do not wish the Templeton name to be besmirched by the gabsters of Bath any more than necessary."

"'Tis not my fault that the *ton* are such chinwaggers," Edmund said hotly.

"Ah, but it is, for you have given them something extra juicy to wag their chins over, have you not?"

Edmund fully hoped that while he was away there would be so many scandals of such mighty proportions that everyone would instantly lose interest in him and he would be ordered to return forthwith.

Or perchance there will be exciting news. There is a rumor abroad that the Prince Regent himself is to attend a ball in Bath soon; what if this turns out to be true?

When Edmund arrived at Selina's house, he did not at first find her as accommodating as he would have hoped, for he had quite thought she would offer to go round to Number 4 and fetch Marianne directly.

"I will not do that," Selina said, "because I am not convinced she wishes to converse with you."

"Why would she not?"

"She is annoyed with you. Angry, even. Surely you realize that? You have not covered yourself in glory today, Edmund. Naturally, we are all mighty pleased that you have not been shot dead with a bullet through your heart, but you have caused Marianne – and everyone else – great worry. Besides, there is no point in my going to fetch her, for I know she is not at home."

"Where has she gone? Is she visiting Captain Windbag?"

"Edmund! I do believe you are jealous. And you have no reason to be, for Captain Wyndham is recently engaged to a lovely young woman. You must know his friendship with Marianne is as that of a sister for a brother."

"I do know that," Edmund said. "But when I think of other men being interested in Marianne, it fair makes my blood boil. And as for the way those officers were talking about her, why, 'tis no wonder I felt compelled to act so rashly."

"Do not fret; 'tis over."

"You have not answered my question, Selina. Where is Marianne? And how come you are so up to date with everything?"

"'Tis for me to know – and for you to find out."

"Is she here? You are tormenting me, Selina! Marianne must be upstairs in your withdrawing room. I know it!"

Edmund raced out of the parlor and began leaping up the stairs, first two at a time, then three.

"Edmund!" Selina called. "Do not upset her again. And watch out for Nelson's claws, for he is there too."

Edmund knocked urgently. "Marianne! Might I come in?"

"Yes – please do."

Edmund opened the door – and felt as if all the breath had been knocked from him. Earlier today, on the fields, he had thought Marianne had never appeared more beautiful, with her long hair shimmering in the dawn light. But now, she looked positively divine, a glowing goddess reclining by the fire, with Nelson on her lap.

Nelson ran to him and licked his boots.

"This is a change, I must say," Edmund said. "What? No growling, little one? What have I done to merit this friendly approach? I have no tidbits about my person, so what is it?"

"Nelson thinks as I do," Marianne said. "Although you went about everything in the wrong way, now we have had a chance to think, we appreciate that you were only trying to do your best. You were defending me – and for that, we thank you."

How glad I am she thinks a little better of me now.

Edmund sat down by the fire next to her. "We have not long together, and there is one thing I must talk to you about. I know you intend to take a position as a governess."

"How do you know that?"

"Something I, er, overheard. Is it true?"

"Yes."

Marianne looks uncomfortable. Perchance she is on the point of changing her mind?

"Will you promise me one thing?" Edmund said.

"That depends on what it is."

"Promise me that you will not rush into a decision. Take your time."

"Ah! This is the same advice Frederick gave me. I do not know why people think I cannot make my own decisions."

"They do not think that," Edmund said. "If people beg caution, 'tis because they care for you and do not want you to be condemned to a life of lonely drudgery."

Should I declare myself here and now? Oh, but 'tis not the right time yet. I want to woo my Marianne properly, with letters and flowers, and let all unfold naturally. But I have to go away first – and make myself worthy of her affection.

"Well, yes, then," Marianne said, "since you mention a life of lonely drudgery, I will take my time before I make any irrevocable decision. That is all I can promise for now. But tell me more of what is happening with you."

"With me? Papa is furious, and Mama is more disappointed than she can express. I am sure you already know what is to happen – I am to be banished."

Marianne sighed. "I am sorry. How long is the punishment for?"

"That is an interesting question – and the answer will depend on my father. He says I am to take responsibility for my life while I am away. And would you believe it, he insists I must live in a worker's cottage that is currently unoccupied."

"Where I have no doubt you will be waited on hand and foot."

"Absolutely not! Voyle is commanded to stay here, and I will have to go up to the main house for my food. Who knows, I might even have to cook for myself."

Marianne's eyes widened. "Cook for yourself?"

Edmund laughed. "Well, maybe not, but that would not be such a hardship for me as you might imagine, for I enjoy the culinary arts."

"The more I know you, Edmund, the more you surprise me."

"The more I know you, the more I want to kiss you again."

Ah! Her lovely eyes! And her luscious lips are drawing me closer and closer.

Selina's head appeared at the door. "You will have to go, Edmund. Lady Barrington has arrived unexpectedly and is in the parlor. I have managed to stall her, but she is fully intent on coming upstairs – she says she has a feeling that Nelson needs her. I think she is looking for information, and if she finds you here, she will interrogate you quite mercilessly."

Edmund grasped Marianne's hands. "Farewell! May I write to you?"

"That would never work," Marianne said. "The maids will find out."

"If 'tis any help, Edmund," Selina said, "you may send letters to Marianne here, addressed to me. I promise I will not read them but will pass them straight on."

Edmund nodded eagerly and Selina then turned to her friend. "And Marianne, if you so wish, it would be possible to send letters back through me, for none of my servants are related to Jane or Martha."

"You are a darling sister," Edmund said as he rushed towards the door.

"Use the back stairs," Selina said, "and be careful."

"I will!" Edmund fled.

I can write to Marianne and she might even write back to me! How this will make the long days fly till we meet again.

THE NEXT MORNING, as Edmund stood shivering in front of the Crescent waiting for the carriage, he felt a shaft of optimism peeping through, just as the sun shows her rays again after a downpour.

I will do my best to make the most of the challenge Papa has set me. I will do it for Marianne.

As he was driven slowly along the front of the Crescent, Edmund spied a single candle shining at a high window – and a small figure with red curls waving at him.

Marianne

MARIANNE PICKED UP the candle and took it back to the desk in her bedchamber.

Is it too soon to write to Edmund?

But what could she possibly write, when her feelings were in such turmoil?

Her mind danced hither and thither, flitting from one thought to the next. She loved Edmund. But did she have the courage to marry again? Perhaps the easiest path, the one she knew she could follow, would be to take a post as a governess, even if Edmund had described such a life as "lonely drudgery."

And was Edmund the right man – would he be a reliable and faithful husband? Challenging Captain Hasket to a duel had been both misjudged and reckless; did this suggest that a union with Edmund was unwise?

And I must not forget that he has not declared himself to me. But how sweet his kisses were! 'Tis a memory I shall treasure forever.

"Are you out of bed already, madam?" Jane was in the chamber doorway.

"Indeed, I am. I wanted to wave to the carriage as it left."

"Is there anything you require?"

"No, thank you." Marianne stifled a yawn. "I think I will snatch another half hour of sleep."

"Very good, madam."

Marianne got into bed, and Jane tidied a few items of clothing before saying, "Although, I have heard some news."

Marianne turned her face away. "I do not want to listen to gossip."

"As you wish." Jane started to make for the door. "But 'tis about Mr. Templeton."

"It is?"

"Yes. My sister told me something that Voyle had told her, and then . . ."

"Jane! I do not wish to hear the full provenance of the information you are about to impart. Pray come here and tell me what you know as quickly and efficiently as possible."

And so Jane explained how yesterday afternoon, when Voyle had been tidying Edmund's room, he had noticed a letter to Marianne on the desk.

"A letter?" Marianne sat up. "But I have not received anything."

"Exactly! 'Tis mysterious! Mr. Templeton did not ask Voyle to deliver it for him, which one might think he should have. Perchance Mr. Templeton has given it to someone else who has yet to deliver it?"

Marianne lay down again. "Well, if that is the case, I will find out what the letter says when it arrives. Thank you, Jane."

"Do you wish to know what the letter said? It had not been folded and sealed, but was open on the desk."

Marianne leapt out of bed, blazing with anger. "Do you mean to say that Voyle actually read my letter? Is nothing sacred?"

Jane flushed deeply. "He only read the last line. Voyle said he knew 'twas wrong – but in his defense, said his eyes could not help but fall upon the page. And 'twas indiscreet of him to tell everyone else about it, too."

"Everyone else? I thought 'twas just your sister, Martha?"

"Yes, at first Martha, and then everyone below stairs at Number 1."

"This gets worse by the minute. I will know what was written! 'Tis only right, when the contents have been revealed to so many others. Tell me at once!"

Tears began to snake their way down Jane's cheeks.

I have frightened her now. Oh, how I struggle to control my passions when Edmund is concerned.

"I am sorry to have overreacted, Jane, and to have caused you distress. Pray tell me – what did Voyle see when his eyes accidentally fell upon the page?"

Jane wiped her face on her apron and sniffed. "The last line was, *Will you do me the honor of becoming my wife?*"

Ah! 'Twas as if the Pump Room band had entered the bed-chamber. The violins played the sweetest, most heartfelt melody of love whilst other instruments provided a soft cushion of harmony.

"That will be all, Jane, thank you," Marianne said dreamily.

Alone in her room, she gently waltzed around the floor, imagining being entwined in Edmund's arms.

He thinks enough of me to have asked for my hand!

When the music came to an end, Marianne curtsied to her vision of Edmund and reached up to kiss him softly upon his chiseled lips. She then went to her writing desk, intending to answer the letter.

Although I do not know what to say. Oh, how I long to accept, but would that not be rash without knowing whether he is truly a reformed character? And what of my plan to move to the Lake District? For a life of lonely drudgery?

It was only when Marianne put pen to paper that she realized quite how forward she was being.

For I have not received the letter from Edmund – yet.

Marianne wondered how long she would have to wait before 'twas delivered. Would the missive be thrust under her bedroom door by the anonymous hand of a servant? Or would it be passed to Jane to give her?

There was another possibility, and one that Marianne would do well to consider. Perchance the letter had never been sent because Edmund had reconsidered his words.

I know that in reality I would have been even more angry at the total lack of privacy, but how I wish Voyle had read the entire page instead of merely the last line, for then I might understand more what prompted Edmund to ask me to marry him.

Marianne sighed, realizing she had no option but to wait.

And even if a letter does arrive, all my previous reservations about Edmund still stand strong, for I do not believe he is yet mature enough to have outgrown his misspent youth.

The best path for Marianne was to make her own way in the world. There was no sense in harboring a romantic dream that might never become reality.

AND SO MARIANNE started assisting Selina with her task of educating the local children. Many times, Marianne accompanied them on nature rambles across the fields, helping them to sketch the tiny spring flowers that were beginning to stud the grass – although she found it hard to concentrate when they wandered near the mighty yew tree where Edmund had kissed her. She played the pianoforte when Selina led the children in their singing, taught the children their letters, and read them stories.

The days dragged past, and still no letter appeared. Was it possible Edmund had penned a proposal in haste, then come to his senses and cast it into the fire to be incinerated? Perhaps it had been an ill-judged jest? Or perchance he had merely been practicing his handwriting.

I can believe that – for his hand resembles nothing more than a demented spider that has inadvertently fallen into an ink pot. I wonder how carefully Edmund listened to his governess as a boy? Could he not have worked harder at his calligraphy?

Then one day, at the beginning of March, Marianne was seated at the pianoforte in Selina's withdrawing room making music with her friend, when George came into the room.

He regards his wife with such devotion. How pleased I am to know they are to be blessed in the autumn.

"The post has arrived, Selina, my dear," George said, "and I believe this letter is in your brother's writing."

"Ah! Because the address is hard to read?" Selina joked. "Yes! That will be from Edmund."

Marianne flushed beetroot. Could this be it, the letter containing the proposal? For Edmund had said he would write to her under cover of writing to his sister. But why would the letter have taken so long to arrive? And why would he have taken it all the way to Templeton Park, only to send it back? Unless perhaps it had not yet been fully completed when Voyle's eyes fell upon it.

"Thank you," Selina said, tucking the letter under some music. "I will look at it later. Will you hear my song, George? Marianne plays so prettily on the pianoforte that she is able to cover up my indifferent performance."

George laughed. "I know full well that both you ladies are superb performers, but sadly the pleasure of an impromptu concert will have to wait for another day, for Lady Barrington has asked for my help regarding a medical matter; she usually consults my father, but he is not available today."

"Oh?" Marianne said. "She seemed very well this morning."

"'Tis not her, I believe, but Nelson who is ailing," George replied.

"George!" Selina said. "Your skills are better employed with humankind, are they not?"

"I am very fond of Nelson," George said, "and am happy to attend. However, if 'tis like the visits my papa has made for the pug in the past, there will be nothing very much wrong. The most likely scenario is that Lady Barrington is merely seeking reassurance."

"I believe she over-indulges that dog by feeding him too many rich things," Selina said.

"I agree," George said, "but fear it might be hard to convey that particular message effectively when conversing with Lady Barrington."

I can believe it, for my aunt has many good qualities, but listening to sound advice is not always one of them.

"I suppose 'tis natural she spoils Nelson a little," Marianne said, "for he has been her constant companion since Lord Barrington died. She regards him as a family member."

"Just as George thinks of his horse, Trigger, as a close friend and a member of our family," Selina said with a smile.

"I admit it!" George said. "Now, farewell ladies. I will let you know how Nelson is later, for I realize how fond you both are of the little scamp."

Once George had left the room, Selina handed the letter to Marianne. "You must open this, for I believe that although addressed to me, 'tis for your eyes only."

Marianne sat down on the sofa next to the fire and broke the seal with trembling fingers.

My dear Marianne, the letter began.

"Yes," she whispered. "'Tis intended for me."

Ah, the use of the word "intended!" How I wish I were Edmund's intended bride.

"In that case I will leave you alone for a few minutes," Selina said. "My brother has certainly taken his time to write, but no doubt Papa has given him plenty of tasks to undertake at Templeton Park. And Edmund never was a very regular correspondent."

Once Selina had left, Marianne began to read.

I hope this letter finds you well and that you have remembered your promise not to become a governess before you have had sufficient time for reflection.

I am staying alone in a worker's cottage and go up to the main house for my meals. After a few uncomfortable instances of being served stone cold food in the dining hall with myself as the only person at the table, I have come to an agreement with Cook that I shall eat in the kitchen with her and the other servants and estate workers. 'Tis far more sociable and jolly, and I have been able to practice my cooking skills a little too. Yesterday I helped make a stew, and the day before, a fruit crumble.

I am sorry it has taken me such a while to write, but I have been kept busy from morn till night. The steward Mr. Grant has been ill for some time and much has been neglected, so I have been helping out with administrative work as well as physical.

Added to which, Papa has set me a task; he wants me to suggest how the workers' cottages might be renovated and improved. This is why he insisted I stay in one of the dwellings, so that I might experience the living conditions first-hand. I have been spending my evenings drafting design plans, which I am more than happy to do – in truth, I have found the whole process immensely rewarding.

Marianne skimmed through the rest of the letter. How strange! Edmund wrote mostly about his plans for new accommodation, with details of weatherproofing and avoiding areas prone to flooding. 'Twas so very technical.

I can see that 'tis an admirable idea to provide better accommodation for the workers at Templeton Park – but is this all that Edmund is going to say to me? Is his mind totally consumed with thoughts of ditches and drains, water tables, and wells?

Marianne's heart contracted with pain as she forced herself to consider the strong possibility that their turbulent – and possibly imagined – romance had finally given up the ghost.

And yet my whole being longs for him most ardently.

After some while, Selina came back into the room. "How was it? What does my brother have to say?"

Marianne passed Selina the letter. "You may read it for yourself. He says at the end he would like me to share his news with you as it saves him from having to write another missive."

Selina began reading. "Ah! I see he is enjoying helping in the kitchen. How useful it is to know that I could ask Edmund to stand in for my cook if she were taken ill when I have planned a dinner party."

"Indeed," Marianne said with a forced smile.

"And I note he misses certain aspects of his former luxurious lifestyle – like Voyle providing a bath full of hot water at the end of a long day."

"I can see that must be a hardship."

Selina frowned. "But wait. This is not right. There should be something more personal, for you alone. When Edmund asked if he could write to you here, I had thought that signified a particular preference."

"I do not know why you would have thought that," Marianne said stiffly. "I myself was not expecting anything beyond simple friendship from your brother. No, nothing!"

"I hate to see you so upset." Selina put her arm on Marianne's shoulder. "If I tell you that Edmund is possibly the worst letter writer in the world, one who has always found it difficult to express his feelings on paper, does that make the situation any easier to bear? And look here, at the beginning – see how he urges you not to leave in a hurry to be a governess? That surely means something."

"As I said before, 'tis of no consequence to me. In reality, this letter helps me greatly by allowing me to finalize the plans for my own future. I have much enjoyed helping you with the children; it has been a useful experience for the next phase of my life."

Before Selina could reply, George rushed into the room.

"I am sorry to be the bearer of bad tidings," he said, "but for once it looks as if poor Nelson is in quite a bad way. Lady Barrington is asking for you, Marianne, for there is every possibility her dear pug will not last till the morrow."

CHAPTER TEN

Edmund

MEANWHILE, EDMUND HAD settled into his new life at Templeton Park. His habit was to rise before dawn, work for several hours in the grounds with the other men, and then walk up to the main house with his new friends to break his fast.

One particular morning, sitting at breakfast in the large kitchen with such a merry crowd, Edmund felt both relaxed and useful. The latter was a strange sensation, and not one that he had ever experienced in Bath. There, he was a figure who was recognized by all in the street, but as a useless ornament, the heir to the Templeton fortune and title, not as a man who had earned the right to anything through honest hard work or merit.

Edmund looked around the table at the smiling faces, the plain plates filled with fresh bread, cheese, and meat, and felt content.

I must tell Marianne more about my life here in my next letter. I had no idea work could be so much fun! And I am pleased every day to remember she has promised to wait before making any decision about being a governess. Oh, Lord, how I miss her! I wish I could have found the words to express how much I long for her in my last letter, but such sentiments are far better expressed face to face. There will be time enough for that when I return.

One of the men started ribbing Edmund about his work that

morning. "You did not dig the hole for the fence post deep enough," he said. "Could you not find the strength?"

"I tried my best," Edmund said, "but 'twas slow going as there was a vast tree root blocking the hole and I had difficulty breaking through it."

"Weakling!" another said.

"Do not worry Templeton," the first man said, "we will make a proper man of you yet."

Edmund grinned. "All the work I have already done digging ditches and putting up fences is making me feel more muscular." He flexed a bicep ostentatiously.

The men started cheering at the sight and banged their cups on the table.

"Enough!" Cook said. "You men need to learn how to behave yourselves in my kitchen."

The men all assumed expressions of contrition – and then burst into raucous laughter.

They are a merry bunch! I am enjoying working with them – and learning from them.

Then Mr. Grant appeared. "If I might have a word, Mr. Templeton, when you have breakfasted?"

"I will come now." Edmund stood and followed Mr. Grant to his room.

"Pray sit down, sir," the steward said. "I want to start by thanking you for all the help you have given us thus far."

"I have done no more than your other workers," Edmund said.

"You have done much more. 'Tis not only your physical labor that you have offered, but you have scrutinized many documents and suggested efficiencies and improvements."

"Helping with the administrative paperwork of Templeton Park has given me much pleasure."

I can scarce believe I am saying this, but 'tis true.

"Although," Edmund continued, "I sincerely hope I have not been guilty of interference?"

"No, quite the reverse," Mr. Grant said. "Your contribution has been invaluable, especially as I have not been on top of things since my illness, which, thank the Lord, is lifting at last. And I have looked at the plans for the new workers' cottages that you gave me yesterday. You have indeed been burning the midnight oil."

"What do you think of the designs?" Edmund asked.

"They are inspired! These new cottages will have more light, and by virtue of their modern construction will be warmer and less damp than the present dwellings, many of which are sadly not fit for purpose, particularly for those workers with families."

"I am glad! And I think 'tis important to site the cottages in a more suitable area, for it does not matter how perfectly they are designed if they are too near the river and will flood – oh, please accept my hearty apologies for babbling on, but I find I have developed a passion for design and long for the plans to become reality."

"Well," Mr. Grant said, "a letter came from your father this morning, to say he will visit us later this afternoon. I will show him your drawings."

"Papa is coming here? How wonderful!"

And how terrifying. I wonder if he is still angry with me. I wonder, too, how much he told Mr. Grant of the real reason I came here – that I was in disgrace and had to be sent away until the gossip died down.

As Edmund walked back to join the men, a footman handed him a letter with a small bow.

'Twill be another from Mama, no doubt urging me to learn important lessons from my enforced exclusion from the season.

Edmund shoved the letter into the pocket of the rough jacket he had taken to wearing every day.

If my friends in Bath could but see me now, sporting these practical but far from stylish garments! I have not worn my usual tailored jackets and skin-tight pantaloons since my arrival, nor a fancy cravat, for such attire would have invited more teasing from the men, as well as being supremely impractical for the physical tasks I have been undertaking.

Edmund spent the rest of the morning working outside. In his next break, he remembered what was in his pocket and sat away from the others as he pulled out the crumpled paper.

Ah! This is not from Mama. 'Tis from Selina. The hand is similar, for sure, but Selina is wont to write the E of my name rather more flamboyantly. She started to do this when we were children, to tease me, and now it has become a habit. But wait! I must look inside, for the letter could be from Marianne.

Edmund tore open the seal and looked at the end.

Yours,
Mrs. Marianne Pembroke.

How formal! That did not bode well. But there was a whole letter to read before Edmund might be forced to give up hope.

Dear Mr. Templeton,

I thank you for your letter. 'Twas fascinating to hear about all you have been doing, and kind of you to share details of your new life with me.

That was more like it! *Fascinating* was an appreciative word, was it not? So was *kind*. Edmund felt exceedingly pleased that Marianne appreciated how diligently he had thrown himself into his new work.

For I am determined to make her proud of me, particularly as she was rightly disappointed by my recent behavior in Bath.

"Templeton!" came a shout. "Five minutes, then back to work. We must finish the fence."

Edmund gave a cheery wave of acquiescence and returned to the letter.

Poor Nelson has been very ill, but George has worked his medical magic . . . I have recently received a letter from my friend Charlotte in the Lake District; she has found me a position in a household nearby. I am not at liberty to delay, as the family are keen to appoint a governess as soon as possible. First, I will travel to my parents' house in Clifton, to sort out various books and necessities, then I plan to proceed to the Lakes by stagecoach.

Edmund's heart sank – oh, why had Marianne not waited as she had promised?

Perchance she rates me very low, especially when compared to her husband, the gallant war hero.

Edmund stuffed the note in his pocket and ran back to his work. Never had he worked so fast or furiously. He dug holes, rammed in posts, and pounded with a hammer as if his life depended on it.

"Careful, Templeton!" one of the other men said. "You will split the fence post with that sort of treatment."

How has everything gone so wrong? Did Marianne not realize that 'twould take time for me to adjust and make myself worthy of her love? For I certainly said as much – did I not?

Edmund put his hammer down. What had he said? He had asked her not to make a quick decision about becoming a governess, yes – but had he begged her not to leave because he loved her with all his heart, body, and soul?

But surely she must have known that any talk of love had to wait till I was completely worthy to seek her hand?

The scales fell from Edmund's eyes.

Marianne can have no idea of the depth of my affection! She must be thoroughly confused, for all she has heard from me is a criticism of her choice of employment, which I described as "lonely drudgery" – and the arrant nonsense I spouted about desiring to remain unwed for years, if not forever.

Besides, a young woman in her position is not afforded the luxury of waiting; not all are born with a silver spoon in their mouths. How blind I have been, in so many ways. And what a fool I am.

"Edmund, my boy! There you are!" Lord Templeton stood beside the fence. "Mr. Grant said you would be out here. I must say I am impressed to see you doing an honest day's work as part of a team. How does it feel?"

"It feels like something I ought to have done a long time ago, Papa."

Lord Templeton looked him up and down. "And you are looking well! All this fresh air – and daylight – is agreeing with you."

'Tis true about the daylight – it does make one feel more alive. Why, in my former Bath life there were sometimes days when I scarcely caught an hour or two of natural light by rising so late.

"Come back to the house with me, my boy. We should talk."

Edmund and Lord Templeton walked to the main parlor where a footman served them with a glass of Madeira.

"I have seen your plans for the new workers' cottages," Lord Templeton said.

"I know they would be costly," Edmund said, "but when I think of the conditions that people have been living in, it does not seem right – not when we have so much."

"I heartily agree with you. And 'tis exactly for this sort of reason that I want you to work closely with me, for a younger pair of eyes and a more modern approach is what the estate needs and deserves."

"I would be honored to work with you, Papa. I admire you greatly. And I apologize for not fulfilling my duty before."

"Ah, Edmund, you are turning into a young man of whom I can be rightly proud."

The two men drank in silence for a few minutes. They had not been in the habit of talking in this manner before, and to Edmund, and perchance to Lord Templeton too, the situation was feeling a little odd.

"But what is the news from Bath?" Edmund said. "How is everyone? I hear Nelson has not been at all well."

"Nelson is much recovered, I am glad to say. 'Twas touch and go for a while, and there was one night in particular when the pug ran such a high fever that George was afeared he could do nothing for him. But he pulled through."

"And Mrs. Pembroke?" Edmund said. "I believe she is to leave the Crescent? Or has she already left?"

"She has plans to leave; however, Lady Barrington is not at all pleased and every day finds a fresh excuse to detain her, usually to do with Nelson's health."

Marianne is still in Bath! Oh, how I long to see her to put things right. And to tell her how much I ardently love and adore her and wish her to become my wife.

"Edmund," Lord Templeton said, "we must arrange your return to Bath. I think you have done enough here for now and should come back with me tomorrow morning."

"You want me to return? But what about my duties at Templeton Park?"

"Of course I want you to return! As for your duties, there are many business documents at home I would like to mull over with you, and we can search for an architect in the city to build these workers' cottages of yours. We will be a team. What say you?"

"I accept! Joyfully!"

I have found my purpose at last – and now I am ready to follow my heart.

"Excellent news!" Lord Templeton said. "And there is another reason you must return to Bath forthwith. The Prince Regent himself is to attend a ball in the Upper Rooms soon, and your mama is most keen that all the family should be there."

"How marvelous! 'Twill be wonderful to see everyone gathered together again. But Papa, would you grant me a small favor?"

"Name it, dear boy."

"Would it be possible to visit Clifton on our way back to Bath? I have a call I wish to pay – and a question I must ask Mr. Oakley."

Lord Templeton raised an enquiring eyebrow – and then a broad beam of approval spread across his face.

Marianne

THAT EVENING, MARIANNE was trying to reason with Lady Barrington.

"Aunt! There is nothing wrong with Nelson; he has almost fully recovered. I must be allowed to prepare for my return to Clifton, and thence to the Lake District. I cannot let Charlotte down, nor the family I am to work for. I have given my word!"

But Lady Barrington continued to refuse to countenance the suggestion that she would be able to manage Nelson in his convalescence without Marianne to aid her.

"And 'tis not only Nelson who needs your help," Lady Barrington said, "for there is my knee to consider."

"Your knee?"

"Yes. It has been troubling me much of late."

Marianne regarded Lady Barrington most severely. "I saw you chasing after Nelson on the lawn this morning – your knee was not troubling you then."

"The stiffness comes on very suddenly – and have I mentioned the excruciating pain?" Lady Barrington screwed her eyes up. "Ouch! Like that! As if from nowhere."

From nowhere, indeed.

THE NEXT MORNING, Marianne and Lady Barrington were at breakfast in the parlor when Jane appeared.

"Excuse me, Lady Barrington; Madame Dubonnet is at the door."

"Pray show her in," Lady Barrington said. "Ah! Madame Dubonnet. Thank you for visiting."

This is an early call. I wonder what she wants? And why is her servant carrying an enormous box?

"I have here your ball gown, Mrs. Pembroke. I hope you will be pleased with it."

"My ball gown?" Marianne said. "Aunt! I do not understand. I was not expecting any further generous gifts."

"As soon as I heard the Prince Regent would be attending a ball in Bath, I took the liberty of asking Madame Dubonnet to make you another frock."

"'Tis cut from the emerald silk you so admired in my shop on your first visit," Madame Dubonnet said.

"Yes, and will match your eyes perfectly," Lady Barrington said.

"Perhaps I might see the gown on you?" Madame Dubonnet said. "There could be last-minute alterations needed."

"Of course," Lady Barrington said. "We will go up to Marianne's chamber for the fitting."

Soon Marianne had been helped into the dress and was standing in front of her mirror with Lady Barrington, Madame Dubonnet, and Jane around her. She moved gently from side to side, feeling the material of the bell-like skirt swish against her legs, while the beads and spangles on the hemline glinted softly.

Marianne imagined herself at the ball. But with whom would she dance? Edmund was far away at Templeton Park. Perchance Captain Wyndham would take pity on her, although now he was engaged, he should perhaps save all his dances for his intended.

"Well, what do you think of the fit?" Lady Barrington said to Madame Dubonnet.

"Very good," she said, "although I believe Mrs. Pembroke has lost a little weight since I first measured her in January. I always allow for some adjustment in the bodice, so if I could just tighten this here – ah! That is better."

Madame Dubonnet stood back to admire her handiwork, and then a roguish smile came to her face. "Sometimes I find my ladies lose weight when they are pining for a certain someone."

Lady Barrington raised her eyebrows and smiled – while Marianne struggled not to show her annoyance at Madame Dubonnet's over-personal remark.

'Tis not surprising my form has changed, for my appetite has deserted me of late and I have spent many nights tossing and turning, wondering what is to become of me.

Marianne stood up straight and regarded herself again in the mirror.

But all is well now. 'Tis merely last-minute nerves. I am to have a new life in the Lakes; all is settled, and I shall enjoy it. I am determined to.

"But what is this?" Madame Dubonnet said, looking around the room. "I see you are in the midst of packing."

"Yes," Marianne said. "I have accepted a position as governess with a family."

Madame Dubonnet's hand flew to her mouth a second too late to stifle her exclamation of horror. Then she recovered her powers of speech. "But Mrs. Pembroke! You will have no need to do this if you wear this beautiful dress at the ball, for every young man will be pursuing you. Why, the Prince Regent himself . . ."

Madame Dubonnet stopped dead, perhaps realizing that 'twas not quite appropriate to talk of the Prince Regent in so familiar a manner, nor to speculate as to what he might or might not do if he saw a beautiful woman at a ball.

"Marianne will shine like a diamond," Lady Barrington said. "And for that reason, I know she will manage to delay her journey for a few more days – for 'twould be criminal to miss the ball of the season. Especially after Madame Dubonnet has gone to all this trouble with the emerald silk."

Marianne bit her lip. Her wishes had been overruled yet again by the whims and caprices of others. She had been thwarted in her desire to control her own destiny; she had been defeated.

Yet should she not surrender gracefully? For all things considered, would it hurt that much to delay her journey by mere days? Hopefully her new employers would be understanding. And the dress was certainly very beautiful – and she did so love dancing.

Marianne nodded.

"That is settled, then," Lady Barrington said. "And pray show us what else is in your box, Madame Dubonnet, for I believe I ordered matching gloves and dancing shoes."

"Oh yes, and something for the hair," Madame Dubonnet

said. "Mrs. Pembroke's curls are her crowning glory. See here; I have had a seamstress stitch this stunning green silk band, fully embellished with a floral design to match the decorations on the dress. And I have taken the liberty of adding a few extra spangles and some feathers."

"The embellishments are simply stunning," Lady Barrington said. "Marianne, you will shine brightly like a tropical bird, as I predicted."

Marianne examined the delicate creation. "Thank you – 'tis enchanting."

I dread to think how many hours the poor seamstresses must have had to spend on this – let alone the whole outfit. Ah! How fortunate I am.

"And now I must leave you," Madame Dubonnet said.

"I expect there are many others in Bath who are desirous of your services," Marianne said.

"Yes, indeed. I have had orders from ladies all over the city, but I promise you one thing – not one of them will outshine you."

I cannot believe that is true – this must be the sort of flattery Madame Dubonnet is wont to dish out. But I do adore the outfit and look forward to wearing it.

"Jane," Lady Barrington said, "could you help Mrs. Pembroke out of her dress while I go downstairs with Madame Dubonnet? Thank you, my dear. And dress warmly, Marianne, for we shall be on our way soon."

"On our way?"

"Yes, to Molland's. I thought we would go there for coffee this morning. Did I not mention this before?"

"No, Aunt; you did not."

Madame Dubonnet and Lady Barrington swept away, and Marianne surveyed the room in dismay.

I had anticipated a morning at home to continue my packing.

'Twas proving very difficult for Marianne to decide what to take with her for her new life. She had no wish to offend Lady

Barrington by leaving some of her new garments, but her trunk had limited space – nor would she have much need for fashion or flamboyance in the future.

Oh! I should have asked Madame Dubonnet to make me a sober and plain outfit, befitting the station of a governess – although I still have all my old mourning clothes I can use up. I wonder where they are?

"Jane," Marianne said, "have you seen the gowns I had when I first arrived in Bath? My black, gray, and lavender frocks? I wondered if you had taken them to launder and press, for I have not seen them for a while."

"Oh, no, madam," Jane said. "All those gowns have gone."

"Gone? What do you mean?"

"Not long ago, when you were out one day, Lady Barrington asked me to help her go through your wardrobe. We removed all the drab colors, boxed them up, and they have been given to the poor."

Without asking me?

"I did notice some reorganization of my wardrobe but thought 'twas part of a general tidy up. I had no idea my possessions had been disposed of."

I have been so distracted with myriad new outfits that I quite forgot about my mourning clothes.

"I am so sorry, Mrs. Pembroke. I did not realize this was done without your permission. Lady Barrington said you were quite happy for her to cull your garments – or did she perchance say you *would* be quite happy for her to do so? I cannot remember."

Marianne sighed. "No matter. I will have to manage the best I can. 'Tis not your fault, Jane."

Very soon Marianne was racing down Milsom Street with Lady Barrington and Nelson.

"We need to get to Molland's quickly," Lady Barrington puffed, "before they run out of my beloved marchpane cakes."

"Is your knee not troubling you now?" Marianne asked innocently.

"Oh, no. As I explained before, it comes and goes. I shall

probably suffer for this haste later in the day, though."

Thankfully, there were still plenty of marchpane cakes left for Lady Barrington, and she was thrilled when she managed to secure her favorite table in the bay window upstairs.

"I always like to sit here," Lady Barrington confided. "It has by far the best view of the street. And we are lucky – we have the room to ourselves, so Nelson is free to scamper about while we chat."

Marianne peered down onto the street while the maid came to take their order. There were throngs of people shopping today, a positive riot of color – and so many adorable hats, many with the most delightful decorations.

I am going to miss the hustle and bustle of a city, for the family I am to work for lives in quite an isolated house.

Charlotte had done as Marianne asked and found her a family in need of a governess, but she had not been as enthusiastic about the whole business as Marianne would have liked. In her letter, she had written,

> *The family I have found will, I know, be kind to you, and their children are very dear – yet I still believe that being a governess is not your ultimate destiny. 'Tis not too late to change your mind, dearest Marianne.*

"Ah!" Lady Barrington applied her quizzing glass to her eye as she peered out of the window. "Here is someone we know. Captain Wyndham! And the young lady must be his intended. I will go down and ask them to join us at our table."

Before Marianne could stop her aunt and suggest that perhaps Captain Wyndham and his intended might have other plans, Lady Barrington had run into the street and accosted them.

"Come here, Nelson," Marianne said. "You stay with me. Oh, 'tis wonderful to see you fully restored to health. I could not have born it if you had not survived."

Marianne buried her face in Nelson's neck to hide her emotions. Why was she so close to tears these days? And, sometimes, to anger?

As if I do not know! Oh, Edmund, how I long for you to return and take me in your arms. I wish I had never spoken to you unkindly – and I do not want you to change your character in any way, for I love you as you are.

But most of all, I wish you wanted to marry me. For I would accept you in a trice.

"What a shame," Lady Barrington said as she returned. "Captain Wyndham and his intended are on their way to the Pump Room to meet with friends. But he was able to tell me some interesting news. I will ask for more refreshments and then tell you what I have discovered."

Soon, more coffee and marchpane cake were brought to the table, and Lady Barrington fed Nelson sugary tidbits while she enlightened Marianne.

"I have it on good authority that many more officers from Captain Wyndham's regiment will soon be arriving in Bath; 'tis the excitement of the Prince Regent's visit that is acting as a draw. Anyhow, this means there will be positively hordes of eligible young men at the ball. Oh, my dear Marianne, I do hope I am not speaking out of turn, but would it not be marvelous if one of them could sweep you off your feet? And I do not mean simply for a dance."

Aunt never stops with her scheming! If she thinks that I will have my head turned by an army officer at a ball, then she misjudges me. I am not that shallow.

Yet, was that not what happened once? For I met dear Richard at a ball. Oh, how muddled I feel! I do believe I have a megrim brewing.

"Do not look so disapproving, my dear," Lady Barrington said, reaching out to smooth the lines between Marianne's brows. She was always concerned to see a frown, and oft warned it could mar a beautiful face if worn frequently. "'Twill be fun for you to meet some more eligible young men; you could do with fresh blood to peruse."

"But Aunt! That is not what I desire."

"Well, what is? I know you say you want to become a governess, but I have never believed that for a moment. I think you are trying to punish yourself."

"Punish myself?"

"Yes! You are punishing yourself for surviving when your husband – and the babe – did not. You might have cast off your widow's weeds, yet you are still mourning."

This is not fair! My aunt is completely impossible. And that reminds me.

"Who gave you the right to dispose of my old clothes? They will be useful to me as a governess."

"You mean when you bury yourself in the middle of no-where, and turn your back on fun and society? Do you seriously want to wear those dreadfully dull colors again – the ones you wore when first you arrived? The ones that did you no favors."

Marianne sprang to her feet. "I will not stay to listen to this!"

"I know you think I am being cruel, my dear, but I have your best interests at heart. Why, I have even been pretending that Nelson was not fully recovered and that my knee was playing up again to get you to stay but a few more days so that you could attend the ball."

"Where, no doubt, you want me to flaunt myself in front of these officers to encourage them to ask me to dance. Well, I am not going to! There is only one person I wish to marry, er, I mean to dance with."

Lady Barrington smiled. "Admit it! You love Edmund and have loved him for a long time."

Marianne felt as if she were simultaneously diving into a burning volcano and chiseling her way out of an icy glacier. Her resolve to keep her romantic sufferings to herself was finally broken, and she gave a great cry of anguish, then sat down and whispered, "Yes, I love him; I have always loved him," before dissolving into a torrent of tears.

Lady Barrington rushed to cradle her niece, holding her tight-ly and patting her rhythmically on her back. "There, there, my dear, sweet child. I am sorry to have resorted to goading you in the way I did – but someone had to break through the carapace you had constructed around your feelings. I know how much you love Edmund – and I know you have loved him since the day you met. Even when you thought you were pretending to love him so that you would not be pushed to look elsewhere for a husband, even then I knew he had already captured your heart. Your aunt is not such a daft old fool as you think. Now, dry your eyes."

"But what shall I do?" Marianne sobbed. "For he is far away, and I told him I hated him. And when Edmund wrote to me, he said nothing of what I had hoped to hear. Besides, he is banished to Templeton Park, who knows for how long? Perhaps forever?"

"I have it on very good authority," Lady Barrington said, "that Lord and Lady Templeton sent him away not only as a punishment for his unfortunate high spirits in provoking a duel, but also because they wanted him to come to his senses concerning you, my dear. You are not the only person who has been denying their feelings and playacting, believe me! Both myself and Lady Templeton are fully convinced Edmund loves you just as much as you love him. Now, dry your eyes. Lord Templeton made a visit to Templeton Park yesterday, intending to collect his son and return today. What have you got to say about that?"

Marianne was entirely struck dumb.

A gigantic weight has been lifted from my mind – and I can hear a choir of angels singing the Hallelujah Chorus high in the sky above Molland's. Oh, dare I hope there is a happy ending waiting for me after all?

Edmund

THE SUN WAS shining when Edmund and his father reached Clifton. As they drove through the streets on their way to Sion Hill, Edmund felt happier than he had done for a long time – and yet more apprehensive too.

Asking Mr. Oakley's permission to address Marianne is a terrifying prospect. I do not know what she might have told her parents about me; would she, for instance, have mentioned my irresponsibility? My lack of purpose and my poor judgement? I tremble to think in what light they regard me. And yet Mr. Oakley was extremely friendly when I met him before – he even said I could be relied upon, did he not?

"Do not look so worried, Edmund," Lord Templeton said. "Mr. Oakley will give you his blessing – of that I am sure."

"'Tis by no means certain, Papa," Edmund said. "I fear I have lived a very superficial life until now, and Mr. Oakley might be rightly cautious."

"We will see. I say, the views of the Gorge are quite splendid, are they not?"

"They are extraordinary! Might we stop for a minute here, Papa? I would like time to collect my thoughts."

"Of course, dear boy. I will stay in the carriage. Take all the time you need."

Edmund looked over the plunging ravine, the turbulent water down below glimmering in the sunshine. He had previously wondered whether he should try to secure Marianne's affections before talking to her father, but in view of her great losses in the past, he thought the traditional way would be more respectful and proper.

And this is just the beginning of my quest, for I fully realize that even if Mr. Oakley gives his blessing, I still have to win Marianne's heart. We have much to resolve.

The carriage made the very short journey from the Gorge to the Oakleys' house, and while Lord Templeton knocked at the door, Edmund looked up at the ironwork balcony on the first floor. He had not taken much notice of this on his previous visit, but now he could see how closely it resembled the balcony Romeo had stood under when he had declared his love for Juliet.

Contemplating Romeo's fate is making me a trifle uneasy; I must concentrate on the romance of Shakespeare's great play, not the tragedy.

Betsy showed Edmund and his father into the parlor where the Oakleys were sitting.

"Mr. Templeton! What a pleasant surprise," Mr. Oakley said.

Once introductions had been made, Edmund expressed how pleased he was to see Mrs. Oakley restored to health.

"Why, thank you. I am fully recovered now and can undertake all my usual activities. This morning I have spent time in my herb garden, which I always enjoy."

A silence descended upon the room.

This is awkward! The Oakleys must be wondering why on earth we are here. How should we proceed?

Lord Templeton cleared his throat. "Mrs. Oakley, I wonder if you would do me the great honor of showing me your herb garden? I am particularly interested in horticulture – especially herbs – and I believe that Edmund has something he wishes to say privately to Mr. Oakley."

Mrs. Oakley beamed – and she and Lord Templeton left the room.

Edmund need not have worried, for once he was alone with the man he hoped to call his father-in-law, Mr. Oakley made everything easy. 'Twas almost as if he had longed for this moment. And after a decent interval, Lord Templeton and Mrs. Oakley returned to find Mr. Oakley's face suffused with joy, and Edmund's with relief.

"But remember, Mr. Templeton," Mr. Oakley said, "though I have given my blessing, 'tis absolutely Marianne's choice whether she accepts you or not."

"I take nothing for granted," Edmund said, "and know full well I am not worthy to be accepted by your daughter – for she is perfection."

"She is our dear Marianne and the best daughter anyone could ever wish for," Mrs. Oakley said. "And we are so proud to know you intend to ask her to become your wife."

"Well," Lord Templeton said, "once we have the good news we joyfully anticipate, I do hope you will both do us the honor of staying with us in Bath."

"As it happens, we are going to Bath in a couple of days," Mr.

Oakley said. "Our good friends the Radcliffes are there for the season and have asked us to join them in their lodgings in Norfolk Crescent for a while. We are thrilled, because they have managed to obtain tickets for the ball everyone is talking about."

"Ah! The one the Prince Regent is to attend," Lord Templeton said. "We look forward to seeing you there; all our family will be in attendance."

Well, perhaps not all our family, for if Marianne turns me down, I will not be at the ball. I will instead return to Clifton and, in a fit of melancholy, throw myself into the Gorge – or at least retire to Templeton Park for the rest of my life to nurse my broken heart.

As the Templeton carriage traveled through Bristol on its way to Bath, Edmund spied a particular lady in the street; this caused him to rap on the roof of the carriage with his cane.

"Stop, driver, if you please."

"What is it?" Lord Templeton asked.

"I have seen Miss Steele," Edmund said, "and I am keen to have a word with her."

"Very well," Lord Templeton said.

"Miss Steele! 'Tis I – Edmund Templeton."

"I know who you are, sir," Miss Steele said. "What a surprise to see you here."

"'Tis a happy coincidence," Edmund said. "My father and I are travelling back to Bath, and I happened to see you from the carriage. Miss Steele, I simply wish to thank you for traveling to Bath recently to warn Mrs. Pembroke of possible danger."

"I felt compelled to do so, sir," Miss Steele said, "for I did not like to think of a lady in peril. But I know now I was mistaken, for Mr. Teysen did not, after all, wish her harm."

"Nevertheless, you wanted to help Mrs. Pembroke, and for that I am grateful. I expect you also know that Mr. Teysen intends to live a better life than he lived as Lord Steyne?"

"I do, sir, for the full story, including the tale of your bravery in chasing him across the roof of the Royal Crescent, is well known all over this city."

"Well, I do not think he will be long in gaol," Edmund said. "I wonder where he will go next?"

"He is out already, sir. He is here, in Bristol." Miss Steele blushed deeply, and the rather hideous brooch she was wearing sparkled in the morning light.

Could it be that Miss Steele still has feelings for the old rogue? I see she is wearing the jewelry he gave her and did not sell it after all.

"I wish you well, Miss Steele." Edmund doffed his hat and returned to the carriage.

She will need all the luck in the world!

ONCE EDMUND ARRIVED home, he wasted no time before going round to Number 4.

"I am afraid Marianne is not at home at the moment," Lady Barrington said.

"Will she be long?"

I cannot wait to see her and learn my fate.

"She is out on the Crescent Fields with Jane and Nelson. Would you care to join them?"

"I would! Thank you, Lady B."

Edmund ran to the fields. How glorious the world looked today! The crocuses were all open, and the trees displayed buds with their promise of summer around the corner; verily, the golden late afternoon light was magical in its intensity.

Marianne stood in the very center of the fields by an oak tree, throwing a stick for Nelson. How beauteous she was in her scarlet cloak, with cheeks aglow, sparkling eyes, and radiant visage.

I pray God she will accept me, for I think I will die if I have to live without her.

"I will go back to the house now, if you will excuse me, Mr. Templeton," Jane said. "Lady Barrington told me earlier that when you arrived, I was to return immediately with Nelson, leaving you and Mrs. Pembroke to sort out the silly tangle. Oh, beg pardon, sir!"

Jane flushed scarlet and ran across the grass with Nelson yapping at her heels.

And so, we are alone at last.

"I must say what is in my heart," Edmund said. "I cannot wait any longer."

"But first I must speak," Marianne said. "Oh, Edmund! I have not been fair towards you."

"Me neither!"

After a rather topsy-turvy conversation about all the various ways the pair had misunderstood situations, said things they didn't mean, assumed things that were not true, and made regrettable mistakes, they enfolded each other within an embrace so close 'twas as if they had become one person. Then Edmund declared his love, which was joyfully reciprocated.

And thus it was that in the middle of the Crescent Fields, in the very heart of Bath, Edmund and Marianne exchanged a heavenly series of kisses which felt radically different from all the ones before, for these kisses anticipated the joy they would have in their lives together and celebrated the lifelong commitment they had just made.

"Dash it all!" Edmund said, as they walked back to Number 4. "Can you see what I can?"

Marianne chuckled. "'Tis Lady B with her telescope. We should have expected it."

THE DAY OF the ball dawned, and the whole of Bath was in a frenzy of excitement to think that the Prince Regent would soon be amongst them in the Upper Rooms. Not for a long time had the *ton* turned out in such numbers, resplendent in their finery and eager to enjoy the music, dancing, refreshments – and the presence of royalty.

As Edmund enjoyed the first dance with his intended, his heart swelled with pride and love.

"You look more beautiful than any lady here," he whispered in Marianne's ear.

"And you look divinely handsome," she answered. "Even more so than usual. Perchance 'tis a result of all that fence building and ditch digging."

"I fully intend to carry on with physical work from time to time," Edmund replied, "for to manage an estate properly, one should not be afraid to get one's hands dirty. I am changing, dear Marianne."

"But Edmund, I love you just as you are – and always will."

"Well, perhaps I have not altered that much," Edmund said, "for I would still like to swim in the river from time to time at midnight. Will that be acceptable?"

"Yes, as long as you take me with you. I have always wondered what it would be like to bathe by moonlight. But only if 'tis a boiling hot summer night."

"We have not had a boiling hot summer for quite a few years – but perchance 1817 will surprise us."

Edmund imagined frolicking with Marianne in the river, holding her gently to protect her from any fierce currents, and smoothing droplets from her divine countenance – until the rules of the dance caused her to link arms with another man and be whisked away.

Ah! Tis Captain Wyndham. 'Tis lucky I no longer feel jealous of this gentleman. He is a decent sort, and I wish him well. And now he is back dancing with his intended, and Marianne is opposite me again in the set.

"I have not told you Charlotte's good news yet," Marianne said to Edmund. "I heard this morning she has been brought to bed of a healthy son. All is well – and I am a godmother."

"How pleased I am! I look forward to visiting the Lake District and admiring your godson in the years to come."

And one day, God willing, Marianne will hold her own babe in her arms. What a fine life we will have together.

Soon it was time for refreshments, and all went to the tea room, with the Prince Regent leading the way.

"I see Carter on the other side of the room, with Henry and

Kitty," Edmund said to Marianne. "I have an important question for him."

"Do not be long!" Marianne said. "I will join my parents and the Radcliffes. Ah! There is Selina too, and George. I am so pleased I will soon be able to call Selina my sister."

Edmund strode over to Carter, who was looking a little ill at ease wearing an exceedingly smart evening suit which Lady Templeton had insisted on having made for him especially for the occasion.

"I am not sure why I am here," Carter said. "I feel like a tailor's dummy."

"You look very elegant," Kitty said.

"Yes, and you are here because you are part of our family," Henry said.

"Exactly!" Edmund said. "And now I have something most particular to ask. Will you be best man at my wedding?"

"Why, I thank you," Carter said, "but I must decline, for what would people say?"

"I care not for tittle-tattle and gossip – you know that," Edmund replied. "'Tis time you took your rightful place in the family as Mama's brother in the full gaze of the world, not merely behind closed doors. My wedding will be a good time to make this clear to the *ton*. And Mama and Papa are in total agreement."

"As are we," Henry and Kitty chorused.

"In that case, I would be honored." Carter raised his glass of Negus. "Edmund – your very good health. I know you and Mrs. Pembroke will be exceedingly happy."

When Edmund returned to Marianne's side, she was chatting to Lady Barrington.

"I will be moving out of Number 4 soon," Lady Barrington said.

"Moving out? Why?" Edmund said.

"Oh, did you not know?" Lady Barrington said. "Have I spoilt the surprise?"

"Possibly," Edmund said, "but as I do not know the nature of the surprise, I cannot say for definite. Pray, reveal all."

"Well, everyone knows that I will relocate to the north this summer. With Augusta and Amabella both expecting blessed events, it makes sense. And 'twill not be long before Aurelia and Alicia follow suit, I am sure. Anyhow, I am selling Number 4 to your dear papa."

Ah, I think I begin to realize where this is going.

"The seed of this idea was planted a long time ago," Lady Barrington said, "when we were in the Pump Room, back in January. I told your parents then that I would be spending most of my time in the north once my grandchildren arrived, and your papa was most interested in what I might want to do with Number 4. He thought it might be the ideal home for you and Marianne."

What! But I had only known Marianne a few days. Papa certainly wasted no time in planning for our union.

"I have found a suitable new home near all four of my daughters – for they live so close to each other 'tis but a five-minute carriage ride between their dwellings. I will be able to offer help and advice, but return to my own house at the end of each day – this will suit us all splendidly. Oh, look! Here is your papa approaching now, Edmund."

"What a splendid evening, is it not?" Lord Templeton said. "What have you been discussing? Everyone has gone very quiet."

"I have to apologize," Lady Barrington said, "for the mention of my imminent move has inadvertently let the cat out of the bag, thus spoiling the wondrous surprise of your wedding gift to the young pair here."

"'Tis time they knew, so I thank you.," Lord Templeton said. "And Edmund and Marianne, to make it crystal clear, I am presenting you with Number 4 to celebrate your forthcoming nuptials. Will that be acceptable?"

Marianne's eyes grew large and moist, and Edmund thanked his father profusely.

"Of course, you will both spend time at Templeton Park

too," Lord Templeton said, "but Number 4 will be your home in Bath."

"And I will continue to live there with Marianne till the very day of your wedding in June, for she must be chaperoned," Lady Barrington said, "then I will stay for a short time with Lord and Lady Templeton before finally moving to the north to be with my dear daughters."

"We will miss you, Aunt," Marianne said, "and Nelson, too."

"You will not," Lady Barrington said, "for you will be far too busy filling the house with children for that."

Marianne blushed as scarlet as a military uniform.

"I insist you stay with us whenever you visit Bath, Lady B," Edmund said. "You will always be welcome."

"I thank you – and will take you up on your kind offer."

Lord Templeton gazed across the room. "There is a crush at the door, and I see the Prince Regent is on the move. Let us return to the ballroom, for the music must be about to begin. Now, where is Lady Templeton? For she has promised me the next dance. Ah! There you are, my dear. Please, take my arm."

The Prince Regent seemed in good spirits after the refreshment break and spent some time watching the revelry, tapping his foot to the rhythm of the country dances. As Edmund and Marianne twirled past, they were close enough to hear His Highness's comment to his companion.

"I say – who is that handsome couple? They look very much in love."

EPILOGUE

AFTER THEIR WEDDING reception at Number 1 in the blazing summer of 1817, the bride and groom walked to their married home upon a carpet of fresh herbs strewn along the pavement.

Once inside the entrance hall, Edmund lifted Marianne into his arms and began to carry her upstairs while she caressed the dark curls at the back of his neck. Then he slowly released her and they walked hand in hand to their newly furnished chamber.

A fire burned in the grate, and candles cast a soft, tender glow; the covers had been turned down invitingly, and fragrant rose petals lay scattered upon the sheets in the shape of a heart.

The pair embraced passionately, sharing a lingering kiss full of promise.

"You have changed my life, dearest Marianne. How I love thee!"

"And I thee, Edmund – you are my new world."

Then Marianne slowly closed the door.

The End

Jenny grew up in Bath, in the west of England, and spent much of her childhood exploring this beautiful city and wondering about the kind of people who lived there centuries ago. She was an avid reader from an early age, inheriting the love of a good story from her Irish grandmother.

After studying music at college, teaching in secondary schools for a number of years, and starting a family, Jenny finally found the time to pursue her dream of writing.

She now lives in London with her husband, writes short stories for UK women's magazines, and has had a number of romantic comedy novels published.

Website – jennyworstall.wordpress.com
Facebook – facebook.com/jennyworstall
Twitter – x.com/JennyWorstall
Amazon – amazon.co.uk/stores/Jenny-Worstall/author/B007IVNY1G
Instagram – instagram.com/jennyworstall